NORA ROBERTS

Dream Makers

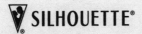

Silhouette and Colophon are registered trademarks of Harlequin Books S.A., used under licence.
Silhouette Books, Eton House, 18-24 Paradise Road, Richmond, Surrey TW9 1SR

DREAM MAKERS © Harlequin Books S.A. 2006

The publisher acknowledges the copyright holder of the individual works as follows:

Untamed © Nora Roberts 1983
Less of a Stranger © Nora Roberts 1984

ISBN: 978 0 263 85008 6

025-0807

Printed and bound in Spain
by Litografia Rosés S.A., Barcelona

CONTENTS

Untamed

For my sons,
Life's a circus.
Go for it!

Chapter 1

At the crack of the whip, twelve lions stood on their haunches and pawed the air. On command, they began to leap from pedestal to pedestal in a quick, close-formation, figure-eight pattern. This required split-second timing. With voice and hand commands the trainer kept the tawny, springing bodies moving.

"Well done, Pandora."

At her name and the signal, the muscular lioness leaped to the ground and lay down on her side. One by one the others followed suit, until, snarling and baring their teeth, they stretched across the tanbark. A male was positioned beside each female; at a sharp reproof from the trainer, Merlin ceased nibbling on Ophelia's ear.

"Heads up!" They obeyed as the trainer walked briskly in front of them. The whip was tossed aside with a flourish, then, with apparent nonchalance, the trainer reclined lengthwise across the warm bodies. The center cat, a full-maned African, let out a great, echoing bellow. As a reward for his response to the cue, his ear was given a good scratching. The trainer rose from the feline couch, clapped hands and brought the lions to their feet. Then, with a hand signal, each was called by name and sent through the chute and into their cages. One stayed behind, a huge, black-maned cat who, like an ordinary tabby, circled and rubbed up against his trainer's legs.

Deftly, a rope was attached to a chain that was hidden under his mane. Then, with swift agility, the trainer mounted the lion's back. As the door of the big cage opened, lion and rider passed through for a tour of the practice ring. When they reached the back door of the ring barn, Merlin, the obliging lion, was transferred to a wheel cage.

"Well, Duffy." Jo turned after the cage was secured. "Are we ready for the road?"

Duffy was a small, round man with a monk's fringe of chestnut hair and a face that exploded with ginger freckles. His open smile and Irish blue eyes gave him the look of an aging choirboy. His mind was sharp, shrewd and scrappy. He was the best manager Prescott's Circus Colossus could have had.

"Since we open in Ocala tomorrow," he replied in a raspy voice, "you'd better be ready." He shifted his fat cigar stump from the right side of his mouth to the left.

Jo merely smiled, then stretched to loosen muscles grown taut during the thirty minutes in the cage. "My cats are ready, Duffy. It's been a long winter. They need to get back on the road as much as the rest of us."

Duffy frowned. As circumstances had it, he stood only inches higher than his animal trainer. Widely spaced, almond-shaped eyes stared back at him. They were as sharp and green as emeralds, surrounded by thick, inky lashes. At the moment they were fearless and amused, but Duffy had seen them frightened, vulnerable and lost. He shifted his cigar again and took two quick puffs as Jo gave a cage hand instructions.

He remembered Steve Wilder, Jo's father. He had been one of the best cat men in the business. Jo was as good with the cats as Wilder had been. In some ways, Duffy acknowledged, even better. But she had the traits of her mother: delicate build; dark, passionate looks. Jolivette Wilder was as slender as her aerialist mother had been, with bold green eyes and straight, raven black hair that fell to just below her waist. Her brows were delicately arched, her nose small and straight, her cheekbones high and elegant,

while her mouth was full and soft. Her skin was
tawny from the Florida sun; it added to her gypsy-
like appearance. Confidence added spark to the
beauty.

Finishing her instructions, Jo tucked her arm
through Duffy's. She had seen that frown before.
"Somebody quit?" she asked as they began to walk
toward Duffy's office.

"Nope."

His monosyllabic reply caused Jo to lift a brow.
It was not often Duffy answered any question briefly.
Years of experience told her to hold her tongue as
they moved across the compound.

Rehearsals were going on everywhere. Vito the
wire walker informally sharpened his act on a cable
stretched between two trees. The Mendalsons called
out to each other as they tossed their juggling pins
high in the air, while the equestrian act led their
horses into the ring barn. She saw one of the Stevenson girls walking on stilts. She'd be six now, Jo
mused, tossing the hair from her eyes as she watched
the young girl's wavering progress. Jo remembered
the year she had been born. It had been that same
year that she had been allowed to work the big cage
alone. She had been sixteen, and it had been another
full year before she had been permitted to work an
audience.

For Jo, there had never been any home but the

circus. She had been born during the winter break, had been tucked into her parents' trailer the following spring to spend her first year and each subsequent one of her life thereafter on the road. She had inherited both her fascination and her flair with animals from her father, her style and grace of movement from her mother. Though she had lost both parents fifteen years before, they continued to influence her. Their legacy to her had been a world of restlessness, a world of fantasies. She had grown up playing with lion cubs, riding elephants, wearing spangles and traveling like a gypsy.

Jo glanced down at a cluster of daffodils growing by the side of Prescott's winter office and smiled. She remembered planting them when she had been thirteen and in love with a tumbler. She remembered, too, the man who had stooped beside her, offering advice on bulb planting and broken hearts. As Jo thought of Frank Prescott, her smile grew sad.

"I still can't believe he's gone," she murmured as she and Duffy moved inside.

Duffy's office was sparsely furnished with a wooden desk, metal filing cabinets and two spindly chairs. A collage of posters adorned the walls. They promised the amazing, the astounding, the incredible: elephants that danced, men who flew through the air, beautiful girls who spun by their teeth, raging tigers that rode horseback. Tumblers, clowns, lions, strong men, fat ladies, boys who could balance on their forefingers; they brought the magic of the circus into the drab little room.

As Jo glanced over at a narrow pine door, Duffy followed her gaze. "I keep expecting him to come busting through there with some crazy new idea," he mumbled as he began to fiddle with his prize possession, an automatic coffee maker.

"Do you?" With a sigh Jo straddled a chair, then rested her chin on its back. "We all miss him. It's not going to seem the same without him this year." She looked up suddenly, and her eyes were angry. "He wasn't an old man, Duffy. Heart attacks should be for old men." She brooded into space, touched again with the injustice of Frank Prescott's death.

He had been barely into his fifties and full of laughter and simple kindness. Jo had loved him and trusted him without reservation. At his death she had grieved for him more acutely than she had for her own parents. In her longest memory he had been the core of her life.

"It's been nearly six months," Duffy said gruffly as he studied her face. When Jo glanced up, he stuck out a mug of coffee.

"I know." She took the mug, letting it warm her hands in the chilly March morning. Resolutely, she shook off the mood. Frank would not have wanted to leave sadness behind. Jo studied the coffee, then sipped. It was predictably dreadful. "Rumor has it we're following last year's route to the letter. Thirteen states." Jo smiled, watching Duffy wince over his coffee before he downed it. "Not superstitious, are you?" She grinned, knowing he kept a four-leaf clover in his billfold.

"Pah!" he said indignantly, coloring under his freckles. He set down his empty cup, then moved around his desk and sat behind it. When he folded his hands on the yellow blotter, Jo knew he was getting down to business. Through the open window she could hear the band rehearsing. "We should be in Ocala by six tomorrow," he began. Dutifully, Jo nodded. "Should have the tents up before nine."

"The parade should be over by ten, and the matinee will start at two," Jo finished with a smile. "Duffy, you're not going to ask me to work the menagerie in the side show again, are you?"

"Should be a good crowd," he replied, adroitly skirting her question. "Bonzo predicts clear skies."

"Bonzo should stick with pratfalls and unicycles." She watched as Duffy chewed on the stub of a now dead cigar. "Okay," she said firmly, "let's have it."

"Someone's going to be joining us in Ocala, at least temporarily." He pursed his lips as his eyes met Jo's. His were blue, faded with age. "I don't know if he'll finish out the season with us."

"Oh, Duffy, not some first of mayer we have to break in this late?" Jo demanded, using the circus term for novice. "What is he, some energetic writer who wants an epic on the vanishing tent circus? He'll spend a few weeks as a roustabout and swear he knows all there is to know about it."

"I don't think he'll be working as a roustabout," Duffy muttered. Striking a match, he coaxed the cigar back to life. Jo frowned, watching the smoke struggle toward the ceiling.

"It's a bit late to work in a new act now, isn't it?"

"He's not a performer." Duffy swore lightly under his breath, then met Jo's eyes again. "He owns us."

For a moment Jo said nothing. She sat unmoving, as Duffy had seen her from time to time when she trained a young cat. "No!" She rose suddenly, shaking her head. "Not him. Not now. Why does he have to come? What does he want here?"

"It's his circus," Duffy reminded her. His voice was both rough and sympathetic.

"It'll never be his circus," Jo retorted passionately. Her eyes lit and glowed with a temper she rarely let have sway. "It's Frank's circus."

"Frank's dead," Duffy stated in a quiet, final tone. "Now the circus belongs to his son."

"Son?" Jo countered. She lifted her fingers to

press them against her temple. Slowly, she moved to the window. Outside, the sun was pouring over the heads of troupers. She watched the members of the trapeze act, in thick robes worn over their tights, head toward the ring barn. The chatter of mixed languages was so familiar she failed to notice it. She placed her palms on the window sill and with a little sigh, steadied her temper. "What sort of son is it who never bothers to visit his father? In thirty years he never came to see Frank. He never wrote. He didn't even come to the funeral." Jo swallowed the tears of anger that rose to her throat and thickened her voice. "Why should he come now?"

"You've got to learn that life's a two-sided coin, kiddo," Duffy said briskly. "You weren't even alive thirty years ago. You don't know why Frank's wife up and left him or why the boy never visited."

"He's not a boy, Duffy, he's a man." Jo turned back, and he saw that she again had herself under control. "He's thirty-one, thirty-two years old now, a very successful attorney with a fancy Chicago office. He's very wealthy, did you know?" A small smile played on her lips but failed to reach her eyes. "And not just from court cases and legal fees; there's quite a lot of money on his mother's side. Nice, quiet, old money. I can't understand what a rich city lawyer would want with a tent circus."

Duffy shrugged his broad, round shoulders.

"Could be he wants a tax shelter. Could be he wants to ride an elephant. Could be anything. He might want to take inventory and sell us off, piece by piece."

"Oh, Duffy, no!" Emotion flew back into Jo's face. "He couldn't do that."

"The heck he couldn't," Duffy muttered as he stubbed out his cigar. "He can do as he pleases. If he wants to liquidate, he liquidates."

"But we have contracts through October...."

"You're too smart for that, Jo." Duffy frowned, scratching his rim of hair. "He can buy them off or let them play through. He's a lawyer. He can figure the way out of a contract if he wants to. He can wait till August when we start to negotiate again and let them all lapse." Seeing Jo's distress, he backpedaled. "Listen, kiddo, I didn't say he was going to sell, I said he *could*."

Jo ran a hand through her hair. "There must be something we can do."

"We can show a profit by the end of the season," Duffy said wryly. "We can show the new owner what we have to offer. I think it's important that he sees we're not just a mud show but a profitable three-ring circus with class acts. He should see what Frank built, how he lived, what he wanted to do. I think," Duffy added, watching Jo's face, "that you should be in charge of his education."

"Me?" Jo was too incredulous to be angry. "Why? You're better qualified in the public relations department than I am. I train lions, not lawyers." She could not keep the hint of scorn from her voice.

"You were closer to Frank than anyone. And there isn't anyone here who knows this circus better than you." Again he frowned. "And you've got brains. Never thought much use would come of all those fancy books you read, but maybe I was wrong."

"Duffy." Her lips curved into a smile. "Just because I like to read Shakespeare doesn't mean I can deal with Keane Prescott. Even thinking about him makes me furious. How will I act when I meet him face to face?"

"Well." Duffy shrugged before he pursed his lips. "If you don't think you can handle it…"

"I didn't say I *couldn't* handle it," Jo muttered.

"Of course, if you're afraid…"

"I'm not afraid of anything, and I'm certainly not afraid of some Chicago lawyer who doesn't know sawdust from tanbark." Sticking her hands in her pockets, she paced the length of the small room. "If Keane Prescott, attorney-at-law, wants to spend his summer with the circus, I'll do my best to make it a memorable one."

"Nicely," Duffy cautioned as Jo moved to the door.

''Duffy,'' she paused and gave him an innocent smile. ''You know what a gentle touch I have.'' To prove it, Jo slammed the door behind her.

Dawn was hovering over the horizon as the circus caravan drew up in a large, grassy field. Colors were just a promise in a pale gray sky. In the distance was grove upon grove of orange trees. As Jo stepped from the cab of her truck, the fragrance met her. It's a perfect day, she decided, then took a long, greedy breath. To her, there was no more beautiful sight than dawn struggling to life.

The air was vaguely chilly. She zipped up her gray sweat jacket as she watched the rest of the circus troupe pouring out of their trucks and cars and trailers. The morning quiet was soon shattered by voices. Work began immediately. As the Big Top canvas was being unrolled out of the spool truck, Jo went to see how her lions had fared the fifty-mile journey.

Three handlers unloaded the traveling cages. Buck had been with Jo the longest. He had worked for her father, and during the interim between his death and Jo's professional debut, he had worked up a small act with four male lions. His shyness had made his retirement from performing a relief. To Buck, two people were a crowd. He stood six-feet-four, and his build was powerful enough for him to pad the side-show from time to time as Hercules the Strong

Man. He had an impressive head of wild blond hair and a full, curling beard. His hands were wide, with thick, strong fingers, but Jo remembered their gentleness when the two of them had delivered a lioness of a pair of cubs.

Pete's small frame seemed puny beside Buck's. He was of indeterminable age. Jo guessed between forty and fifty, but she was never certain. He was a quiet man with skin like polished mahogany and a rich, low-pitched voice. He had come to Jo five years before, asking for a job. She had never asked where he had come from, and he had never told her. He wore a fielder's cap and was never seen without a wad of gum moving gently in his teeth. He read Jo's books and was the undisputed king of the poker table.

Gerry was nineteen and eager. He was nearly six feet and still carried the lankiness of his youth. His mother sewed, and his father was a souvenir salesman, or a candy butcher, as circus jargon had it. Working the big cage was Gerry's dream, and because it had been hers, Jo had finally agreed to tutor him.

"How are my babies?" she demanded as she approached. At each cage she paused and soothed a nervous cat, calling each by name until they had settled. "They've traveled well. Hamlet's still edgy, but it's his first year on the road."

"He's a mean one," Buck muttered, watching Jo move from cage to cage.

"Yes, I know," she replied absently. "He's smart, too." She had twisted her hair into one thick braid and now tossed it to her back. "Look, here come some towners." A few cars and a smattering of bikes drew into the field.

These were the people from the outlying towns who wanted to see a Big Top raised, who wanted to see the circus, if only for a moment, from the other side. Some would watch while others would lend a hand with tent poles, stretching canvas and rigging. They would earn a show pass and an unforgettable experience.

"Keep them clear of the cages," Jo ordered, nodding to Pete before she moved toward the still flaccid canvas. Buck lumbered beside her.

The field was alive with ropes and wire and people. Six elephants were harnessed but idle, with their handlers standing by the stake line. As workers pulled on guy ropes, the dusky brown canvas billowed up like a giant mushroom.

The poles were positioned—side, quarter, center—while the canvas muffled the sounds of scrambling workers. In the east the sun was rising fast, streaking the sky with pink. There were shouted instructions from the head canvas man, laughter from adventuresome boys and an occasional oath. As the quarter poles were driven into the sag of canvas, Jo signaled Maggie, the large African elephant. Obligingly, Maggie lowered her trunk. Jo stepped nimbly into the *u,* then scrambled onto the wide, gray back.

The sun grew higher by the second, shooting the first streams of light onto the field. The scent of orange blossoms mingled with the odor of leather harnesses. Jo had watched the canvas rise under a lightening sky countless times. Each time it was special, and the first raising each season was the most special of all. Maggie lifted her head and trumpeted as if pleased to be around for another season. With a laugh Jo reached back and swatted her rough, wrinkled rump. She felt free and fresh and incredibly alive. If there were a moment, she thought suddenly, that I could capture and bottle, it would be this one. Then, when I'm very old, I could take it out and feel young again. Smiling, she glanced down at the people swarming below her.

Her attention was caught by a man who stood by a coil of cable. Typically, she noted his build first. A well-proportioned body was essential to a performer. He was lean and stood straight. She noted he had good shoulders but doubted if there was much muscle in his arms. Though he was dressed casually in jeans, *city* stood out all over him. His hair was a dark, rich blond, and the early breeze had disturbed it so that it teased his forehead. He was clean-shaven, with a narrow, firm-jawed face. It was an attractive face. It was not, Jo mused, smoothly handsome like Vito the wire walker's but more aware, more demanding. Jo liked the face, liked the shape of the long, unsmiling mouth, liked the hint of bone beneath his tawny skin. Most of all she liked the directness of the amber eyes that stared back at her. They're like Ari's, she observed, thinking of her favorite lion. She was certain that he had been watching her long before she had looked down. Knowing this, Jo was impressed with his unself-consciousness. He continued to stare, making no effort to camouflage his interest. She laughed, unperturbed, and tossed her braid from her shoulder.

"Want a ride?" she called out. Too many strangers had walked in and out of her world for her to be aloof. She watched his brow lift in acknowledgment of her offer. She would see if it was only his eyes that were like Ari's. "Maggie won't hurt you. She's gentle as a lamb, just bigger." Instantly, she saw he had understood the challenge. He walked across the grass until he stood beside her. He moved well, she noted. Jo tapped Maggie's side with the bull hook she carried. Wearily, the elephant knelt down on her trunklike front legs. Jo held out her hand. With an agility that surprised her, the man mounted the elephant and slid into place behind her.

For a moment she said nothing, a bit stunned by

the trembling that had coursed up her arm as her palm had met his. The contact had been brief. Jo decided she had imagined it. "Up, Maggie," she said, giving her mount another tap. With an elephantine sigh, Maggie obeyed, rocking her passengers gently from side to side.

"Do you always pick up strange men?" the voice behind her inquired. It was a smooth, well-keyed voice, a good pitchman's voice.

Jo grinned over her shoulder. "Maggie's doing the picking up."

"So she is. Are you aware that she's remarkably uncomfortable?"

Jo laughed with genuine enjoyment. "You should try riding her a few miles in a street parade while keeping a smile on your face."

"I'll pass. Are you in charge of her?"

"Maggie? No, but I know how to handle her. You have eyes like one of my cats," she told him. "I like them. And since you seemed to be interested in Maggie and me, I asked you up."

This time it was he who laughed. Jo twisted her head, wanting to see his face. There was humor in his eyes now, and his teeth were white and straight. Liking his smile, she answered with one of her own. "Fascinating. You asked me to take a ride on an elephant because I have eyes like your cat's. And no offense to the lady beneath me, but I was looking at you."

"Oh?" Jo pursed her lips in thought. "Why?"

For several seconds he studied her in silence. "Strange, I believe you really don't know."

"I wouldn't ask if I did," she returned, shifting her weight slightly. "It would be a waste of time to ask a question if I knew the answer." She shifted again and turned away from him. "Hold on now. Maggie's got to earn her bale of hay."

The poles hung between the canvas and the ground at forty-five degree angles. Quickly the elephant's chains were hooked to the metal rings at the base of the quarter poles. Jo urged Maggie forward in unison with her coworkers. Poles skidded along the ground, then up into place, pushing the canvas with it. The Big Top billowed to life under the early morning sky.

Her job done, Maggie moved through the flaps and into the light. "Beautiful, isn't it?" Jo murmured. "It's born fresh every day."

Vito walked by, calling out to Jo in Italian. Sending him a wave, she called back in his own language, then signaled to Maggie to kneel again. Jo waited until her passenger had dismounted before she slid off. It surprised her, when they stood face to face, that he was so tall. Tilting back her head, she judged him to be only two inches shy of Buck.

"You looked shorter when I was up on Maggie," she told him with her usual candor.

"You looked taller."

Jo chuckled, patting Maggie behind the ear. "Will you see the show?" She knew that she wanted him to, knew as well that she wanted to see him again. She found this both strange and intriguing. Men had always taken a second place to her cats, and towners had never interested her.

"Yes, I'm going to see the show." There was a slight smile on his face, but he was studying her thoughtfully. "Do you perform?"

"I have an act with my cats."

"I see. Somehow I pictured you in an aerial act, flying from the trapeze."

She sent him an easy smile. "My mother was an aerialist." Someone called her name, and looking, Jo saw Maggie was needed for raising the sideshow tent. "I have to go. I hope you like the show."

He took her hand before she could lead Maggie away. Jo stood still, again surprised by a trembling up her arm. "I'd like to see you tonight."

Glancing up, she met his eyes. They were direct and unselfconscious. "Why?" The question was sincere. Jo knew she wanted to see him as well but was unsure why.

This time he did not laugh. Gently, he ran a finger

down the length of her braid. "Because you're beautiful, and you intrigue me."

"Oh." Jo considered. She had never thought of herself as beautiful. Striking, perhaps, in her costume, surrounded by her cats, but in jeans, without makeup, she doubted it. Still, it was an interesting thought. "All right, if there's no trouble with the cats. Ari hasn't been well."

A smile played at the corners of his mouth. "I'm sorry to hear that."

There was another loud summons for Jo, and both looked toward it. "I see you're needed," he said with a nod. "Perhaps you could point out Bill Duffy for me before you go."

"Duffy?" Jo repeated, surprised. "You can't be looking for a job?" There was incredulity in her voice, and he grinned.

"Why can't I?"

"Because you don't fit any of the types."

"Are there types?" he asked, both interested and amused. Jo shook her head in annoyance.

"Yes, of course, and you don't fit into any of them."

"Actually, I'm not looking for a job, so to speak," he told her, still smiling. "But I am looking for Bill Duffy."

It was against Jo's nature to probe. Privacy was both guarded and respected in the circus. Shielding her eyes with her hand, Jo looked around until she spotted Duffy supervising the raising of the cookhouse tent. "There," she said, pointing. "Duffy's the one with the red checked jacket. He still dresses like an outside talker."

"A what?"

"You'd call it a barker, I imagine." With easy grace she mounted the patient Maggie. "That's a towner's term, not a circus one." She smiled at him, then urged Maggie into a walk. "Tell Duffy Jo said to give you a pass," she called over her shoulder, then waved and turned away.

Dawn was over, and it was morning.

Chapter 2

Jo stood at the back door of the Big Top waiting for her cue. Beside her was Jamie Carter, alias Topo. He was a third generation clown and wore his bright face and orange wig naturally. He was young and limber and used these traits as well as his makeup to bring enthusiasm to his craft. To Jo, Jamie was more brother than friend. He was tall and thin, and under his greasepaint his face was mobile and pleasant. He and Jo had grown up together.

"Did she say anything?" Jamie demanded for the third time. With a sigh, Jo tossed closed the flap of the tent. Inside, clowns were performing around the hippodrome track while hands set up the big cage.

"Carmen said nothing. I don't know why you

waste your time." Her voice was sharp, and Jamie bristled.

"I don't expect you to understand," he said with great dignity. His thin shoulders drew straight under his red polka dot shirt. "After all, Ari's the closest you've come to being involved with the opposite sex."

"That's very cute," Jo replied, unoffended by the jibe. Her annoyance stemmed from seeing Jamie make a fool of himself over Carmen Gribalti, the middle sister of the flying Gribaltis. She was darkly beautiful, graceful, talented, selfish and sublimely indifferent to Jamie. Looking into his happy, painted face and moody eyes, Jo's irritation dissipated. "She probably hasn't had a chance to answer the note you sent her," she soothed. "The first day of a new season's always wild."

"I suppose," Jamie muttered with a grudging shrug. "I don't know what she sees in Vito."

Jo thought of the wire walker's dark, cocky looks and rippling muscles. Wisely, she refrained from mentioning them. "Who can account for taste?" She gave him a smacking kiss on his round, red nose. "Personally, I get all wobbly when I see a man with thick, orange hair."

Jamie grinned. "Proves you know what to look for in a man."

Turning, Jo lifted the flap again, noting Jamie's

cue was nearly upon them. "Did you happen to notice a towner hanging around today?"

"Only a couple dozen of them," Jamie answered
dryly as he lifted the pail of confetti he used to finish
the gag now being performed inside.

Jo shot him a half-hearted glare. "Not the usual
type. About thirty, I think," she continued. "Wearing jeans and a T-shirt. He was tall, six-one, six-
two," she went on as laughter poured out of the open
flap to drown out her words. "He had dark blond
straight hair."

"Yeah, I saw him." Jamie nudged her out of his
way and prepared to make his entrance. "He was
going into the red wagon with Duffy." With a wild,
high-pitched scream, Topo the clown bounded into
the Big Top in size fifteen tennis shoes, brandishing
his bucket of confetti.

Thoughtfully, Jo watched Jamie chase three other
clowns around the track. It was odd, she thought, for
Duffy to take a towner into the administration trailer.
He had said he wasn't looking for a job. He wasn't
a drifter; there was an unmistakable air of stability
about him. He wasn't a circus hand from another
show, either. His palm had been too smooth. And,
her mind added as she vaulted onto Babette, a pure
white mare, there had been an undeniable aura of
urbanity about him. Success, as well, she thought.

And authority. No, he had not been looking for a job.

Jo shrugged, annoyed that a stranger was crowding into her thoughts. It irritated her further that she had scanned the crowds for him during the parade and that even now she wondered if he sat somewhere in the circular arena. He hadn't been at the matinee. Jo patted the mare's neck absently, then straightened as she heard the ringmaster's whistle.

"Ladies and gentlemen," he called in deep, musical tones. "Presenting the most spectacular exhibition of animal subjugation under the Big Top. Jovilette, Queen of the Jungle Cats!"

Jo nudged Babette with her heels and raced into the arena. The applause rose to meet her as the audience appreciated the dashing figure she cut. Swathed in a black cape, raven hair flying free under a glittering tiara, she galloped bareback on the snow white mare. In each hand she held a long, thin whip, which she cracked alternately overhead. At the entrance to the big cage she leaped from the still racing horse. While Babette galloped out of the back door and into the care of a handler, Jo shifted both whips into one hand, then removed the cape with a flourish. Her costume was a close-fitting, one-piece jumpsuit, dazzling in white and spangled with gold sequins. In dramatic contrast, her hair hung straight and severe down her back.

Make an entrance, Frank had always said. And Jovilette made an entrance.

The twelve cats were already in the cage, banding its inside edge as they perched on blue and white pedestals. Entering the main cage appeared routine to the audience, but Jo knew it was one of the most dangerous moments of the act. To enter, she had to pass directly between two cats as she moved from the safety cage to the main arena. She always stationed her best behaved cats there, but if one was irritated, or even playful, he could easily strike out with a powerful paw. Even with sharp claws retracted, the damage could be deadly.

She entered swiftly and was surrounded by cats on all sides. Her spangles and tiara caught the lights and played with them as she began to move around the cage, cracking the whip for showmanship while using her voice to command the cats to rise on their haunches. She moved them through their routine, adjusting the timing to compensate for any feline reluctance, letting one trick begin where the last ended.

Jo disliked overdone propping, preferring action and movement. The contrast of the big, tawny cats and the small white and gold woman were the best props available to her. She used them well. Hers was a *picture act,* relying on style and flash, rather than a *fighting act,* which emphasized the ferocity of the big cats by employing blank-bulleted guns and rehearsed charges, or *bounces*. Her confidence transmitted itself to the audience, making her handling of the cats appear effortless. In truth, her body was coiled for any danger, and her mind was focused so intently on her cats, there might have been no audience at all.

She stood between two high pedestals as the cats leaped over her head from both directions. They set up a light breeze, which stirred her hair. They roared when she cued them, setting up an echoing din. Now and then one reached out to paw at the stock of her whip, and she stopped him with a quick command. She sent her best leaper through a hoop of flame and coaxed her best balancer to walk on a glistening silver ball. She ended to waves of applause by trotting Merlin around the hippodrome track.

At the back door Merlin jumped into a wheel cage and was turned over to Pete. "Nice show," he said as he handed her a long chenille robe. "Smooth as silk."

"Thanks." Cold, she bundled into the robe. The spring night was frigid in contrast to the hot lights and heat in the big cage. "Listen, Pete, tell Gerry he can feed the cats tonight. They're behaving themselves."

Pete snapped his gum and chuckled. "Won't he be riding high tonight." As he moved to the truck that would pull the cage to the cat area, Jo called after him.

"Pete." She bit her lip, then shrugged when he twisted his head. "You'll keep an eye on him, won't you?"

Pete grinned and climbed into the cab of the truck. "Who you worried about, Jo? Those big cats or that skinny boy?"

"Both," she answered. The rhinestones in her tiara sparkled as she tossed her head and laughed. Knowing she had nearly an hour before the finale parade, Jo walked away from the Big Top. She thought of wandering to the cookhouse for some coffee. Mentally, she began replaying every segment of her act. It had gone well, she thought, pleased with the timing and the flow. If Pete had said it had been smooth, Jo knew it had. She had heard his criticisms more than once over the past five years. True, Hamlet had tested her once or twice, but no one knew that but Jo and the cat. She doubted if anyone but Buck would have seen that he had given her trouble. Closing her eyes a moment, Jo rolled her shoulders, loosening tight, tensed muscles.

"That's quite an act you have."

Jo whirled around at the sound of the voice. She could feel her heart rate accelerate. Though she wondered at her interest in a man she barely knew, Jo was aware that she had been waiting for him. There was a quick surge of pleasure as she watched him approach, and she allowed it to show on her face.

"Hello." She saw that he smoked a cigar, but unlike Duffy's, his was long and slim. Again she admired the elegance of his hands. "Did you like the show?"

He stopped in front of her, then studied her face with a thoroughness that made her wonder if her makeup had smeared. Then he gave a small, surprised laugh and shook his head. "Do you know," he began, "when you told me this morning that you did an act with cats, I had Siamese in mind rather than African."

"Siamese?" Jo repeated blankly, then laughed. "House cats?" He brushed her hair behind her back while Jo giggled at the thought of coaxing a Siamese to jump through a flaming hoop.

"From my point of view," he told her as he let a strand of her hair linger between his fingers, "it made more sense than a little thing like you walking into a cage with a dozen lions."

"I'm not little," Jo corrected good-naturedly. "Besides, size hardly matters to twelve lions."

"No, I suppose it doesn't." He lifted his eyes from her hair and met hers. Jo continued to smile, enjoying looking at him. "Why do you do it?" he asked suddenly.

Jo gave him a curious look. "Why? Because it's my job."

By the way he studied her, Jo could see that he was not satisfied with the simplicity of her answer. "Perhaps I should ask *how* you became a lion tamer."

"Trainer," Jo corrected automatically. To her left, she could hear the audience's muffled applause. "The Beirots are starting," she said with a glance toward the sound. "You shouldn't miss their act. They're first-rate acrobats."

"Don't you want to tell me?" His voice was soft.

She lifted a brow, seeing that he truly wanted to know. "Why, it's not a secret. My father was a trainer, and I have a knack for working with cats. It just followed." Jo had never thought about her career past this point, and she shrugged it aside. "You shouldn't waste your ticket standing out here. You can stand by the back door and watch the rest of the act." Jo turned to lead the way to the performer's entrance but stopped when his hand took hers.

He stepped forward until their bodies were nearly touching. Jo could feel the heat from his as she watched his face. Her heart was thudding in a quick, steady rhythm. She could hear it vibrate through her the same way it did when she approached a new cat for the first time. Here was something new, something untested. She tingled with the excitement of the unknown when he lifted his hand to touch her cheek. She did not move but let the warmth spread while she watched him carefully, gauging him. Her eyes were wide, curious and unafraid.

"Are you going to kiss me?" she asked in a tone that expressed more interest than desire.

His eyes lit with humor and glittered in the dim light. "I had given it some thought," he answered. "Do you have any objections?"

Jo considered a moment, dropping her eyes to his mouth. She liked its shape and wondered how it would feel against hers. He brought her no closer. One hand still held hers while the other slid around to cradle her neck. Jo shifted her gaze until their eyes met again. "No," she decided. "I haven't any objections."

The corners of his mouth twitched as he tightened his hold slightly on the base of her neck. Slowly, he lowered his head toward hers. Curious and a bit wary, Jo kept her eyes open, watching his. She knew from experience that you could tell more about people and about cats from the eyes. To her surprise, his remained open as well, even as their lips met.

It was a gentle kiss, without pressure, only a whisper of a touch. Amazed, Jo thought she felt the ground tremble under her feet. Dimly, she wondered if the elephants were being led by. But it can't be time, she thought in confusion. His lips moved lightly over hers, and his eyes remained steady. Jo's pulse drummed under her skin. They stood, barely touching, as the Big Top throbbed with noise behind them. Lazily, he traced her lips with the tip of his tongue, teasing them open. Still there was no demand in the kiss, only testing. Unhurried, confident, he explored her mouth while Jo felt her breath accelerating. A soft moan escaped her as her lids fluttered down.

For an instant she surrendered utterly to him, to the new sensations swimming through her. She leaned against him, straining toward pleasure, sighing with it as the kiss lingered.

He drew her away, but their faces remained close. Dizzily, Jo realized that she had risen to her toes to compensate for their difference in height. His hand was still light on the back of her neck. His eyes were gold in the darkening night.

"What an incredible female you are, Jovilette," he murmured. "One surprise after another."

Jo felt stunningly alive. Her skin seemed to tingle with new feelings. She smiled. "I don't know your name."

He laughed, releasing her neck to take her other hand in his. Before he could speak, Duffy called out from the direction of the Big Top. Jo turned to watch as he moved toward them in his quick, rolling walk.

"Well, well, well," he said in his jolly, rough

voice. "I didn't know you two had met. Has Jo been showing you around already?" Reaching them, he squeezed Jo's shoulder. "Knew I could count on you, kiddo." Jo glanced at him in puzzlement, but he continued before she could form a question. "Yes, sir, this little girl puts on quite a show, doesn't she? Always a grabber. And she knows this circus like the back of her hand. Born and raised to it," he continued. Jo relaxed. She recognized that Duffy was into one of his spiels, and there was no stopping him. "Yessiree, any questions you got, you just ask our Jo, and she'll tell you. 'Course, I'm always at your disposal, too. Anything I can tell you about the books or accounts or contracts and the like, you just let me know." Duffy puffed twice on his cigar as Jo felt her first hint of unease.

Why was Duffy rambling about books and contracts? Jo glanced at the man who still held her hands in his. He was watching Duffy with an easy, amused smile.

"Are you a bookkeeper?" Jo asked, perplexed. Duffy laughed and patted her head.

"You know Mr. Prescott's a lawyer, Jo. Don't miss your cue." He gave them both a friendly nod and toddled off.

Jo had stiffened almost imperceptibly at Duffy's offhand information, but Keane had felt it. His brows lowered as he studied her. "Now you know my name."

"Yes." All warmth fled from Jo. Her voice was as cool as her blood. "Would you let go of my hands, Mr. Prescott?"

After a brief hesitation Keane inclined his head and obliged. Jo stuffed her hands quickly into the pockets of her robe. "Don't you think we've progressed to the first name stage of our relationship, Jo?"

"I assure you, Mr. Prescott, if I had known who you were, we wouldn't have progressed at all." Jo's words were stiff with dignity. Inside, though she tried to ignore it, she felt betrayal, anger, humiliation. All pleasure had died from the evening. Now the kiss that had left her feeling clean and alive seemed cheap and shabby. No, she would not use his first name, she vowed. She would never use it. "If you'll excuse me, I have some things to do before my cue."

"Why the turnaround?" he asked, halting her with a hand on her arm. "Don't you like lawyers?"

Coldly, Jo studied him. She wondered how it was possible that she had completely misjudged the man she had met that morning. "I don't categorize people, Mr. Prescott."

"I see." Keane's tone became detached, his eyes assessing. "Then it would appear that you have an aversion to my name. Should I assume you hold a grudge against my father?''

Jo's eyes glittered with quick fury. She jerked her arm from his hold. ''Frank Prescott was the most generous, the kindest, most unselfish man I've ever known. I don't even associate you with Frank, Mr. Prescott. You have no right to him.'' Though it was nearly impossible, Jo forced herself to speak in a normal tone of voice. She would not shout and draw anyone's attention. This would be kept strictly between Keane Prescott and herself. ''It would have been much better if you had told me who you were right away, then there would have been no mix-up.''

''Is that what we've had?'' he countered mildly. ''A mix-up?''

His cool tone was nearly Jo's undoing. He watched her with a dispassionate curiosity that tempted her to slap him. She fought to keep her fury from spilling over into her voice. ''You have no right to Frank's circus, Mr. Prescott,'' she managed quietly. ''Leaving it to you is the only thing I've ever faulted him for.'' Knowing her control was slipping, Jo whirled, running across the grass until she merged with the darkness.

Chapter 3

The morning was surprisingly warm. There were no trees to block the sun, and the smell of the earth was strong. The circus had moved north in the early hours. All the usual scents merged into the aroma of circus: canvas, leather, sweating horses, greasepaint and powder, coffee and oilcloth. The trailers and trucks sat in the accustomed spots, forming the "back yard" that would always take the same formation each time the circus made a stop along the thousands of miles it traveled. The flag over the cookhouse tent signaled that lunch was being served. The Big Top stood waiting for the matinee.

Rose hurried along the midway toward the animal cages. Her dark hair was pinned neatly in a bun at the back of her neck. Her big brown eyes darted about searchingly, while her mouth sat softly in a pout. She was wrapped in a terry cloth robe and wore tennis shoes over her tights. When she saw Jo standing in front of Ari's cage, she waved and broke into a half-run. Watching her, Jo shifted her attention from Ari. Rose was always a diversion, and Jo felt in need of one.

"Jo!" She waved again as if Jo had not seen her the first time, then came to a breathless halt. "Jo, I only have a few minutes. Hello, Ari," she added out of politeness. "I was looking for Jamie."

"Yes, I gathered." Jo smiled, knowing Rose had set her heart on capturing Topo's alter ego. And if he had any sense, she thought, he'd let himself be caught instead of pining over Carmen. Silly, she decided, dismissing all affairs of the heart. Lions were easier to understand. "I haven't seen him all morning, Rose. Maybe he's rehearsing."

"Drooling over Carmen, more likely," Rose muttered, sending a sulky glare in the direction of the Gribalti trailer. "He makes a fool of himself."

"That's what he's paid for," Jo reminded her, but Rose did not respond to the humor. Jo sighed. She had a true affection for Rose. She was bright and fun and without pretentions. "Rose," she said, keeping her voice both light and kind. "Don't give up on him. He's a little slow, you know," she explained. "He's just a bit dazzled by Carmen right now. It'll pass."

"I don't know why I bother," she grumbled, but Jo saw the dark mood was already passing. Rose was a creature of quick passions that flared and soon died. "He's not so very handsome, you know."

"No," Jo agreed. "But he has a cute nose."

"Lucky for him I like red," Rose returned and grinned. "Ah, now we're speaking of handsome," she murmured as her eyes drifted from Jo. "Who is this?"

At the question, Jo glanced over her shoulder. The humor fled from her eyes. "That's the owner," she said colorlessly.

"Keane Prescott? No one told me he was so handsome. Or so tall," she added, admiring him openly as he crossed the back yard. Jo noted that Rose always became more Mexican around men. "Such shoulders. Lucky for Jamie I'm a one-man woman."

"Lucky for you your mama can't hear you," Jo muttered, earning an elbow in the ribs.

"But he comes here, *amiga,* and he looks at you. La, la, my papa would have Jamie to the altar *pronto* if he looked at me that way."

"You're an idiot," Jo snapped, annoyed.

"Ah, Jo," Rose said with mock despair. "I am a romantic."

Jo was helpless against the smile that tugged at her lips. Her eyes were laughing when she glanced up and met Keane's. Hastily, she struggled to dampen their brilliance, turning her mouth into a sober line.

"Good morning, Jovilette." He spoke her name too easily, she thought, as if he had been saying it for years.

"Good morning, Mr. Prescott," she returned. Rose gave a loud, none-too-subtle cough. "This is Rose Sanches."

"It's a pleasure, Mr. Prescott." Rose extended a hand, trying out a smile she had been saving for Jamie. "I heard you were traveling with us."

Keane accepted the hand and smiled in return. Jo noticed with annoyance that it was the same easy, disarming smile of the stranger she had met the morning before. "Hello, Rose, it's nice to meet you."

Seeing her friend's Mexican blood heat her cheeks, Jo intervened. She would not permit Keane Prescott to make a conquest here. "Rose, you only have ten minutes to get back and into makeup."

"Holy cow!" she said, forgetting her attempt at sophistication. "I've got to run." She began to do so, then called over her shoulder, "Don't tell Jamie I was looking for him, the pig!" She ran a little further, then turned and ran backwards. "I'll look for him later," she said with a laugh, then turned back and streaked toward the midway.

Keane watched her dart across the compound

while holding up the long skirts of her robe in one hand. "Charming."

"She's only eighteen," Jo offered before she could stop herself.

When Keane turned to her, his look was one of amusement. "I see," he said. "I'll take that information under advisement. And what does the eighteen-year-old Rose do?" he asked, slipping his thumbs into the front pockets of his jeans. "Wrestle alligators?"

"No." Jo returned without batting an eye. "Rose is Serpentina, your premier sideshow attraction. The snake charmer." She was pleased with the incredulous look that passed over his face. It was replaced quickly, however, with one of genuine humor.

"Perfect." He brushed Jo's hair from her cheek before she could protest by word or action. "Cobras?" he asked, ignoring the flash in her eyes.

"And boa constrictors," she returned sweetly. Jo brushed the dust from the knees of her faded jeans. "Now, if you'll excuse me…"

"No, I don't think so." Keane's voice was cool, but she recognized the underlying authority. She did her best not to struggle against it. He *was* the owner, she reminded herself.

"Mr. Prescott," she began, banking down hard on the urge to mutiny. "I'm very busy. I have to get ready for the afternoon show."

"You've got an hour and a half until you're on,"

he countered smoothly. "I think you might spare me a portion of that time. You've been assigned to show me around. Why don't we start now?" The tone of the question left room for only one answer. Jo's mind fidgeted in search of a way out.

Tilting her head back, she met his eyes. He won't be easy to beat, she concluded, studying his steady, measuring gaze. I'd better study his moves more carefully before I start a battle. "Where would you like to begin?" she asked aloud.

"With you."

Keane's easy answer brought a deep frown to Jo's brows. "I don't understand what you mean."

For a moment Keane watched her. There was no coyness or guile in her eyes as they looked into his. "No, I can see you don't," he agreed with a nod. "Let's start with your cats."

"Oh." Jo's frown cleared instantly. "All right." She watched as he pulled out a thin cigar, waiting until the flame of his lighter licked the tip before speaking. "I have thirteen—seven males, six females. They're all African lions between four-and-a-half and twenty-two years."

"I thought you worked with twelve," Keane commented as he dropped his lighter into his pocket.

"That's right, but Ari's retired." Turning, Jo indicated the large male lion dozing in a cage. "He travels with me because he always has, but I don't work him anymore. He's twenty-two, the oldest. My father kept him, even though he was born in captivity, because he was born the same day I was." Jo sighed, and her voice became softer. "He's the last of my father's stock. I couldn't sell him to a zoo. It seemed like shoving an old relative into a home and abandoning him. He's been with this circus every day of his life, just as I have. His name is Hebrew for *lion*." Jo laughed, forgetting the man beside her as she sifted through memories. "My father always gave his cats names that meant lion somehow or other. Leo, Leonard, Leonara. Ari was a first-class leaper in his prime. He could climb, too; some cats won't. I could teach Ari anything. Smart cat, aren't you, Ari?" The altered tone of her voice caused the big cat to stir. Opening his eyes, he stared back at Jo. The sound he made was more grumble than roar before he dozed again. "He's tired," Jo murmured, fighting a shaft of gloom. "Twenty-two's old for a lion."

"What is it?" Keane demanded, touching her shoulder before she could turn away. Her eyes were drenched with sadness.

"He's dying," she said unsteadily. "And I can't stop it." Stuffing her hands in her pockets, Jo moved away to the main group of cages. To steady herself, she took two deep breaths while waiting for Keane to join her. Regaining her composure, she began again. "I work with these twelve," she told him, making a sweeping gesture. "They're fed once a day, raw meat six days a week and eggs and milk on the seventh. They were all imported directly from Africa and were cage broken when I got them.''

The faint sound of a calliope reached them, signaling the opening of the midway. ''This is Merlin, the one I ride out on at the finish. He's ten, and the most even-tempered cat I've ever worked with. Heathcliff,'' she continued as she moved down the line of cages, ''he's six, my best leaper. And this is Faust, the baby at four and a half.'' The lions paced their cages as Jo walked Keane down the line. Unable to prevent herself, Jo gave Faust a signal by raising her hand. Obediently, he sent out a huge, deafening roar. To Jo's disappointment, Keane did not scramble for cover.

''Very impressive,'' he said mildly. ''You put him in the center when you lie down on them, don't you?''

''Yes.'' She frowned, then spoke her thoughts candidly. ''You're very observant—and you've got steady nerves.''

''My profession requires them, too, to an extent,'' he returned.

Jo considered this a moment, then turned back to the lions. ''Lazareth, he's twelve and a natural ham. Bolingbroke, he's ten, from the same lioness as Merlin. Hamlet,'' she said stopping again, ''he's five. I bought him to replace Ari in the act.'' Jo stared into the tawny eyes. ''He has potential, but he's arrogant.

Patient, too. He's just waiting for me to make a mistake.''

"Why?" Keane glanced over at Jo. Her eyes were cool and steady on Hamlet's.

"So he can get a good clean swipe at me," she told him without altering her expression. "It's his first season in the big cage. Pandora," Jo continued, pointing out the females. "A very classy lady. She's six. Hester, at seven, my best all-around. And Portia; it's her first year, too. She's mostly a seat-warmer."

"Seat-warmer?"

"Just what it sounds like," Jo explained. "She hasn't mastered any complicated tricks yet. She evens out the act, does a few basics and warms the seat." Jo moved on. "Dulcinea, the prettiest of the ladies. Ophelia, who had a litter last year; and Abra, eight, a bit bad-tempered but a good balancer."

Hearing her name, the cat rose, stretched her long, golden body, then began to rub it against the bars of the cage. A deep sound rumbled in her throat. Jo scowled and jammed her hands into her pockets. "She likes you," she muttered.

"Oh?" Lifting a brow, Keane studied the three-hundred-pound Abra more carefully. "How do you know?"

"When a lion likes you, it does exactly what a house cat does. It rubs against you. Abra's rubbing against the bars because she can't get any closer."

"I see." Humor touched his mouth. "I must ad-

mit, I'm at a loss on how to return the compliment.''
He drew on his cigar, then regarded Jo through a
haze of smoke. ''Your choice of names is fascinating.''

''I like to read,'' she stated, leaving it at that. ''Is
there anything else you'd like to know about the
cats?'' Jo was determined to keep their conversation
on a professional level. His smile had reminded her
all too clearly of their encounter the night before.

''Do you drug them before a performance?''

Fury sparked Jo's eyes. ''Certainly not.''

''Was that an unreasonable question?'' Keane
countered. He dropped his cigar to the ground, then
crushed it out with his heel.

''Not for a first of mayer,'' Jo decided with a sigh.
She tossed her hair carelessly behind her back.
''Drugging is not only cruel, it's stupid. A drugged
animal won't perform.''

''You don't touch the lions with that whip,''
Keane commented. He watched the light breeze
tease a few strands of her hair. ''Why do you use
it?''

''To get their attention and to keep the audience
awake.'' She smiled reluctantly.

Keane took her arm. Instantly, Jo stiffened. ''Let's
walk,'' he suggested. He began to lead her away
from the cages. Spotting several people roaming the
back yard, Jo refrained from pulling away. The last
thing she wanted was the story spreading that she

was having a tiff with the owner. "How do you tame them?" he asked her.

"I don't. They're not tame, they're trained." A tall blond woman walked by carrying a tiny white poodle. "Merlin's hungry today," Jo called out with a grin.

The woman bundled the dog closer to her breast in mock alarm and began a rapid scolding in French. Jo laughed, telling her in the same language that Fifi was too tough a mouthful for Merlin.

"Fifi can do a double somersault on the back of a moving horse," Jo explained as they began to walk again. "She's trained just as my cats are trained, but she's also domesticated. The cats are wild." Jo turned her face up to Keane's. The sun cast a sheen over her hair and threw gold flecks into her eyes. "A wild thing can never be tamed, and anyone who tries is foolish. If you take something wild and turn it into a pet, you've stolen its character, blanked out its spark. And still, there's always an essence of the wild that can come back to life. When a dog turns on his master, it's ugly. When a lion turns, it's lethal." She was beginning to become accustomed to his hand on her arm, finding it easy to talk to him because he listened. "A full-grown male stands three feet at the shoulder and weighs over five hundred pounds. One well-directed swipe can break a man's neck, not to mention what teeth and claws can do."

Jo gave a smile and a shrug. "Those aren't the virtues of a pet."

"Yet you go into a cage with twelve of them, armed with a whip?"

"The whip's window dressing." Jo discounted it with a gesture of her hand. "It would hardly be a defense against even one cat at full charge. A lion is a very tenacious enemy. A tiger is more bloodthirsty, but it normally strikes only once. If it misses, it takes it philosophically. A lion charges again and again. Do you know the line Byron wrote about a tiger's spring? 'Deadly, quick and crushing.'" Jo had completely forgotten her animosity and began to enjoy her walk and conversation with this handsome stranger. "It's a true description, but a lion is totally fearless when he charges, and stubborn. He's not the razzle-dazzle fighter the tiger is, just accurate. I'd bet on a lion against a tiger any day. And a man simply hasn't a prayer against one."

"Then how do you manage to stay in one piece?"

The calliope music was just a hint in the air now. Jo turned, noting with surprise that they had walked a good distance from camp. She could see the trailers and tents, hear occasional shouts and laughter, but she felt oddly separated from it all. She sat down cross-legged on the grass and plucked a blade. "I'm smarter than they are. At least I make them think so. And I dominate them, partly by a force of will. In training, you have to develop a rapport, a mutual respect, and if you're lucky, a certain affection. But you can't trust them to the point where you grow careless. And above all," she added, glancing over as he sat down beside her, "you have to remember the basic rule of poker. Bluff." Jo grinned, leaning back on her elbows. "Do you play poker?"

"I've been known to." Her hair trailed out along the grass, and he lifted a strand. "Do you?"

"Sometimes. My assistant handler, Pete..." Jo scanned the back yard, then smiled and pointed. "There he is, by the second trailer, sitting with Mac Stevenson, the one with the fielder's cap. Pete organizes a game now and then."

"Who's the little girl on stilts?"

"That's Mac's youngest, Katie. She wants to walk on them in the street parade. She's getting pretty good. There's Jamie," she said, then laughed as he did a pratfall and landed at Katie's wooden stilts.

"Rose's Jamie?" Keane asked, watching the impromptu show in the back yard.

"If she has her way. He's currently dazzled by Carmen Gribalti. Carmen won't give Jamie the time of day. She bats her lashes at Vito, the wire walker. He bats his at everyone."

"A complicated state of affairs," Keane commented. He twisted Jo's hair around his fingers. "Romance seems to be very popular in circus life."

"From what I read," she countered, "it's popular everywhere."

"Who dazzles you, Jovilette?" He gave her hair a tug to bring her face around to his.

Jo hadn't realized he was so close. She need do no more than sway for her mouth to touch his. Her eyes measured his while she waited for her pulse to calm. It was odd, she thought, that he had such an effect on her. With sudden clarity, she could smell the grass, a clean, sweet scent, and feel the sun. The sounds of the circus were muted in the background. She could hear birds call out with an occasional high-pitched trill. She remembered the taste of his mouth and wondered if it would be the same.

"I've been too busy to be dazzled," she replied. Her voice was steady, but her eyes were curious.

For the first time, Jo truly *wanted* to be kissed by a man. She wanted to feel again what she had felt the night before. She wanted to be held, not lightly as he had held her before, but close, with his arms tight around her. She wanted to renew the feeling of weightlessness. She had never experienced a strong physical desire, and for a moment she explored the sensation. There was a quiver in her stomach which was both pleasant and disturbing. Throughout her silent contemplations Keane watched her, intrigued by the intensity of her eyes.

"What are you thinking of?"

"I'm wondering why you make me feel so odd," she told him with simple frankness. He smiled, and she noticed that it grew in his eyes seconds before it grew on his mouth.

"Do I?" He appeared to enjoy the information. "Did you know your hair catches the sunlight?" Keane took a handful, letting it spill from between his fingers. "I've never seen another woman with hair like this. It's a temptation all in itself. In what way do I make you feel odd, Jovilette?" he asked as his eyes trailed back up to hers.

"I'm not sure yet." Jo found her voice husky. Abruptly, she decided it would not do to go on feeling odd or to go on wanting to be kissed by Keane Prescott. She scrambled up and brushed off the seat of her pants.

"Running away?" As Keane rose, Jo's head snapped up.

"I never run away from anything, Mr. Prescott." Ice sharpened her voice. She was annoyed that she had allowed herself to fall under his charm again. "I certainly won't run from a city-bred lawyer." Her words were laced with scorn. "Why don't you go back to Chicago and get someone thrown in jail?"

"I'm a defense attorney," Keane countered easily. "I get people out of jail."

"Fine. Go put a criminal back on the streets, then."

Keane laughed, bringing Jo's temper even closer to the surface. "That covers both sides of the issue, doesn't it? You dazzle me, Jovilette."

"Well, it's strictly unintentional." She took a step back from the amusement in his eyes. She would not tolerate him making fun of her. "You don't belong here," she blurted out. "You have no business here."

"On the contrary," he disagreed in a cool, untroubled voice. "I have every business here. I own this circus."

"Why?" she demanded, throwing out her hands as if to push his words aside. "Because it says so on a piece of paper? That's all lawyers understand, I imagine—pieces of paper with strange little words. Why did you come? To look us over and calculate the profit and loss? What's the liquidation value of a dream, Mr. Prescott? What price do you put on the human spirit? Look at it!" she demanded, swinging her arm to encompass the lot behind them. "You only see tents and a huddle of trailers. You can't possibly understand what it all means. But Frank understood. He loved it."

"I'm aware of that." Keane's voice was still calm but had taken on a thin edge of steel. Jo saw that his eyes had grown dark and guarded. "He also left it to me."

"I don't understand why." In frustration, Jo stuffed her hands in her pockets and turned away.

"Neither do I, I assure you, but the fact remains that he did."

"Not once in thirty years did you visit him." Jo

whirled back around. Her hair followed in a passionate arch. "Not once."

"Quite true," Keane agreed. He stood with his weight even on both legs and watched her. "Of course, some might look at it differently. Not once in thirty years did he visit me."

"Your mother left him and took you to Chicago—"

"I won't discuss my mother," Keane interrupted in a tone of clipped finality.

Jo bit off a retort, spinning away from him again. Still she could not find the reins to her control. "What are you going to do with it?" she demanded.

"That's my business."

"Oh!" Jo spun back, then shut her eyes and muttered in a language he failed to understand. "Can you be so arrogant? Can you be so dispassionate?" Her lashes fluttered up, revealing eyes dark with anger. "Do the lives of all those people mean nothing to you? Does Frank's dream mean nothing? Haven't you enough money already without hurting people to get more? Greed isn't something you inherited from Frank."

"I'll only be pushed so far," Keane warned.

"I'd push you all the way back to Chicago if I could manage it," she snapped.

"I wondered how much of a temper there was behind those sharp green eyes," Keane commented, watching her passion pour color into her cheeks. "It appears it's a full-grown one.'' Jo started to retort, but Keane cut her off. ''Just hold on a minute,'' he ordered. ''With or without your approval, I own this circus. It might be easier for you if you adjusted to that. Be quiet,'' he added when her mouth opened again. ''Legally, I can do with my—'' He hesitated a moment, then continued in a mordant tone. ''—inheritance as I choose. I have no obligation or intention of justifying my decision to you.''

Jo dug her nails into her palms to help keep her voice from shaking. ''I never knew I could grow to dislike someone so quickly.''

''Jovilette.'' Keane dipped his hands into his pockets, then rocked back on his heels. ''You disliked me before you ever saw me.''

''That's true,'' she replied evenly. ''But I've learned to dislike you in person in less than twenty-four hours. I have a show to do,'' she said, turning back toward the lot. Though he did not follow, she felt his eyes on her until she reached her trailer and closed the door behind her.

Thirty minutes later Jamie sprang through the back door of the Big Top. He was breathless after a lengthy routine and hooked one hand through his purple suspenders as he took in gulps of air. He spotted Jo standing beside the white mare. Her eyes were dark and stormy, her shoulders set and rigid. Jamie recognized the signs. Something or someone had put

Jo in a temper, and she had barely ten minutes to work her way out of it before her cue.

He crossed to her and gave a tug on her hair. "Hey."

"Hello, Jamie." Jo struggled to keep her voice pleasant, but he heard the traces of emotion.

"Hello, Jo," he replied in precisely the same tone.

"Cut it out," she ordered before taking a few steps away. The mare followed docilely. Jo had been trying for some time to put her emotions back into some semblance of order. She was not succeeding.

"What happened?" Jamie asked from directly behind her.

"Nothing," Jo snapped, then hated herself for the short nastiness of the word.

Jamie persisted, knowing her too well to be offended. "Nothing is one of my favorite topics of conversation." He put his hands on her shoulders, ignoring her quick, bad-tempered jerk. "Let's talk about it."

"There's nothing to talk about."

"Exactly." He began massaging the tension in her shoulders with his white gloved hands.

"Oh, Jamie." His good-heartedness was irresistible. Sighing, she allowed herself to be soothed. "You're an idiot."

"I'm not here to be flattered."

"I had an argument with the owner." Jo let out a long breath and shut her eyes.

"What're you doing having arguments with the owner?"

"He infuriates me." Jo whirled around. Her cape whipped and snapped with the movement. "He shouldn't be here. If he were back in Chicago…"

"Hold it." With a slight shake of her shoulders, Jamie halted Jo's outburst. "You know better than to get yourself worked up like this right before a show. You can't afford to have your mind on anything but what you're doing when you're in that cage."

"I'll be all right," she mumbled.

"Jo." There was censure in his voice mixed with affection and exasperation.

Reluctantly, Jo brought her gaze up to his. It was impossible to resist the grave eyes in the brightly painted face. With something between a sigh and a moan, she dropped her forehead to his chest. "Jamie, he makes me so mad! He could ruin everything."

"Let's worry about it when the time comes," Jamie suggested, patting her hair.

"But he doesn't understand us. He doesn't understand anything."

"Well, then it's up to us to make him understand, isn't it?"

Jo looked up and wrinkled her nose. "You're so logical."

"Of course I am," he agreed and struck a pose.

As he wiggled his orange eyebrows, Jo laughed. "Okay?" he asked, then picked up his prop bucket.

"Okay," she agreed and smiled.

"Good, 'cause there's my cue."

When he disappeared behind the flap, Jo leaned her cheek against the mare and nuzzled a moment. "I don't think I'm the one to make him understand, though."

I wish he'd never come, she added silently as she vaulted onto the mare's back. I wish I'd never noticed how his eyes are like Ari's and how nice his mouth is when he smiles, she thought. Jo ran the tip of her tongue gingerly over her lips. I wish he'd never kissed me. *Liar.* Her conscience spoke softly in her ear: *Admit it, you're glad he kissed you. You've never felt anything like that before, and no matter what, you're glad he kissed you last night. You even wanted him to kiss you again today.*

She forced her mind clear, taking deep, even breaths until she heard the ringmaster announce her. With a flick of her heels, she sent the mare sprinting into the tent.

It did not go well. The audience cheered her, oblivious to any problem, but Jo was aware that the routine was far from smooth. And the cats sensed her preoccupation. Again and again they tested her, and again and again Jo was forced to alter her timing to compensate. When the act was over, her head throbbed from the strain of concentration. Her hands were clammy as she turned Merlin over to Buck.

The big man came back to her after securing the cage. "What's the matter with you?" he demanded without preamble. By the underlying and very rare anger in his voice, Jo knew he had observed at least a portion of her act. Unlike the audience, Buck would note any deviation. "You go in the cage like that again, one of those cats is going to find out what you taste like."

"My timing was a little off, that's all." Jo fought against the trembling in her stomach and tried to sound casual.

"A little?" Buck glowered, looking formidable behind the mass of blond beard. "Who do you think you're fooling? I've been around these ugly cats since before you were born. When you go in the cage, you've got to take your brain in with you."

Only too aware that he was right, Jo conceded. "I know, Buck. You're right." With a weary hand she pushed back her hair. "It won't happen again. I guess I was tired and a little off-balance." She sent him an apologetic smile.

Buck frowned and shuffled. Never in his forty-five years had he managed to resist feminine smiles. "All right," he muttered, then sniffed and made his voice firm. "But you go take a nap right after the finale. No coffee. I don't want to see you around again until dinner time."

"Okay, Buck." Jo kept her voice humble, though she was tempted to grin. The weakness was going out of her legs, and the dull buzz of fear was fading from between her temples. Still she felt exhausted and agreeable to Buck's uncharacteristic tone of command. A nap, she decided as Buck drove Merlin away, was just what she needed, not to mention that it was as good a way as any to avoid Keane Prescott for the rest of the day. Shooing this thought aside, Jo decided to while away the time until the finale in casual conversation with Vito the wire walker.

Chapter 4

It rained for three days. It was a solid downpour, not heavy but insistent. As the circus wound its way north, the rain followed. Nevertheless, canvas men pitched the tents in soggy fields and muddy lots while straw was laid on the hippodrome track and performers scurried from trailers to tents under dripping umbrellas.

The lot near Waycross, Georgia, was scattered with puddles under a thick, gray sky. Jo could only be grateful that no evening show had been scheduled. By six, it was nearly dark, with a chill teasing the damp air. She hustled from the cookhouse after an early supper. She would check on the cats, she decided, then closet herself in her trailer, draw the curtains against the rain and curl up with a book. Shivering, she concluded that the idea was inspired.

She carried no umbrella but sought questionable shelter under a gray rolled-brimmed hat and thin windbreaker. Keeping her head lowered, she jogged across the mud, skimming around or hopping over puddles. She hummed lightly, anticipating the simple pleasures of an idle evening. Her humming ended in a muffled gasp as she ran into a solid object. Fingers wrapped around her upper arms. Even before she lifted her head, Jo knew it was Keane who held her. She recognized his touch. Through some clever maneuvering, she had managed to avoid being alone with him since they had walked together and looked back on the circus.

"Excuse me, Mr. Prescott. I'm afraid I wasn't looking where I was going."

"Perhaps the weather's dampened your radar, Jovilette." He made no move to release her. Annoyed, Jo was forced to hold her hat steady with one hand as she tilted her head to meet his eyes. Rain fell cool on her face.

"I don't know what you mean."

"Oh, I think you do," Keane countered. "There's not another soul around. You've been careful to keep yourself in a crowd for days."

Jo blinked rain from her lashes. She admitted ruefully that it had been foolish to suppose he wouldn't notice her ploy. She saw he carried no umbrella either, nor did he bother with a hat. His hair was darkened with rain, much the same color that one of her cats would be if caught in an unexpected shower. It was difficult, in the murky light, to clearly make out his features, but the rain could not disguise his mockery.

"That's an interesting observation, Mr. Prescott," Jo said coolly. "Now, if you don't mind, I'm getting wet." She was surprised when she remained in his hold after a strong attempt on her part to pull away. Frowning, she put both hands against his chest and pushed. She discovered that she had been wrong; under the lean frame was an amazing amount of strength. Infuriated that she had misjudged him and that she was outmatched, Jo raised her eyes again. "Let me go," she demanded between clenched teeth.

"No," Keane returned mildly. "I don't believe I will."

Jo glared at him. "Mr. Prescott, I'm cold and wet and I'd like to go to my trailer. Now, what do you want?"

"First, I want you to stop calling me Mr. Prescott." Jo pouted but she kept silent. "Second, I'd like an hour of your time for going over a list of personnel." He paused. Through her windbreaker Jo could feel his fingers unyielding on her arms.

"Is there anything else?" she demanded, trying to sound bored.

For a moment there was only the sound of rain drumming on the ground and splashing into puddles. "Yes," Keane said quietly. "I think I'll just get this out of my system."

Jo's instincts were swift but they were standing too close for her to evade him. And he was quick. Her protest was muffled against his mouth. Her arms were pinioned to her sides as his locked around her. Jo had felt a man's body against her own before— working out with the tumblers, practicing with the equestrians—but never with such clarity as this. She was aware of Keane in every fiber of her being. His body was whipcord lean and hard, his arms holding the strength she had discounted the first time she had seen him. But more, it was his mouth that mystified her. Now it was not gentle or testing; it took and plundered and demanded more before she could withhold a response.

Jo forgot the rain, though it continued to fall against her face. She forgot the cold. The warmth spread from inside, where her blood flowed fast, as her body was molded to Keane's. She forgot herself, or the woman she had thought herself to be, and discovered another. When he lifted his mouth, Jo kept her eyes closed, savoring the lingering pleasures, inviting fresh ones.

''More?'' he murmured as his hand trailed up, then down her spine. Heat raced after it. ''Kissing can be a dangerous pastime, Jo.'' He lowered his mouth again, then nipped at her soft bottom lip. ''But you know all about danger, don't you?'' He kissed her hard, leaving her breathless. ''How courageous are you without your cats?''

Suddenly her heart raced to her throat. Her legs became rubbery, and a tingle sprinted up her spine. Jo recognized the feeling. It was the way she felt when she experienced a close call with the cats. Reaction would set in after the door of the safety cage locked behind her and the crisis had passed. It was then that fear found her. She studied Keane's bold, amber eyes, and her mouth went dry. She shuddered.

''You're cold.'' His voice was abruptly brisk. ''Small wonder. We'll go to my trailer and get you some coffee.''

''No!'' Jo's protest was sharp and instantaneous. She knew she was vulnerable and she knew as well that she did not yet possess the experience to fight him. To be alone with him now was too great a risk.

Keane drew her away, but his grip remained firm. She could not read his expression as he searched her face. ''What happened just now was personal,'' he told her. ''Strictly man to woman. I'm of the opinion that love making should be personal. You're an appealing armful, Jovilette, and I'm accustomed to taking what I want, one way or another.''

His words were like a shot of adrenaline. Jo's chin thrust forward, and her eyes flamed. ''No one *takes* me, one way or another.'' She spoke with the deadly calm of fury. ''If I make love with anyone, it's only because I want to.''

''Of course,'' Keane agreed with an easy nod. ''We're both aware you'll be willing when the time comes. We could make love quite successfully tonight, but I think it best if we know each other better first.''

Jo's mouth trembled open and closed twice before she could speak. ''Of all the arrogant, outrageous…''

''Truthful,'' Keane supplied, tossing her into incoherency again. ''But for now, we have business, and while I don't mind kissing in the rain, I prefer to conduct business in a drier climate.'' He held up a hand as Jo started to protest. ''I told you, the kiss was between a man and a woman. The business we have now is between the owner of this circus and a performer under contract. Understood?''

Jo took a long, deep breath to bring her voice to a normal level. ''Understood,'' she agreed. Without another word she let him lead her across the slippery lot.

When they reached Keane's trailer, he hustled Jo

inside without preliminaries. She blinked against the change in light when he hit the wall switch. "Take off your coat," he said briskly, pulling down her zipper before she could perform the task for herself. Instinctively, her hand reached for it as she took a step backward. Keane merely lifted a brow, then stripped off his own jacket. "I'll get the coffee." He moved down the length of the narrow trailer and disappeared around the corner where the tiny kitchen was set.

Slowly, Jo pulled off her dripping hat, letting her hair tumble free from where it had been piled under its confinement. With automatic movements she hung both her hat and coat on the hooks by the trailer door. It had been almost six months since she had stood in Frank's trailer, and like a woman visiting an old friend, she searched for changes.

The same faded lampshade adorned the maple table lamp that Frank had used for reading. The shade sat straight now, however, not at its usual slightly askew angle. The pillow that Lillie from wardrobe had sewn for him on some long-ago Christmas still sat over the small burn hole in the seat cushion of the couch. Jo doubted that Keane knew of the hole's existence. Frank's pipe stand sat, as always, on the counter by the side window. Unable to resist, Jo crossed over to run her finger over the worn bowl of his favorite pipe.

"Never could pack it right," she murmured to his well-loved ghost. Abruptly, her senses quivered. She twisted her head to see Keane watching her. Jo dropped her hand. A rare blush mantled her cheeks as she found herself caught unguarded.

"How do you take your coffee, Jo?"

She swallowed. "Black," she told him, aware that he was granting her the privacy of her thoughts. "Just black. Thank you."

Keane nodded, then turned to pick up two steaming mugs. "Come, sit down." He moved toward the Formica table that sat directly across from the kitchen. "You'd better take off your shoes. They're wet."

After squeaking her way down the length of the trailer, Jo sat down and pulled at the damp laces. Keane set both mugs on the table before disappearing into the back of the trailer. When he returned, Jo was already sipping at the coffee.

"Here." He offered her a pair of socks.

Surprised, Jo shook her head. "No, that's all right. I don't need…"

Her polite refusal trailed off as he knelt at her feet. "Your feet are like ice," he commented after cupping them in his palms. Briskly, he rubbed them while Jo sat mute, oddly disarmed by the gesture. The warmth was spreading dangerously past her ankles. "Since I'm responsible for keeping you out in the rain," he went on as he slipped a sock over her foot, "I'd best see to it you don't cough and sneeze your way through tomorrow's show. Such small feet," he murmured, running his thumb over the curve of her ankle as she stared wordlessly at the top of his head.

Raindrops still clung to and glistened in his hair. Jo found herself longing to brush them away and feel the texture of his hair beneath her fingers. She was sharply aware of him and wondered if it would always be this way when she was near him. Keane pulled on the second sock. His fingers lingered on her calf as he lifted his eyes. Hers were darkened with confusion as they met his. The body over which she had always held supreme control was journeying into frontiers her mind had not yet explored.

"Still cold?" Keane asked softly.

Jo moistened her lips and shook her head. "No. No, I'm fine."

He smiled a lazy, masculine smile that said as clearly as words that he was aware of his effect on her. His eyes told her he enjoyed it. Unsmiling, Jo watched him rise to his feet.

"It doesn't mean you'll win," she said aloud in response to their silent communication.

"No, it doesn't." Keane's smile remained as his gaze roamed possessively over her face. "That only makes it more interesting. Open and shut cases are invariably boring, hardly worth the trouble of going on if you've won before you've finished your opening statement."

Jo lifted her coffee and sipped, taking a moment to settle her nerves. "Are we here to discuss the law or circus business, counselor?" she asked, letting her eyes drift to his again as she set the mug back on the table. "If it's law, I'm afraid I'm going to disappoint you. I don't know much about it."

"What do you know about, Jovilette?" Keane slid into the chair beside hers.

"Cats," she said. "And Prescott's Circus Colossus. I'll be glad to let you know whatever I can about either."

"Tell me about you," he countered, and leaning back, pulled a cigar from his pocket.

"Mr. Prescott—" Jo began.

"Keane," he interrupted, flicking on his lighter. He glanced at the tip of his cigar, then back up at her through the thin haze of smoke.

"I was under the impression you wanted to be briefed on the personnel."

"You are a member of this circus, are you not?" Casually, Keane blew smoke at the ceiling. "I have every intention of being briefed on the entire troupe and see no reason why you shouldn't start with yourself." His eyes traveled back to hers. "Humor me."

Jo decided to take the line of least resistance. "It's

a short enough story," she said with a shrug. "I've been with the circus all my life. When I was old enough, I started work as a generally useful."

"A what?" Keane paused in the action of reaching for the coffeepot.

"Generally useful," Jo repeated, letting him freshen her cup. "It's a circus term that means exactly what it says. Rose's parents, for instance, are generally usefuls. We get a lot of drifters who work that way, too. It's also written into every performer's contract, after the specific terms, that they make themselves generally useful. There isn't room in most circuses, and certainly not in a tent circus, for performers with star complexes. You do what's necessary, what's needed. Buck, my handler, fills in during a slump at the sideshow, and he's one of the best canvas men around. Pete is the best mechanic in the troupe. Jamie knows as much about lighting as most shandies—electricians," she supplied as Keane lifted a brow. "He's also a better-than-average tumbler."

"What about you?" Keane interrupted the flow of Jo's words. For a moment she faltered, and the hands that had been gesturing became still. "Besides riding a galloping horse without reins or saddle, giving orders to elephants and facing lions?" He lifted his cup, watching her as he sipped. A smile lurked in his eyes. Jo frowned, studying him.

"Are you making fun of me?"

His smile sobered instantly. "No, Jo, I'm not making fun of you."

She continued. "In a pinch, I run the menagerie in the sideshow or I fill in the aerial act. Not the trap," she explained, relaxing again. "They have to practice together constantly to keep the timing. But sometimes I fill in on the Spanish Web, the big costume number where the girls hang from ropes and do identical moves. They're using butterfly costumes this year."

"Yes, I know the one." Keane continued to watch her as he drew on his cigar.

"But mostly Duffy likes to use girls who are more curvy. They double as showgirls in the finale."

"I see." A smile tugged at the corners of Keane's mouth. "Tell me, were your parents European?"

"No." Diverted, Jo shook her head. "Why do you ask?"

"Your name. And the ease with which I've heard you speak both French and Italian."

"It's easy to pick up languages in the circus," Jo said.

"Your accent was perfect in both cases."

"What? Oh." She shrugged and absently shifted in her chair, bringing her feet up to sit cross-legged. "We have a wide variety of nationalities here. Frank used to say that the world could take a lesson from the circus. We have French, Italian, Spanish, German, Russian, Mexican, Americans from all parts of the country and more.''

"I know. It's like a traveling United Nations.'' He tipped his cigar ash in a glass tray. "So you picked up some French and Italian along the way. But if you've traveled with the circus all your life, what about the rest of your schooling?''

The hint of censure in his voice brought up her chin. "I went to school during the winter break and had a tutor on the road. I learned my ABC's, counselor, and a bit more, besides. I probably know more about geography and world history than you, and from more interesting sources than textbooks. I imagine I know more about animals than a third-year veterinary student and have more practical experience healing them. I can speak seven languages and—''

"Seven?'' Keane interrupted. "Seven languages?''

"Well, five fluently,'' she corrected grudgingly. "I still have a bit of trouble with Greek and German, unless I can really take my time, and I can't read Greek yet at all.''

"What else besides French, Italian and English?''

"Spanish and Russian.'' Jo scowled into her coffee. "The Russian's handy. I use it for swearing at the cats during the act. Not too many people understand Russian cursing, so it's safe.''

Keane's laughter brought Jo's attention from her coffee. He was leaning back in his chair, his eyes gold with their mirth. Jo's scowl deepened. ''What's so funny?''

''You are, Jovilette.'' Stung, she started to scramble up, but his hands on her shoulders stopped her. ''No, don't be offended. I can't help but find it amusing that you toss out so offhandedly an accomplishment that any language major would brag about.'' Carelessly, he ran a finger over her sulky mouth. ''You continually amaze me.'' He brushed a hand through her hair. ''You mumbled something at me the other day. Were you swearing at me in Russian?''

''Probably.''

Grinning, Keane dropped his hand and settled into his chair again. ''When did you start working with the cats?''

''In front of an audience? When I was seventeen. Frank wouldn't let me start any earlier. He was my legal guardian as well as the owner, so he had me both ways. I was ready when I was fifteen.''

''How did you lose your parents?''

The question caught her off guard. ''In a fire,'' she said levelly. ''When I was seven.''

''Here?''

She knew Keane was not referring to their locale but to the circus. Jo sipped her cooling coffee. "Yes."

"Didn't you have any other family?"

"The circus is a family," she countered. "I was never given the chance to be an orphan. And I always had Frank."

"Did you?" Keane's smile was faintly sarcastic. "How was he as a father figure?"

Jo studied him for a moment. Was he bitter? she wondered. Or amused? Or simply curious? "He never took my father's place," she replied quietly. "He never tried to, because neither of us wanted it. We were friends, as close as I think it's possible for friends to be, but I'd already had a father, and he'd already had a child. We weren't looking for substitutes. You look nothing like him, you know."

"No," Keane replied with a shrug. "I know."

"He had a comfortable face, all creases and folds." Jo smiled, thinking of it while she ran a finger absently around the rim of her mug. "He was dark, too, just beginning to gray when..." She trailed off, then brought herself back with a quick shake of her head. "Your voice is rather like his, though; he had a truly beautiful voice. I'll ask you a question now."

Keane's expression became attentive, then he gestured with the back of his hand. "Go ahead."

"Why are you here? I lost my temper when I asked you before, but I do want to know." It was against her nature to probe, and some of her discomfort found its way into her voice. "It must have caused you some difficulty to leave your practice, even for a few weeks."

Keane frowned at the end of his cigar before he slowly crushed it out. "Let's say I wanted to see firsthand what had fascinated my father all these years."

"You never came when he was alive." Jo gripped her hands together under the table. "You didn't even bother to come to his funeral."

"I would've been the worst kind of hypocrite to attend his funeral, don't you think?"

"He was your father." Jo's eyes grew dark and her tone sharp in reproof.

"You're smarter than that, Jo," Keane countered calmly. "It takes more than an accident of birth to make a father. Frank Prescott was a complete stranger to me."

"You resent him." Jo felt suddenly torn between loyalty for Frank and understanding for the man who sat beside her.

"No." Keane shook his head thoughtfully. "No, I believe I actively resented him when I was growing up, but…" He shrugged the thought aside. "I grew rather ambivalent over the years."

"He was a good man," Jo stated, leaning forward as she willed him to understand. "He only wanted to give people pleasure, to show them a little magic. Maybe he wasn't made to be a father—some men aren't—but he was kind and gentle. And he was proud of you."

"Of me?" Keane seemed amused. "How?"

"Oh, you're hateful," Jo whispered, hurt by his careless attitude. She slipped from her chair, but before she could step away, Keane took her arm.

"No, tell me. I'm interested." His hold on her arm was light, but she knew it would tighten if she resisted.

"All right." Jo tossed her head to send her hair behind her back. "He had the Chicago paper delivered to his Florida office. He always looked for any mention of you, any article on a court case you were involved in or a dinner party you attended. Anything. You have to understand that to us a write-up is very important. Frank wasn't a performer, but he was one of us. Sometimes he'd read me an article before he put it away. He kept a scrapbook."

Jo pulled her arm away and strode past Keane into the bedroom. The oversize wooden chest was where it had always been, at the foot of Frank's bed. Kneeling down, Jo tossed up the lid. "This is where he kept all the things that mattered to him." Jo began to shift through papers and mementos quickly; she had not been able to bring herself to sort through the chest before. Keane stood in the doorway and watched her. "He called it his memory box." She pushed at her hair with an annoyed hand, then continued to search. "He said memories were the rewards for growing old. Here it is." Jo pulled out a dark green scrapbook, then sat back on her heels. Silently, she held it out to Keane. After a moment he crossed the room and took it from her. Jo could hear the rain hissing on the ground outside as their eyes held. His expression was unfathomable as he opened the book. The pages rustled to join the quiet sound of the rain.

"What an odd man he must have been," Keane murmured, "to keep a scrapbook on a son he never knew." There was no rancor in his voice. "What was he?" he asked suddenly, shifting his eyes back to Jo.

"A dreamer," she answered. "His watch was always five minutes slow. If he hung a picture on the wall, it was always crooked. He'd never straighten it because he'd never notice. He was always thinking about tomorrow. I guess that's why he kept yesterday in this box." Glancing down, she began to straighten the chaos she had caused while looking for the book. A snatch of red caught her eye. Reaching for it, her fingers found a familiar shape. Jo hesitated, then drew the old doll out of the chest.

It was a sad piece of plastic and faded silk with its face nearly washed away. One arm was broken off, leaving an empty sleeve. The golden hair was straggled but brave under its red cap. Ballet shoes were painted on the dainty feet. Tears backed up behind Jo's eyes as she made a soft sound of joy and despair.

"What is it?" Keane demanded, glancing down to see her clutching the battered ballerina.

"Nothing." Her voice was unsteady as she scrambled quickly to her feet. "I have to go." Though she tried, Jo could not bring herself to drop the doll back into the box. She swallowed. She did not wish to reveal her emotions before his intelligent, gold eyes. Perhaps he would be cynical, or worse, amused. "May I have this, please?" She was careful with the tone of the request.

Slowly, Keane crossed the distance between them, then cradled her chin in his hand. "It appears to be yours already."

"It was." Her fingers tightened on the doll's waist. "I didn't know Frank had kept it. Please," she whispered. Her emotions were already dangerously heightened. She could feel a need to rest her head against his shoulder. The evening had been a roller coaster for her feelings, climaxing now with the discovery of her most prized childhood possession. She knew that if she did not escape, she would

seek comfort in his arms. Her own weakness frightened her. "Let me by."

For a moment, Jo read refusal in his eyes. Then
he stepped aside. Jo let out a quiet, shaky breath.
"I'll walk you back to your trailer."

"No," she said quickly, too quickly. "It isn't necessary," she amended, moving by him and into the
kitchen. Sitting down, she pulled on her shoes, too
distraught to remember she still wore his socks.
"There's no reason for us both to get wet again."
She rambled on, knowing he was watching her hurried movement, but unable to stop. "And I'm going
to check on my cats before I go in, and..."

She stopped short when he took her shoulders and
pulled her to her feet. "And you don't want to take
the chance of being alone in your trailer with me in
case I change my mind."

A sharp denial trembled on her lips, but the
knowledge in his eyes crushed it. "All right," she
admitted. "That, too."

Keane brushed her hair from her neck and shook
his head. He kissed her nose and moved down to
pluck her hat and coat from their hooks. Cautiously,
Jo followed him. When he held out her coat, she
turned and slipped her arms into the sleeves. Before
she could murmur her thanks, he turned her back
and pulled up the zipper. For a moment his fingers
lingered at her neck, his eyes on hers. Taking her

hair into his hand, he piled it atop her head, then dropped on her hat. The gestures were innocent, but Jo was rocked by a feeling of intimacy she had never experienced.

"I'll see you tomorrow," he said, pulling the brim of her hat down further over her eyes.

Jo nodded. Holding the doll against her side, she pushed open the door. The sound of rain was amplified through the trailer. "Good night," she murmured, then moved quickly into the night.

Chapter 5

The morning scent was clean. In the new lot rainbows glistened in puddles. At last the sky was blue with only harmless white puffs of clouds floating over its surface. In the cookhouse a loud, crowded breakfast was being served. Finding herself without appetite, Jo skipped going to the cookhouse altogether. She was restless and tense. No matter how she disciplined her mind, her thoughts wandered back to Keane Prescott and to the evening they had spent together. Jo remembered it all, from the quick passion of the kiss in the rain to the calmness of his voice when he had said good-night. It was odd, she mused, that whenever she began to talk to him, she forgot he was the owner, forgot he was Frank's son.

Always she was forced to remind herself of their positions.

Deep in thought, Jo slipped into tights and a leotard. It was true, she admitted, that she had failed to keep their relationship from becoming personal. She found it difficult to corral her urge to laugh with him, to share a joke, to open for him the doorway to the magic of the circus. If he could feel it, she thought, he would understand. Though she could admit her interest in him privately, she could not find a clear reason for his apparent interest in her.

Why me? she wondered with a shake of her head. Turning, she opened her wardrobe closet and studied herself in the full-length glass on the back of the door. There she saw a woman of slightly less-than-average height with a body lacking the generous curves of Duffy's showgirls. The legs, she decided, were not bad. They were long and well-shaped with slim thighs. The hips were narrow, more, she thought with a pout, like a boy's than a woman's; and the bustline was sadly inadequate. She knew many women in the troupe with more appeal and a dozen with more experience.

Jo could see nothing in the mirror that would attract a sophisticated Chicago attorney. She did not note the honesty that shone from the exotically shaped green eyes or the strength in her chin or the full promise of her mouth. She saw the touch of gypsy in the tawny complexion and raven hair but remained unaware of the appeal that came from the hint of something wild and untamed just under the surface. The plain black leotard showed her firm, lithe body to perfection, but Jo thought nothing of the smooth satiny sheen of her skin. She was frowning as she pulled her hair back and began to braid it.

He must know dozens of women, she thought as her hands worked to confine her thick mane of hair. He probably takes a different one to dinner every night. They wear beautiful clothes and expensive perfume, she mused, torturing herself with the thought. They have names like Laura and Patricia, and they have low, sophisticated laughs. Jo lifted a brow at the reflection in the mirror and gave a light, low laugh. She wrinkled her brow at the hollowness of the sound. They discuss mutual friends, the Wallaces or the Jamesons, over candlelight and Beaujolais. And when he takes the most beautiful one home, they listen to Chopin and drink brandy in front of the fire. Then they make love. Jo felt an odd tightening in her stomach but pursued the fantasy to the finish. The lovely lady is experienced, passionate and worldly. Her skin is soft and white. When he leaves, she is not devastated but mature. She doesn't even care if he loves her or not.

Jo stared at the woman in the glass and saw her

cheeks were wet. On a cry of frustration, she slammed the door shut. *What's wrong with me?* she demanded, brushing all traces of tears from her face. I haven't been myself for days! I need to shake myself out of this—this...whatever it is that I'm in. Slipping on gymnastic shoes and tossing a robe over her arm, Jo hustled from the trailer.

She moved carefully, avoiding puddles and any further speculation on Keane Prescott's romantic life. Before she was halfway across the lot, she saw Rose. From the expression on her face, Jo could see she was in a temper.

"Hello, Rose," she said, strategically stepping aside as the snake charmer splashed through a puddle.

"He's hopeless," Rose tossed back. "I tell you," she continued, stopping and wagging a finger at Jo, "I'm through this time. Why should I waste my time?"

"You've certainly been patient," Jo agreed, deciding that sympathy was the wisest course. "It's more than he deserves."

"Patient?" Rose raised a dramatic hand to her breast. "I have the patience of a saint. Yet even a saint has her limits!" Rose tossed her hair behind her shoulders. She sighed heavily. "*Adios*. I think I hear Mama calling me."

Jo continued her walk toward the Big Top. Jamie

walked by, his hands in his pockets. "She's crazy," he muttered. He stopped and spread his arms wide. His look was that of a man ill-used and innocent. Jo shrugged. Shaking his head, Jamie moved away. "She's crazy," he said again.

Jo watched him until he was out of sight, then darted to the Big Top.

Inside, Carmen watched adoringly while Vito practiced a new routine on the incline wire. The tent echoed with the sounds of rehearsals: voices and thumps, the rattle of rigging, the yapping of clown dogs. In the first ring Jo spotted the Six Beirots, an acrobatic act that was just beginning its warm-ups. Pleased with her timing, Jo walked the length of the arena. A raucous whistle sounded over her head, and she glanced up to shake a friendly fist at Vito. He called from fifteen feet above her as he balanced on a slender wire set at a forty-five-degree angle.

"Hey, chickie, you have a nice rear view. You're almost as cute as me."

"No one's as cute as you, Vito," she called back.

"Ah, I know." With a weighty sigh, he executed a neat pivot. "But I have learned to live with it." He sent down a lewd wink. "When you going into town with me, chickie?" he asked as he always did.

"When you teach my cats to walk the wire," Jo answered as she always did. Vito laughed and began a light-footed cha-cha. Carmen fired Jo a glare. She must have it bad, Jo decided, if she takes Vito's harmless flirting seriously. Stopping beside her, Jo leaned close and spoke in a conspirator's whisper. "He'd fall off his wire if I said I'd go."

"I'd go," Carmen said with a lovely pout, "if he'd just ask me."

Jo shook her head, wondering why romances were invariably complicated. She was lucky not to have the problem. Giving Carmen an encouraging pat on the shoulder, Jo set off toward the first ring.

The Six Beirots were brothers. They were all small-statured, dark men who had immigrated from Belgium. Jo worked out with them often to keep herself limber and to keep her reflexes sharp. She liked them all, knew their wives and children, and understood their unique blending of French and English. Raoul was the oldest, and the stockiest of the six brothers. Because of his build and strength, he was the under-stander in their human pyramid. It was he who spotted Jo and first lifted a hand in greeting.

"Halo." He grinned and ran his palm over his receding hairline. "You gonna tumble?"

Jo laughed and did a quick handspring into the ring. She stuck out her tongue when the unanimous critique was "sloppy." "I just need to warm up," she said, assuming an air of injured dignity. "My muscles need tuning."

For the next thirty minutes Jo worked with them, doing muscle stretches and limbering exercises, rib stretches and lung expanders. Her muscles warmed and loosened, her heart pumped steadily. She was filled with energy. Her mind was clear. Because of her lightened mood, Jo was easily cajoled into a few impromptu acrobatics. Leaving the more complicated feats to the experts, she did simple back flips, handsprings or twists at Raoul's command. She did a brief, semi-successful thirty seconds atop the rolling globe and earned catcalls from her comrades at her dismount.

She stood back as they began the leaps. One after another they lined up to take turns running along a ramp, bounding upon a springboard and flying up to do flips or twists before landing on the mat. There was a constant stream of French as they called out to each other.

"Hokay, Jo." Raoul gestured with his hand. "Your turn."

"Oh, no." She shook her head and reached for her robe. "Uh-uh." There was a chorus of coaxing, teasing French. "I've got to give my cats their vitamins," she told them, still shaking her head.

"Come on, Jo. It's fun." Raoul grinned and wiggled his eyebrows. "Don't you like to fly?" As she glanced at the ramp, Raoul knew she was tempted. "You take a good spring," he told her. "Do one forward somersault, then land on my shoulders.'' He patted them to show their ability to handle the job.

Jo smiled and nibbled pensively on her lower lip. It had been a long while since she had taken the time to go up on the trapeze and really fly. It did look like fun. She gave Raoul a stern look. ''You'll catch me?''

''Raoul never misses,'' he said proudly, then turned to his brothers. *''Ne c'est pas?''* His brothers shrugged and rolled their eyes to the ceiling with indistinguishable mutters. ''Ah.'' He waved them away with the back of his hand.

Knowing Raoul was indeed a top flight understander, Jo approached the ramp. Still she gave him one last narrow-eyed look. ''You catch me,'' she ordered, shaking her finger at him.

''Cherie.'' He took his position with a stylish movement of his hand. ''It's a piece of pie.''

''Cake,'' Jo corrected, took a deep breath, held it and ran. When she came off the springboard, she tucked into the somersault and watched the Big Top turn upside down. She felt good. As the tent began to right itself, she straightened for her landing, keeping herself loose. Her feet connected with Raoul's powerful shoulders, and she tilted only briefly before he took her ankles in a firm grip. Straightening her poor posture, Jo styled elaborately with both arms while she received exaggerated applause and whis-

tles. She leaped down nimbly as Raoul took her
waist to give her landing bounce.

"When do you want to join the act?" he asked
her, giving her a friendly pat on the bottom. "We'll
put you up on the sway pole."

"That's okay." Grinning, Jo again reached for her
robe. "I'll stick with the cats." After a cheerful
wave, she slipped one arm into a sleeve and started
back down the hippodrome track. She pulled up
short when she spotted Keane leaning up against the
front seat rail.

"Amazing," he said, then straightened to move
to her. "But then, the circus is supposed to be amazing, isn't it?" He lifted the forgotten sleeve to her
robe, then slipped her other arm into it. "Is there
anything here you can't do?"

"Hundreds of things," Jo answered, taking him
seriously. "I'm only really proficient with animals.
The rest is just show and play."

"You looked amazingly proficient to me for the
last half hour or so," he countered as he pulled out
her braid from where it was trapped by her robe.

"Have you been here that long?"

"I walked in as Vito was commenting on your
rear view."

"Oh." Jo laughed, glancing back to where Vito
now stood flirting with Carmen. "He's crazy."

"Perhaps," Keane agreed, taking her arm. "But

his eyesight's good enough. Would you like some coffee?''

Jo was reminded instantly of the evening before. Leery of being drawn to his charms again, she shook her head. ''I've got to change,'' she told him, belting her robe. ''We've got a show at two. I want to rehearse the cats.''

''It's incredible how much time you people devote to your art. Rehearsals seem to run into the beginning of a show, and a show seems to run into more rehearsals.''

Jo softened when he referred to circus skills as art. ''Performers always look for just a bit more in themselves. It's a constant struggle for perfection. Even when a performance goes beautifully and you know it, you start thinking about the next time. How can I do it better or bigger or higher or faster?''

''Never satisfied?'' Keane asked as they stepped out into the sunlight.

''If we were, we wouldn't have much of a reason to come back and do it all over again.''

He nodded, but there was something absent in the gesture, as if his mind was elsewhere. ''I have to leave this afternoon,'' he said almost to himself.

''Leave?'' Jo's heart skidded to a stop. Her distress was overwhelming and so unexpected that she was forced to take an extra moment to steady herself. ''Back to Chicago?''

"Hmm?" Keane stopped, turning to face her. "Oh, yes."

"And the circus?" Jo asked, thoroughly ashamed that it had not been her first concern. She didn't want him to leave, she suddenly realized.

Keane frowned a moment, then continued to walk. "I see no purpose in disrupting this year's schedule." His voice was brisk now and businesslike.

"This year's?" Jo repeated cautiously.

Keane turned and looked at her. "I haven't decided its ultimate fate, but I won't do anything until the end of the summer."

"I see." She let out a long breath. "So we have a reprieve."

"In a manner of speaking," Keane agreed.

Jo was silent for a moment but could not prevent herself from asking, "Then you won't—I mean, you'll be staying in Chicago now; you won't be traveling with us?"

They negotiated their way around a puddle before Keane answered. "I don't feel I can make a judicious decision about the circus after so brief an exposure. There's a complication in one of my cases that needs my personal attention, but I should be back in a week or two."

Relief flooded through her. He would be back, a voice shouted in her ear. It shouldn't matter to you, another whispered. "We'll be in South Carolina in a couple of weeks,'' Jo said casually. They had reached her trailer, and she took the handle of her door before she turned to face him. *It's just that I want him to understand what this circus means,* she told herself as she looked up into his eyes. *That's the only reason I want him to come back.* Knowing she was lying to herself made it difficult to keep her gaze steady.

Keane smiled, letting his eyes travel over her face. ''Yes, Duffy's given me a route list. I'll find you. Aren't you going to ask me in?''

''In?'' Jo repeated. ''Oh, no, I told you, I have to change, and…'' He stepped forward as she talked. Something in his eyes told her a firm stand was necessary. She had seen a similar look in a lion's eyes while he contemplated taking a dangerous liberty. ''I simply don't have time right now. If I don't see you before you go, have a good trip.'' She turned and opened the door. Aware of a movement, she turned back, but not before he had nudged her through the door and followed. As it closed at his back, Jo bristled with fury. She did not enjoy being outmaneuvered. ''Tell me, counselor, do you know anything about a law concerning breaking and entering?''

''Doesn't apply,'' he returned smoothly. ''There was no lock involved.'' He glanced around at the attractive simplicity of Jo's trailer. The colors were restful earth tones without frills. The beige- and brown-flecked linoleum floor was spotlessly clean. It was the same basic floorplan as Frank's trailer, but here there were softer touches. There were curtains rather than shades at the windows; large, comfortable pillows tossed onto a forest green sofa; a spray of fresh wildflowers tucked into a thin, glass vase. Without comment Keane wandered to a black lacquer trunk that sat directly opposite the door. On it was a book that he picked up while Jo fumed. *"The Count of Monte Cristo,"* he read aloud and flipped it open. "In French," he stated, lifting a brow.

"It was written in French," Jo muttered, pulling it from his hand. "So I read it in French." Annoyed, she lifted the lid on the trunk, preparing to drop the book inside and out of his reach.

"Good heavens, are those all yours?" Keane stopped the lid on its downswing, then pushed books around with his other hand. "Tolstoy, Cervantes, Voltaire, Steinbeck. When do you have time in this crazy, twenty-four-hour world you live in to read this stuff?"

"I make time," Jo snapped as her eyes sparked. "My *own* time. Just because you're the owner doesn't mean you can barge in here and poke through my things and demand an account of my time. This is my trailer. I own everything in it."

"Hold on." Keane halted her rushing stream of words. "I wasn't demanding an account of your time, I was simply astonished that you could find enough of it to do this type of reading. Since I can't claim to be an expert on your work, it would be remarkably foolish of me to criticize the amount of time you spend on it. Secondly,'' he said, taking a step toward her—and though Jo stiffened in anticipation, he did not touch her—''I apologize for 'poking through your things,' as you put it. I was interested for several reasons. One being I have quite an extensive library myself. It seems we have a common interest, whether we like it or not. As for barging into your trailer, I can only plead guilty. If you choose to prosecute, I can recommend a couple of lousy attorneys who overcharge.''

His last comment forced a smile onto Jo's reluctant lips. ''I'll give it some thought.'' With more care than she had originally intended, Jo lowered the lid of the trunk. She was reminded that she had not been gracious. ''I'm sorry,'' she said as she turned back to him.

His eyes reflected curiosity. ''What for?''

''For snapping at you.'' She lifted her shoulders, then let them fall. ''I thought you were criticizing me. I suppose I'm too sensitive.''

Several seconds passed before he spoke. ''Unnecessary apology accepted if you answer one question.''

Mystified, Jo frowned at him. ''What question?''

"Is the Tolstoy in Russian?"

Jo laughed, pushing loose strands of hair from her face. "Yes, it is."

Keane smiled, enjoying the two tiny dimples that flickered in her cheeks when she laughed. "Did you know that though you're lovely in any case, you grow even more so when you smile?"

Jo's laughter stilled. She was unaccustomed to this sort of compliment and studied him without any idea of how to respond. It occurred to her that any of the sophisticated women she had imagined that morning would have known precisely what to say. She would have been able to smile or laugh as she tossed back the appropriate comment. That woman, Jo admitted, was not Jovilette Wilder. Gravely, she kept her eyes on his. "I don't know how to flirt," she said simply.

Keane tilted his head, and an expression came and went in his eyes before she could analyze it. He stepped toward her. "I wasn't flirting with you, Jo, I was making an observation. Hasn't anyone ever told you that you're beautiful?"

He was much too close now, but in the narrow confines of the trailer, Jo had little room to maneuver. She was forced to tilt back her head to keep her eyes level with his. "Not precisely the way you did." Quickly, she put her hand to his chest to keep the slight but important distance between them. She knew she was trapped, but that did not mean she was defeated.

Gently, Keane lifted her protesting hand, turning it palm up as he brought it to his lips. An involuntary breath rushed in and out of Jo's lungs. "Your hands are exquisite," he murmured, tracing the fine line of blue up the back. "Narrow-boned, long-fingered. And the palms show hard work. That makes them more interesting." He lifted his eyes from her hand to her face. "Like you."

Jo's voice had grown husky, but she could do nothing to alter it. "I don't know what I'm supposed to say when you tell me things like that." Beneath her robe her breasts rose and fell with her quickening heart. "I'd rather you didn't."

"Do you really?" Keane ran the back of his hand along her jaw line. "That's a pity, because the more I look at you, the more I find to say. You're a bewitching creature, Jovilette."

"I have to change," she said in the firmest voice she could muster. "You'll have to go."

"That's unfortunately true," he murmured, then cupped her chin. "Come, then, kiss me goodbye."

Jo stiffened. "I hardly think that's necessary...."

"You couldn't be more wrong," he told her as he lowered his mouth. "It's extremely necessary." In a light, teasing whisper, his lips met hers. His arms encircled her, bringing her closer with only the slightest pressure. "Kiss me back, Jo," he ordered softly. "Put your arms around me and kiss me back."

For a moment longer she resisted, but the lure of his mouth nibbling at hers was too strong. Letting instinct rule her will, Jo lifted her arms and circled his neck. Her mouth grew mobile under his, parting and offering. Her surrender seemed to lick the flames of his passion. The kiss grew urgent. His arms locked, crushing her against him. Her quiet moan was not of protest but of wonder. Her fingers found their way into his hair, tangling in its thickness as they urged him closer. She felt her robe loosen, then his hands trail up her rib cage. At his touch, she shivered, feeling her skin grow hot, then cold, then hot again in rapid succession.

When his hand took her breast, she shied, drawing in her breath quickly. "Steady," he murmured against her mouth. His hands stroked gently, coaxing her to relax again. He kissed the corners of her mouth, waiting until she quieted before he took her deep again. The thin leotard molded her body. It created no barrier against the warmth of his searching fingers. They moved slowly, lingering over the peak of her breast, exploring its softness, wandering to her waist, then tracing her hip and thigh.

No man had ever touched her so freely. Jo was helpless to stop him, helpless against her own growing need for him to touch her again. Was this the passion she had read of so often? The passion that drove men to war, to struggle against all reason, to risk everything? She felt she could understand it now. She clung to him as he taught her—as she learned—the demands of her own body. Her mouth grew hungrier for the taste of him. She was certain she remained in his arms while seasons flew by, while decades passed, while worlds were destroyed and built again.

But when he drew away, Jo saw the same sun spilling through her windows. Eternity had only been moments.

Unable to speak, she merely stared up at him. Her eyes were dark and aware, her cheeks flushed with desire. But somehow, though it still tingled from his, her mouth maintained a youthful innocence. Keane's eyes dropped to it as his hands loitered at the small of her back.

"It's difficult to believe I'm the first man to touch you," he murmured. His eyes roamed to hers. "And quite desperately arousing. Particularly when I find you've passion to match your looks. I think I'd like to make love with you in the daylight first so that I can watch that marvelous control of yours slip away layer by layer. We'll have to discuss it when I get back."

Jo forced strength back into her limbs, knowing

she was on the brink of losing her will to him. "Just because I let you kiss me and touch me doesn't mean I'll let you make love to me." She lifted her chin, feeling her confidence surging back. "If I do, it'll be because it's what I want, not because you tell me to."

The expression in Keane's eyes altered. "Fair enough," he agreed and nodded. "It'll simply be my job to make it what you want." He took her chin in his hand and lowered his mouth to hers for a brief kiss. As she had the first time, Jo kept her eyes open and watched him. She felt him grin against her mouth before he raised his head. "You are the most fascinating woman I've ever met." Turning, he crossed to the door. "I'll be back," he said with a careless wave before it closed behind him. Dumbly, Jo stared into empty space.

Fascinating? she repeated, tracing her still warm lips with her fingertips. Quickly, she ran to the window, and kneeling on the sofa below it, watched Keane stride away.

She realized with a sudden jolt that she missed him already.

Chapter 6

Jo learned that weeks could drag like years. During the second week of Keane's absence she had searched each new lot for a sign of him. She had scanned the crowds of towners who came to watch the raising of the Big Top, and as the days stretched on and on, she balanced between anger and despair at his continued absence. Only in the cage did she manage to isolate her concentration, knowing she could not afford to do otherwise. But after each performance Jo found it more and more difficult to relax. Each morning she felt certain he would be back. Each night she lay restless, waiting for the sun to rise.

Spring was in full bloom. The high grass lots

smelled of it. Often there were wildflowers crushed underfoot, leaving their heavy fragrances in the air. Even as the circus caravan traveled north, the days grew warm, sunlight lingering further into evening. While other troupers enjoyed the balmy air and prov- identially sunny skies, Jo lived on nerves.

It occurred to her that after returning to his life in Chicago, Keane had decided against coming back. In Chicago he had comfort and wealth and elegant women. Why should he come back? Jo closed her mind against the ultimate fate of the circus, unwill- ing to face the possibility that Keane might close the show at the end of the season. She told herself the only reason she wanted him to come back was to convince him to keep the circus open. But the mem- ory of being in his arms intruded too often into her thoughts. Gradually, she grew resigned, filling the strange void she felt with her work.

Several times each week she found time to give the eager Gerry more training. At first she had only permitted him to work with the two menagerie cubs, allowing him, with the protection of leather gloves, to play with them and to feed them. She encouraged him to teach them simple tricks with the aid of small pieces of raw meat. Jo was as pleased as he when the cats responded to his patience and obeyed.

Jo saw potential in Gerry, in his genuine affection for animals and in his determination. Her primary concern was that he had not yet developed a healthy fear. He was still too casual, and with casualness, Jo knew, came carelessness. When she thought he had progressed far enough, Jo decided to take him to the next step of his training.

There was no matinee that day, and the Big Top was scattered with rehearsing troupers. Jo was dressed in boots and khakis with a long-sleeved blouse tucked into the waist. She studied Gerry as she ran the stock of her whip through her hand. They stood together in the safety cage while she issued instructions.

"All right, Buck's going to let Merlin through the chute. He's the most tractable of the cats, except for Ari." She paused a moment while her eyes grew sad. "Ari isn't up to even a short practice session." She pushed away the depression that threatened and continued. "Merlin knows you, he's familiar with your voice and your scent." Gerry nodded and swallowed. "When we go in, you're to be my shadow. You move when I move, and don't speak until I tell you. If you get frightened, don't run." Jo took his arm for emphasis. "That's *important*, understand? Don't run. Tell me if you want out, and I'll get you to the safety cage."

"I won't run, Jo," he promised and wiped hands, damp with excitement, on his jeans.

"Are you ready?"

Gerry grinned and nodded. "Yeah."

Jo opened the door leading to the big cage and let Gerry through behind her before securing it. She walked to the center of the arena in easy, confident strides. "Let him in, Buck," she called and heard the immediate rattle of bars. Merlin entered without hurry, then leaped onto his pedestal. He yawned hugely before looking at Jo. "A solo today, Merlin," she said as she advanced toward him. "And you're the star. Stay with me," she ordered as Gerry merely stood still and stared at the big cat. Merlin gave Gerry a disinterested glance and waited.

With an upward move of her arm, she sent Merlin into a sit-up. "You know," she told the boy behind her, "that teaching a cat to take his seat is the first trick. The audience won't even consider it one. The sit-up," she continued while signaling Merlin to bring his front paws back down, "is usually next and takes quite a bit of time. It's necessary to strengthen the cat's back muscles first." Again she signaled Merlin to sit up, then, with a quick command, she had him pawing the air and roaring. "Marvelous old ham," she said with a grin and brought him back down. "The primary move of each cue is always given from the same position with the same tone of voice. It takes patience and repetition. I'm going to bring him down off the pedestal now."

Jo flicked the whip against the tanbark, and Merlin leaped down. "Now I maneuver him to the spot in the arena where I want him to lie down." As she moved, Jo made certain her student moved with her. "The cage is a circle, forty feet in diameter. You have to know every inch of it inside your head. You have to know precisely how far you are from the bars at all times. If you back up into the bars, you've got no room to maneuver if there's trouble. It's one of the biggest mistakes a trainer can make." At her signal Merlin laid down, then shifted to his side. "Over, Merlin," she said briskly, sending him into a series of rolls. "Use their names often; it keeps them in tune with you. You have to know each cat and their individual tendencies."

Jo moved with Merlin, then signaled him to stop. When he roared, she rubbed the top of his head with the stock of her whip. "They like to be petted just like house cats, but they are not tabbies. It's essential that you never give them your complete trust and that you remember always to maintain your dominance. You subjugate not by poking them or beating or shouting, which is not only cruel but makes for a mean, undependable cat, but with patience, respect and will. Never humiliate them; they have a right to their pride. You bluff them, Gerry," she said as she raised both arms and brought Merlin up on his hind legs. "Man is the unknown factor. That's why we use jungle-bred rather than captivity-bred cats. Ari is the exception. A cat born and raised in captivity is too familiar with man, so you lose your edge.'' She moved forward, keeping her arms raised. Merlin followed, walking on his hind legs. He spread seven feet into the air and towered over his trainer. ''They might have a sense of affection for you, but there's no fear and little respect. Unfortunately, this often happens if a cat's been with a trainer a long time. They don't become more docile the longer they're in an act, but they become more dangerous. They test you constantly. The trick is to make them believe you're indestructible.''

She brought Merlin down, and he gave another yawn before she sent him back to his seat. ''If one swipes at you, you have to stop it then and there, because they try again and again, getting closer each time. Usually, if a trainer's hurt in the cage, it's because he's made a mistake. The cats are quick to spot them; sometimes they let them pass, sometimes they don't. This one's given me a good smack on the shoulder now and again. He's kept his claws retracted, but there's always the possibility that one time he'll forget he's just playing. Any questions?''

''Hundreds,'' Gerry answered, wiping his mouth with the back of his hand. ''I just can't focus on one right now.''

Jo chuckled and again scratched Merlin's head

when he roared. "They'll come to you later. It's hard to absorb anything the first time, but it'll come back to you when you're relaxed again. All right, you know the cue. Make him sit up."

"Me?"

Jo stepped to the side, giving Merlin a clear view of her student. "You can be as scared as you like," she said easily. "Just don't let it show in your voice. Watch his eyes."

Gerry rubbed his palm on the thighs of his jeans, then lifted it as he had seen Jo do hundreds of times. "Up," he told the cat in a passably firm voice.

Merlin studied him a moment, then looked at Jo. This, his eyes told her clearly, was an amateur and beneath his notice. Carefully, Jo kept her face expressionless. "He's testing you," she told Gerry. "He's an old hand and a bit harder to bluff. Be firm and use his name this time."

Gerry took a deep breath and repeated the hand signal. "Up, Merlin."

Merlin glanced back at him, then stared with measuring, amber eyes. "Again," Jo instructed and heard Gerry swallow audibly. "Put some authority into your voice. He thinks you're a pushover."

"Up, Merlin!" Gerry repeated, annoyed enough by Jo's description to put some dominance into his voice. Though his reluctance was obvious, Merlin obeyed. "He did it," Gerry whispered on a long, shaky breath. "He really did it."

"Very good," Jo said, pleased with both the lion and her student. "Now bring him down." When this was accomplished, Jo had him bring Merlin from the seat. "Here." She handed Gerry the whip. "Use the stock to scratch his head. He likes it best just behind the ear." She felt the faint tremble in his hand as he took the whip, but he held it steady, even as Merlin closed his eyes and roared.

Because he had performed well, Jo afforded Merlin the liberty of rubbing against her legs before she called for Buck to let him out. The rattle of the bars was the cat's cue to exit, and like a trouper, he took it with his head held high. "You did very well," she told Gerry when they were alone in the cage.

"It was great." He handed her back the whip, the stock damp from his sweaty palms. "It was just great. When can I do it again?"

Jo smiled and patted his shoulder. "Soon," she promised. "Just remember the things I've told you and come to me when you remember all those questions."

"Okay, thanks, Jo." He stepped through the safety cage. "Thanks a lot. I want to go tell the guys."

"Go ahead." Jo watched him scramble away, leaping over the ring and darting through the back door. With a grin, she leaned against the bars. "Was I like that?" she asked Buck, who stood at the opposite end of the cage.

"The first time you got a cat to sit up on your own, we heard about it for a week. Twelve years old and you thought you were ready for the big show."

Jo laughed, and wiping the damp stock of her whip against her pants, turned. It was then she saw him standing behind her. "Keane!" she used the name she had sworn not to use as pleasure flooded through her. It shone on her face. Just as she had given up hope of seeing him again, he was there. She took two steps toward him before she could check herself. "I didn't know you were back." Jo gripped the stock of the whip with both hands to prevent herself from reaching out to touch him.

"I believe you missed me." His voice was as she remembered, low and smooth.

Jo cursed herself for being so naïve and transparent. "Perhaps I did, a little," she admitted cautiously. "I suppose I'd gotten used to you, and you were gone longer than you said you'd be." He looks the same, she thought rapidly, exactly the same. She reminded herself that it had only been a month. It had seemed like years.

"*Mmm,* yes. I had more to see to than I had expected. You look a bit pale," he observed and touched her cheek with his fingertip.

"I suppose I haven't been getting much sun," she said with quick prevarication. "How was Chicago?" Jo needed to turn the conversation away from personal lines until she had an opportunity to gauge her emotions; seeing him suddenly had tossed them into confusion.

"Cool," he told her, making a long, thorough survey of her face. "Have you ever been there?"

"No. We play near there toward the end of the season, but I've never had time to go all the way into the city."

Nodding absently, Keane glanced into the empty cage behind her. "I see you're training Gerry."

"Yes." Relieved that they had lapsed into a professional discussion, Jo let the muscles of her shoulders ease. "This was the first time with an adult cat and no bars between. He did very well."

Keane looked back at her. His eyes were serious and probing. "He was trembling. I could see it from where I stood watching you."

"It was his first time—" she began in Gerry's defense.

"I wasn't criticizing him," Keane interrupted with a tinge of impatience. "It's just that he stood beside you, shaking from head to foot, and you were totally cool and in complete control."

"It's my job to be in control," Jo reminded him.

"That lion must have stood seven feet tall when

he went up on his hind legs, and you walked under him without any protection, not even the traditional chair.''

"I do a picture act," she explained, "not a fighting act."

"Jo," he said so sharply she blinked. "Aren't you ever frightened in there?"

"Frightened?" she repeated, lifting a brow. "Of course I'm frightened. More frightened than Gerry was—or than you would be."

"What are you talking about?" Keane demanded. Jo noted with some curiosity that he was angry. "I could see that boy sweat in there."

"That was mostly excitement," Jo told him patiently. "He hasn't the experience to be truly frightened yet." She tossed back her hair and let out a long breath. Jo did not like to talk of her fears with anyone and found it especially difficult with Keane. Only because she felt it necessary that he understand this to understand the circus did she continue. "Real fear comes from knowing them, working with them, understanding them. You can only speculate on what they can do to a man. I *know*. I know exactly what they're capable of. They have an incredible courage, but more, they have an incredible guile. I've seen what they can do." Her eyes were calm and clear as they looked into his. "My father almost lost a leg once. I was about five, but I remember it perfectly.

He made a mistake, and a five-hundred-pound Nubian sunk into his thigh and dragged him around the arena. Luckily, the cat was diverted by a female in season. Cats are unpredictable when they have sex on their minds, which is probably one of the reasons he attacked my father in the first place. They're fiercely jealous once they've set their minds on a mate. My father was able to get into the safety cage before any of the other cats took an interest in him. I can't remember how many stitches he had or how long it was before he could walk properly again, but I do remember the look in that cat's eyes. You learn quickly about fear when you're in the cage, but you control it, you channel it or you find another line of work.''

''Then why?'' Keane demanded. He took her shoulders before she could turn away. ''Why do you do it? And don't tell me because it's your job. That's not good enough.''

It puzzled Jo why he seemed angry. His eyes were darkened with temper, and his fingers dug into her shoulders. As if wanting to draw out her answer, he gave her one quick shake. ''All right,'' Jo said slowly, ignoring the ache in her flesh. ''That is part of it, but not all. It's all I've ever known, that's part of it, too. It's what I'm good at.'' While she spoke, she searched his face for a clue to his mood. She wondered if perhaps he had felt it wrong of her to take Gerry into the cage. "Gerry's going to be good at it, too," she told him. "I imagine everyone needs to be good—really good—at something. And I enjoy giving the people who come to see me the best show I can. But over all, I suppose it's because I love them. It's difficult for a layman to understand a trainer's feeling for his animals. I love their intelligence, their really awesome beauty, their strength, the unquenchable streak of wildness that separates them from well-trained horses. They're exciting, challenging and terrifying."

Keane was silent for a moment. She saw that his eyes were still angry, but his fingers relaxed on her shoulders. Jo felt a light throbbing where bruises would certainly show in the morning. "I suppose excitement becomes addicting—difficult to live without once it's become a habit."

"I don't know," Jo replied, grateful that his temper was apparently cooling. "I've never thought about it."

"No, I suppose you'd have little reason to." With a nod, he turned to walk away.

Jo took a step after him. "Keane." His name raced through her lips before she could prevent it. When he turned back to her, she realized she could not ask any of the dozens of questions that flew through her mind. There was only one she felt she had any right to ask. "Have you thought any more about what you're going to do with us...with the circus?''

For an instant she saw temper flare again into his eyes. ''No.'' The word was curt and final. As he turned his back on her again, she felt a spurt of anger and reached for his arm.

''How can you be so callous, so unfeeling?'' she demanded. ''How is it possible to be so casual when you hold the lives of over a hundred people in your hands?''

Carefully, he removed her hand from his arm. ''Don't push me, Jo.'' There was warning in his eyes and in his voice.

''I'm not trying to,'' she returned, then ran a frustrated hand through her hair. ''I'm only asking you to be fair, to be...kind,'' she finished lamely.

''Don't ask me anything,'' he ordered in a brisk, authoritative tone. Jo's chin rose in response. ''I'm here,'' he reminded her. ''You'll have to be satisfied with that for now.''

Jo battled with her temper. She could not deny that in coming back he had proved himself true to his word. She had the rest of the season if nothing else. ''I don't suppose I have any choice,'' she said quietly.

''No,'' he agreed with a faint nod. ''You don't.''

Frowning, Jo watched him stride away in a smooth, fluid gait she was forced to admire. She noticed for the first time that her palms were as damp as Gerry's had been. Annoyed, she rubbed them over her hips.

"Want to talk about it?"

Jo turned quickly to find Jamie behind her in full clown gear. She knew her preoccupation had been deep for her to be caught so completely unaware. "Oh, Jamie, I didn't see you."

"You haven't seen anything but Prescott since you stepped out of the cage," Jamie pointed out.

"What are you doing in makeup?" she asked, skirting his comment.

He gestured toward the dog at her feet. "This mutt won't respond to me unless I'm in my face. Do you want to talk about it?"

"Talk about what?"

"About Prescott, about the way you feel about him."

The dog sat patiently at Jamie's heels and thumped his tail. Casually, Jo stopped and ruffled his gray fur.

"I don't know what you're talking about."

"Look, I'm not saying it can't work out, but I don't want to see you get hurt. I know how it is to be nuts about somebody."

"What in the world makes you think I'm nuts about Keane Prescott?" Jo gave the dog her full attention.

"Hey, it's me, remember?" Jamie took her arm and pulled her to her feet. "Not everybody would've noticed, maybe, but not everybody knows you the way I do. You've been miserable since he went back to Chicago, looking for him in every car that drove on the lot. And just now, when you saw him, you lit up like the midway on Saturday night. I'm not saying there's anything wrong with you being in love with him, but—"

"In love with him?" Jo repeated, incredulous.

"Yeah." Jamie spoke patiently. "In love with him."

Jo stared at Jamie as the realization slid over her. "In love with him," she murmured, trying out the words. "Oh, no." She sighed, closing her eyes. "Oh, no."

"Didn't you have enough sense to figure it out for yourself?" Jamie said gently. Seeing Jo's distress, he ran a hand gently up her arm.

"No, I guess I'm pretty stupid about this sort of thing." Jo opened her eyes and looked around, wondering if the world should look any different. "What am I going to do?"

"Heck, I don't know." Jamie kicked sawdust with an oversized shoe. "I'm not exactly getting rave notices myself in that department." He gave Jo a reassuring pat. "I just wanted you to know that you always have a sympathetic ear here." He grinned

engagingly before he turned to walk away, leaving
Jo distracted and confused.

Jo spent the rest of the afternoon absorbed with
the idea of being in love with Keane Prescott. For a
short time she allowed herself to enjoy the sensation,
the novel experience of loving someone not as a
friend but as a lover. She could feel the light and the
power spread through her, as if she had caught the
sun in her hand. She daydreamed.

Keane was in love with her. He'd told her hundreds of times as he'd held her under a moonlit sky.
He wanted to marry her, he couldn't bear to live
without her. She was suddenly sophisticated and
worldly enough to deal with the country club set on
their own ground. She could exchange droll stories
with the wives of other attorneys. There would be
children and a house in the country. How would it
feel to wake up in the same town every morning?
She would learn to cook and give dinner parties.
There would be long, quiet evenings when they
would be alone together. There would be candlelight
and music. When they slept together, his arms would
stay around her until morning.

Idiot. Jo dragged herself back sternly. As she and
Pete fed the cats, she tried to remember that fairy
tales were for children. None of those things are ever

going to happen, she reminded herself. I have to figure out how to handle this before I get in any deeper.

"Pete," she began, keeping her voice conversational as she put Abra's quota of raw meat on a long stick. "Have you ever been in love?"

Pete chewed his gum gently, watching Jo hoist the meat through the bars. "Well, now, let's see." Thrusting out his lower lip, he considered. "Only 'bout eight or ten times, I guess. Maybe twelve."

Jo laughed, moving down to the next cage. "I'm serious," she told him. "I mean *really* in love."

"I fall in love easy," Pete confessed gravely. "I'm a pushover for a pretty face. Matter of fact, I'm a pushover for an ugly face." He grinned. "Yes sir, the only thing like being in love is drawing an ace-high flush when the pot's ripe."

Jo shook her head and continued down the line. "Okay, since you're such an expert, tell me what you do when you're in love with a person and the person doesn't love you back and you don't want that person to know that you're in love because you don't want to make a fool of yourself."

"Just a minute." Pete squeezed his eyes tight. "I got to think this one through first." For a moment he was silent as his lips moved with his thoughts. "Okay, let's see if I've got this straight." Opening his eyes, he frowned in concentration. "You're in love—"

"I didn't say *I* was in love," Jo interrupted hastily.

Pete lifted his brows and pursed his lips. "Let's just use *you* in the general sense to avoid confusion," he suggested. Jo nodded, pretending to absorb herself with the feeding of the cats. "So, you're in love, but the guy doesn't love you. First off, you've got to be sure he doesn't."

"He doesn't," Jo murmured, then added quickly, "let's say he doesn't."

Pete shot her a look out of the corner of his eye, then shifted his gum to the other side of his mouth. "Okay, then the first thing you should do is change his mind."

"Change his mind?" Jo repeated, frowning at him.

"Sure." Pete gestured with his hand to show the simplicity of the procedure. "You fall in love with him, then he falls in love with you. You play hard to get, or you play easy to get. Or you play flutter and smile." He demonstrated by coyly batting his lashes and giving a winsome smile. Jo giggled and leaned on the feeding pole. Pete in fielder's cap, white T-shirt and faded jeans was the best show she'd seen all day. "You make him jealous," he continued. "Or you flatter his ego. Girl, there're so many ways to get a man, I can't count them, and I've been gotten by them all. Yes, sir, I'm a real pushover.'' He looked so pleased with his weakness, Jo smiled. How easy it would be, she thought, if I could take love so lightly.

''Suppose I don't want to do any of those things. Suppose I don't really know how and I don't want to humiliate myself by making a mess of it. Suppose the person isn't—well, suppose nothing could ever work between us, anyway. What then?''

''You got too many supposes,'' Pete concluded, then shook his finger at her. ''And I got one for you. Suppose you ain't too smart because you figure you can't win even before you play.''

''Sometimes people get hurt when they play,'' Jo countered quietly. ''Especially if they aren't familiar with the game.''

''Hurting's nothing,'' Pete stated with a sweep of his hand. ''Winning's the best, but playing's just fine. This whole big life, it's a game, Jo. You know that. And the rules keep changing all the time. You've got nerve,'' he continued, then laid his rough, brown hand on her shoulder. ''More raw nerve than most anybody I've ever known. You've got brains, too, hungry brains. You going to tell me that with all that, you're afraid to take a chance?''

Meeting his eyes, Jo knew hypothetical evasions would not do. ''I suppose I only take calculated risks, Pete. I know my turf; I know my moves. And I know exactly what'll happen if I make a mistake.

I take a chance that my body might be clawed, not my emotions. I've never rehearsed for anything like this, and I think playing it cold would be suicide.''

"I think you've got to believe in Jo Wilder a little more," Pete countered, then gave her cheek a quick pat.

"Hey, Jo." Looking over, Jo saw Rose approaching. She wore straight-leg jeans, a white peasant blouse and a six-foot boa constrictor over her shoulders.

"Hello, Rose." Jo handed Pete the feeding pole. "Taking Baby out for a walk?"

"He needed some air." Rose gave her charge a pat. "I think he got a little carsick this morning. Does he look peaked to you?"

Jo looked down at the shiny, multicolored skin, then studied the tiny black eyes as Rose held Baby's head up for inspection. "I don't think so," she decided.

"Well, it's a warm day," Rose observed, releasing Baby's head. "I'll give him a bath. That might perk him up."

Jo noticed Rose's eyes darting around the compound. "Looking for Jamie?"

"Hmph." Rose tossed her black curls. "I'm not wasting my time on that one." She stroked the latter half of Baby's anatomy. "I'm indifferent."

"That's another way to do it," Pete put in, giving Jo a nudge. "I forgot about that one. It's a zinger."

Rose frowned at Pete, then at Jo. "What's he talking about?"

With a laugh, Jo sat down on a water barrel. "Catching a man," she told her, letting the warm sun play on her face. "Pete's done a study on it from the male point of view."

"Oh." Rose threw Pete her most disdainful look. "You think I'm indifferent so he'll get interested?"

"It's a zinger," Pete repeated, adjusting his cap. "You get him confused so he starts thinking about you. You make him crazy wondering why you don't notice him."

Rose considered the idea. "Does it usually work?"

"It's got an eighty-seven percent success average," Pete assured her, then gave Baby a friendly pat. "It even works with cats." He jerked his thumb behind him and winked at Jo. "The pretty lady cat, she sits there and stares off into space like she's got important things occupying her mind. The boy in the next cage is doing everything but standing on his head to get her attention. She just gives herself a wash, pretending she doesn't even know he's there. Then, maybe after she's got him banging his head against the bars, she looks over, blinks her big yellow eyes and says, 'Oh, were you talking to me?'"

Pete laughed and stretched his back muscles. "He's hooked then, brother, just like a fish on a line."

Rose smiled at the image of Jamie dangling from her own personal line. "Maybe I won't put Baby in Carmen's trailer after all," she murmured. "Oh, look, here comes Duffy and the owner." An inherent flirt, Rose instinctively fluffed her hair. "Really, he is the most handsome man. Don't you think so, Jo?"

Jo's eyes had already locked on Keane's. She seemed helpless to release herself from the gaze. Gripping the edge of the water barrel tightly, she reminded herself not to be a fool. "Yes," she agreed with studied casualness. "He's very attractive."

"Your knuckles are turning white, Jo," Pete muttered next to her ear.

Letting out a frustrated breath, Jo relaxed her hands. Straightening her spine, she determined to show more restraint. Control, she reminded herself, was the basic tool of her trade. If she could train her emotions and outbluff a dozen lions, she could certainly outbluff one man.

"Hello, Duffy." Rose gave the portly man a quick smile, then turned her attention to Keane. "Hello, Mr. Prescott. It's nice to have you back."

"Hello, Rose." He smiled into her upturned face, then lifted a brow as his eyes slid over the reptile around her neck and shoulders. "Who's your friend?"

"Oh, this is Baby." She patted one of the tan-colored saddle marks on Baby's back.

"Of course." Jo noticed how humor enhanced the gold of his eyes. "Hello, Pete." He gave the handler an easy nod before his gaze shifted and then lingered on Jo.

As on the first day they had met, Keane did not bother to camouflage his stare. His look was cool and assessing. He was reaffirming ownership. It shot through Jo that yes, she was in love with him, but she was also afraid of him. She feared his power over her, feared his capacity to hurt her. Still, her face registered none of her thoughts. Fear, she reminded herself as her eyes remained equally cool on his, was something she understood. Love might cause impossible problems, but fear could be dealt with. She would not cower from him, and she would honor the foremost rule of the arena. She would not turn and run.

Silently, they watched each other while the others looked on with varying degrees of curiosity. There was the barest touch of a smile on Keane's lips. The battle of wills continued until Duffy cleared his throat.

"Ah, Jo."

Calmly, without hurry, she shifted her attention. "Yes, Duffy?"

"I just sent one of the web girls into town to see

the local dentist. Seems she's got an abscess. I need you to fill in tonight.''

''Sure.''

''Just for the web and the opening spectacular,'' he continued. Unable to prevent himself, he cast a quick look at Keane to see if he was still staring at her. He was. Duffy shifted uncomfortably and wondered what the devil was going on. ''Take your usual place in the finale. We'll just be one girl shy in the chorus. Wardrobe'll fix you up.''

''Okay.'' Jo smiled at him, though she was very much aware of Keane's eyes on her. ''I guess I'd better go practice walking in those three-inch heels. What position do I take?''

''Number four rope.''

''Duffy,'' Rose chimed in and tugged on his sleeve. ''When are you going to let me do the web?''

''Rose, how's a pint-sizer like you going to stand up with that heavy costume on?'' Duffy shook his head at her, keeping a respectable distance from Baby. After thirty-five years of working carnies, sideshows and circuses, he still was uneasy around snakes.

''I'm pretty strong,'' Rose claimed, stretching her spine in the hope of looking taller. ''And I've been practicing.'' Anxious to demonstrate her accomplishments, Rose deftly unwound Baby. ''Hold him a minute," she requested and dumped several feet of snake into Keane's arms.

"Ah…" Keane shifted the weight in his arms and looked dubiously into Baby's bored eyes. "I hope he's eaten recently."

"He had a nice breakfast," Rose assured him, going into a fluid backbend to show Duffy her flexibility.

"Baby won't eat owners," Jo told Keane. She did not bother to suppress her grin. It was the first time she had seen him disconcerted. "Just a stray towner, occasionally. Rose keeps him on a strict diet."

"I assume," Keane began as Baby slithered into a more comfortable position, "that he's aware I'm the owner."

Grinning at Keane's uncomfortable expression, Jo turned to Pete. "Gee, I don't know. Did anybody tell Baby about the new owner?"

"Haven't had a chance, myself," Pete drawled, taking out a fresh stick of gum. "Looks a lot like a towner, too. Baby might get confused."

"They're just teasing you, Mr. Prescott," Rose told him as she finished her impromptu audition with a full split. "Baby doesn't eat people at all. He's docile as a lamb. Little kids come up and pet him during a demonstration." She rose and brushed off her jeans. "Now, you take a cobra…"

"No, thank you," Keane declined, unloading the six-foot Baby back into Rose's arms.

Rose slipped the boa back around her neck. "Well, Duffy, I'm off. What do you say?"

"Get one of the girls to teach you the routine," he said with a nod. "Then we'll see." Smiling, he watched Rose saunter away.

"Hey, Duffy!" It was Jamie. "There's a couple of towners looking for you. I sent them over to the red wagon."

"Fine. I'll just go right on along with you." Duffy winked at Jo before turning to catch up with Jamie's long stride.

Keane was standing very close to the barrels. Jo knew getting down from her perch was risky. She knew, too, however, that her pulse was beginning to behave erratically despite her efforts to control it. "I've got to see about my costume." Nimbly, she came down, intending to skirt around him. Even as her boots touched the ground, his hands took her waist. Exercising every atom of willpower, she neither jerked nor struggled but lifted her eyes calmly to his.

His thumbs moved in a lazy arch. She could feel the warmth through the fabric of her blouse. With her entire being she wished he would not hold her. Then, perversely, she wished he would hold her closer. She struggled not to weaken as her lips grew warm under the kiss of his eyes. Her heart began to hammer in her ears.

Keane ran a hand down the length of her long, thick braid. Slowly, his eyes drifted back to hers. Abruptly, he released her and backed up to let her pass. ''You'd best go have wardrobe take a few tucks in that costume.''

Deciding she was not meant to decipher his changing moods, Jo stepped by him and crossed the compound. If she spent enough time working, she could keep her thoughts from dwelling on Keane Prescott. Maybe.

Chapter 7

The Big Top was packed for the evening show. Jo watched the anticipation in the range of faces as she took her temporary position in the opening spectacular. The band played jumpy, upbeat music, leaning heavily on brass as the theme parade marched around the hippodrome track. As the substitute Bo Peep, Jo wore a demure mopcap and a wide crinoline skirt and led a baby lamb on a leash. Because her act came so swiftly on the tail of the opening, she rarely participated in the spectacular. Now she enjoyed a close-up look at the audience. In the cage, she blocked them out almost completely.

They were, she decided, a well-mixed group: young babies, older children, parents, grandparents, teenagers. They gave the pageant enthusiastic applause. Jo smiled and waved as she performed the basic choreography with hardly a thought.

After a quick costume change, she took her cue as Queen of the Jungle Cats. After that followed another costume change that transformed her into one of the Twelve Spinning Butterflies.

"Just heard," Jamie whispered in her ear as she took the customary pose by the rope. "You got the job for the next week. Barbara won't be able to handle the teeth grip."

Jo shifted her shoulders to compensate for the weight of her enormous blue wings. "Rose is going to learn the routine," she mumbled back, smiling in the flood of the sunlight. "Duffy's giving her the job if she can stand up under this blasted costume." She made a quick, annoyed sound and smiled brightly. "It weighs a ton."

Slowly, to the beat of the waltz the band played, Jo climbed hand over hand up the rope. "Ah, show biz," she heard Jamie sigh. She vowed to poke him in the ribs when she took her bow. Then, hooking her foot in the hoop, she began the routine, imitating the other eleven Spinning Butterflies.

She was able to share a cup of coffee with Rose's mother when she returned the butterfly costume to wardrobe and changed into her own white and gold jumpsuit. Her muscles complained a bit due to the unfamiliar weight of the wings, and she gave a passing thought to a long, luxurious bath. That was a dream for September, she reminded herself. Showers were the order of the day on the road.

Jo's last duty in the show was to stand on the head of Maggie, the key elephant in the finale's long mount. Sturdy and dependable, Maggie stood firm while four elephants on each side of her rose on their hind legs, resting their front legs on the back of the one in front. Atop Maggie's broad head, Jo stood glittering under the lights with both arms lifted in the air. It was here, more than any other part of the show, that the applause washed over her. It merged with the music, the ringmaster's whistle, the laughter of children. Where she had been weary, she was now filled with energy. She knew the fatigue would return, so she relished the power of the moment all the more. For those few seconds there was no work, no long hours, no predawn drives. There was only magic. Even when it was over and she slid from Maggie's back, she could still feel it.

Outside the tent, troupers and roustabouts and shandies mingled. There were anecdotes to exchange, performances to dissect, observations to be made. Gradually, they drifted away alone, in pairs or in groups. Some would change and help strike the tents, some would sleep, some would worry over their performances. Too energized to sleep, Jo planned to assist in the striking of the Big Top.

She switched on a low light as she entered her trailer, then absently braided her hair as she moved to the tiny bath. With quick moves she creamed off her stage makeup. The exotic exaggeration of her eyes was whisked away, leaving the thick fringe of her lashes and the dark green of her irises unenhanced. The soft bloom of natural rose tinted her cheeks again, and her mouth, unpainted, appeared oddly vulnerable. Accustomed to the change, Jo did not see the sharp contrast between Jovilette the performer and the small, somewhat fragile woman in the glittering jumpsuit. With her face naked and the simple braid hanging down her back, the look of the wild, of the gypsy, was less apparent. It remained in her movements, but her face rinsed of all artifice and unframed, was both delicate and young, part ingenue, part flare. But Jo saw none of this as she reached for her front zipper. Before she could pull it down, a knock sounded on her door.

"Come in," she called out and flicked her braid behind her back as she started down the aisle. She stopped in her tracks as Keane stepped through the door.

"Didn't anyone ever tell you to ask who it is first?" He shut the door behind him and locked it with a careless flick of his wrist. "You might not have to lock your door against the circus people,'' he continued blandly as she remained still, ''but there are several dozen curious towners still hanging around.''

''I can handle a curious towner,'' Jo replied. The offhand quality of his dominance was infuriating. ''I never lock my door.''

There was stiffness and annoyance in her voice. Keane ignored them both. ''I brought you something from Chicago.''

The casual statement succeeded in throwing Jo's temper off the mark. For the first time, she noticed the small package he carried. ''What is it?'' she asked.

Keane smiled and crossed to her. ''It's nothing that bites,'' he assured her, then held it out.

Still cautious, Jo lifted her eyes to his, then dropped her gaze back to the package. ''It's not my birthday,'' she murmured.

''It's not Christmas, either,'' Keane pointed out.

The easy patience in the tone caused Jo to lift her eyes again. She wondered how it was he understood her hesitation to accept presents. She kept her gazed locked on his. ''Thank you,'' she said solemnly as she took the gift.

''You're welcome,'' Keane returned in the same tone.

The amenities done, Jo recklessly ripped the paper. "Oh! It's Dante," she exclaimed, tearing off the remaining paper and tossing it on the table. With reverence she ran her palm over the dark leather binding. The rich scent drifted to her. She knew her quota of books would have been limited to one a year had she bought a volume so handsomely bound. She opened it slowly, as if to prolong the pleasure. The pages were heavy and rich cream in color. The text was Italian, and even as she glanced over the first page, the words ran fluidly through her mind.

"It's beautiful," she murmured, overcome. Lifting her eyes to thank him again, Jo found Keane smiling down at her. Shyness enveloped her suddenly, all the more intense because she had so rarely experienced it. A lifetime in front of crowds had given her a natural confidence in almost any situation. Now color began to surge into her cheeks, and her mind was a jumble of words that would not come to order.

"I'm glad you like it." He ran a finger down her cheek. "Do you always blush when someone gives you a present?"

Because she was at a loss as to how to answer his question, Jo maneuvered around it. "It was nice of you to think of me."

"It seems to come naturally," Keane replied, then watched Jo's lashes flutter down.

"I don't know what to say." She was able to meet

his eyes again with her usual directness, but he had again touched her emotions. She felt inadequate to deal with her feelings or with his effect on her.

"You've already said it." He took the book from Jo's hand and paged through it. "Of course, I can't read a word of it. I envy you that." Before Jo could ponder the idea of a man like Keane Prescott envying her anything, he looked back up and smiled. Her thoughts scattered like nervous ants. "Got any coffee?" he asked and set the book back down on the table.

"Coffee?"

"Yes, you know, coffee. They grow it in quantity in Brazil."

Jo gave him a despairing look. "I don't have any made. I'd fix you a cup, but I've got to change before I help strike the tents. The cookhouse will still be serving."

Keane lifted a brow as he let his eyes wander over her face. "Don't you think that between Bo Peep, lions and butterflies, you've done enough work tonight? By the way, you make a very appealing butterfly."

"Thank you, but—"

"Let's put it this way," Keane countered smoothly. He took the tip of her braid in his fingers. "You've got the night off. I'll make the coffee myself if you show me where you keep it."

Though she let out a windy sigh, Jo was more amused than annoyed. Coffee, she decided, was the least she could do after he had brought her such a lovely present. "I'll make it," she told him, "but you'll probably wish you'd gone to the cookhouse." With this dubious invitation, Jo turned and headed toward the kitchen. He made no sound, but she knew he followed her. For the first time, she felt the smallness of her kitchen.

Setting an undersized copper kettle on one of the two burners, Jo flicked on the power. It was a simple matter to keep her back to him while she plucked cups from the cupboard. She was well aware that if she turned around in the compact kitchen, she would all but be in his arms.

"Did you watch the whole show?" she asked conversationally as she pulled out a jar of instant coffee.

"Duffy had me working props," Keane answered. "He seems to be making me generally useful."

Amused, Jo twisted her head to grin at him. Instantly, she discovered her misstep in strategy. Keane's face was only inches from hers, and in his eyes she read his thoughts. He wanted her, and he intended to have her. Before she could shift her position, Keane took her shoulders and turned her completely around. Jo knew she had backed up against the bars.

Leisurely, he began to loosen her hair, working

his fingers through it until it pooled over her shoulders. "I've wanted to do that since the first time I saw you. It's hair to get lost in." His voice was soft as he took a generous handful. The gesture itself seemed to stake his claim. "In the sun it shimmers with red lights, but in the dark it's like night itself." It came to her that each time she was close to him, she was less able to resist him. She became more lost in his eyes, more beguiled by his power. Already her mouth tingled with the memory of his kiss, with the longing for a new one. Behind them the kettle began a feverish whistle.

"The water," she managed and tried to move around him. With one hand in her hair, Keane kept her still as he turned off the burner. The whistle sputtered peevishly, then died. The sound echoed in Jo's head.

"Do you want coffee?" he murmured as his fingers trailed to her throat.

Jo's eyes clung to his. Hers were enormous and direct, his quiet and searching. "No," she whispered, knowing she wanted nothing more at that moment than to belong to him. He circled her throat with his hand and pressed his fingers against her pulse. It fluttered wildly.

"You're trembling." He could feel the light tremor of her body as he brought her closer. "Is it fear?'' he demanded as his thumbs brushed over her lips. ''Or excitement?''

''Both,'' she answered in a voice thickened with emotion. She made a tiny, confused sound as his palm covered her heart. Its desperate thudding increased. ''Are you...'' She stopped a moment because her voice was breathless and unsteady. ''Are you going to make love to me?'' Did his eyes really darken? she wondered dizzily. Or is it my imagination?

''Beautiful Jovilette,'' he murmured as his mouth lowered to hers. ''No pretentions, no evasions...irresistible.'' The quality of the kiss altered swiftly. His mouth was hungry on hers, and her response leaped past all caution. If loving him was madness, her heart reasoned, could making love take her further beyond sanity? Past wisdom and steeped in sensation, she let her heart rule her will. When her lips parted under his, it was not in surrender but in equal demand.

Keane gentled the kiss. He kept her shimmering on the razor's edge of passion. His mouth teased, promised, then fed her growing need. He found the zipper at the base of her throat and pulled it downward slowly. Her skin was warm, and he sought it, giving a low sound of pleasure as her breast swelled under his hand. He explored without hurry, as if memorizing each curve and plane. Jo no longer trembled but became pliant as her body moved to the rhythm he set. Her sigh was spontaneous, filled with wonder and delight.

With a suddenness that took her breath away, Keane crushed her mouth beneath his in fiery urgency. Jo's instincts responded, thrusting her into a world she had only imagined. His hands grew rougher, more insistent. Jo realized he had relinquished control. They were both riding on the tossing waves of passion. This sea had no horizon and no depth. It was a drowning sea that pulled the unsuspecting under while promising limitless pleasure. Jo did not resist but dove deeper.

At first she thought the knocking was only the sound of her heart against her ribs. When Keane drew away, she murmured in protest and pulled him back. Instantly, his mouth was avid, but as the knocking continued, he swore and pulled back again.

"Someone's persistent," he muttered. Bewildered, Jo stared up at him. "The door," he explained on a long breath.

"Oh." Flustered, Jo ran a hand through her hair and tried to collect her wits.

"You'd better answer it," Keane suggested as he pulled the zipper to her throat in one quick move. Jo broke the surface into reality abruptly. For a moment Keane watched her, taking in her flushed cheeks and tousled hair before he moved aside. Willing her legs to carry her, Jo walked to the front of the trailer. The door handle resisted, then she remembered that Keane had locked it, and she turned the latch.

"Yes, Buck?" she said calmly enough when she opened the door to her handler.

"Jo." His face was in shadows, but she heard the distress in the single syllable. Her chest tightened. "It's Ari."

He had barely finished the name before Jo was out of the trailer and running across the compound. She found both Pete and Gerry standing near Ari's cage.

"How bad?" she demanded as Pete came to meet her.

He took her shoulders. "Really bad this time, Jo."

For a moment she wanted to shake her head, to deny what she read in Pete's eyes. Instead, she nudged him aside and walked to Ari's cage. The old cat lay on his side as his chest lifted and fell with the effort of breathing. "Open it," she ordered Pete in a voice that revealed nothing. There was the jingle of keys, but she did not turn.

"You're not going in there." Jo heard Keane's voice and felt a restraining grip on her shoulders. Her eyes were opaque as she looked up at him.

"Yes, I am. Ari isn't going to hurt me or anyone else. He's just going to die. Now leave me alone." Her voice was low and toneless. "Open it," she ordered again, then pulled out of Keane's loosened hold. The bars rattled as he slid the door open. Hearing it, Jo turned, then hoisted herself into the cage.

Ari barely stirred. Jo saw, as she knelt beside him, that his eyes were open. They were glazed with weariness and pain. "Ari," she sighed, seeing there would be no tomorrow for him. His only answer was a hollow wheezing. Putting a hand to his side, she felt the ragged pace of his breathing. He made an effort to respond to her touch, to his name, but managed only to shift his great head on the floor. The gesture tore at Jo's heart. She lowered her face to his mane, remembering him as he had once been: full of strength and a terrifying beauty. She lifted her face again and took one long, steadying breath. "Buck." She heard him approach but kept her eyes on Ari. "Get the medical kit. I want a hypo of pentobarbital." She could feel Buck's brief hesitation before he spoke.

"Okay, Jo."

She sat quietly, stroking Ari's head. In the distance were the sounds of the Big Top going down, the call of men, the rattle of rigging, the clang of wood against metal. An elephant trumpeted, and three cages down, Faust roared half-heartedly in response.

"Jo." She turned her head as Buck called her and pushed her hair from her eyes. "Let me do it."

Jo merely shook her head and held out her hand.

"Jo." Keane stepped up to the bars. His voice was gentle, but his eyes were so like the cat's at her knees, Jo nearly sobbed aloud. "You don't have to do this yourself."

"He's my cat," she responded dully. "I said I'd do it when it was time. It's time." Her eyes shifted to Buck. "Give me the hypo, Buck. Let's get it done." When the syringe was in her hand, Jo stared at it, then closed her fingers around it. Swallowing hard, she turned back to Ari. His eyes were on her face. After more than twenty years in captivity there was still something not quite tamed in the dying cat. But she saw trust in his eyes and wanted to weep. "You were the best," she told him as she passed a hand through his mane. "You were always the best." Jo felt a numbing cold settling over her and prayed it would last until she had finished. "You're tired now. I'm going to help you sleep." She pulled the safety from the point of the hypodermic and waited until she was certain her hands were steady. "This won't hurt, nothing is going to hurt you anymore."

Involuntarily, Jo rubbed the back of her hand over her mouth, then, moving quickly, she plunged the needle into Ari's shoulder. A quiet whimper escaped her as she emptied the syringe. Ari made no sound but continued to watch her face. Jo offered no words of comfort but sat with him, methodically stroking his fur as his eyes grew cloudy. Gradually, the effort of his breathing lessened, becoming quieter and quieter until it wasn't there at all. Jo felt him grow still, and her hand balled into a fist inside the mass of his mane. One quick, convulsive shudder escaped her. Steeling herself, she moved from the cage, closing the door behind her. Because her bones felt fragile, she kept them stiff, as though they might shatter. Even as she stepped back to the ground, Keane took her arm and began to lead her away.

"Take care of things," he said to Buck as they moved past.

"No." Jo protested, trying and failing to free her arm. "I'll do it."

"No, you won't." Keane's tone held a quiet finality. "Enough's enough."

"Don't tell me what to do," she said sharply, letting her grief take refuge in anger.

"I *am* telling you," he pointed out. His hand was firm on her arm.

"You *can't* tell me what to do," she insisted as tears rose treacherously in her throat. "I want you to leave me alone."

Keane stopped, then took her by the shoulders. His eyes caught the light of a waning moon. "There's no way I'm going to leave you alone when you're so upset."

"My emotions have nothing to do with you." Even as she spoke, he took her arm again and pulled her toward her trailer. Jo wanted desperately to be alone to weep out her grief in private. The mourning belonged to her, and the tears were personal. As if her protests were nonexistent, he pulled her into the trailer and closed the door behind them. "Will you get out of here?" she demanded, frantically swallowing tears.

"Not until I know you're all right." Keane's answer was calm as he walked back to the kitchen.

"I'm perfectly all right." Her breath shuddered in and out quickly. "Or I will be when you leave me alone. You have no right to poke your nose in my business."

"So you've told me before," Keane answered mildly from the back of the trailer.

"I just did what had to be done." She held her body rigid and fought against her own quick, uneven breathing. "I put a sick animal out of his misery; it's as simple as that." Her voice broke, and she turned away, hugging her arms. "For heaven's sake, Keane, go away!"

Quietly, he walked back to her carrying a glass of water. "Drink this."

"No." She whirled back to him. Tears spilled out of her eyes and trickled down her cheeks despite her efforts to banish them. Hating herself, she pressed the heel of her hand between her brows and closed her eyes. "I don't want you here." Keane set down the glass, then gathered her into his arms. "No, don't. I don't want you to hold me."

"Too bad." He ran a hand gently up and down her back. "You did a very brave thing, Jo. I know you loved Ari. I know how hard it was to let him go. You're hurting, and I'm not leaving you."

"I don't want to cry in front of you." Her fists were tight balls at his shoulders.

"Why not?" The stroking continued up and down her back as he cradled her head in the curve of his shoulder.

"Why won't you let me be?" she sobbed as her control slipped. Her fingers gripped his shirt convulsively. "Why am I always losing what I love?" She let the grief come. She let his arms soothe her. As desperately as she had protested against it, she clung to his offer of comfort.

She made no objection as he carried her to the couch and cradled her in his arms. He stroked her hair, as she had stroked Ari, to ease the pain of what couldn't be changed. Slowly, her sobbing quieted. Still she lay with her cheek against his chest, with her hair curtaining her face.

"Better?" he asked as the silence grew calmer. Jo nodded, not yet trusting her voice. Keane shifted her as he reached for the glass of water. "Drink this now."

Gratefully, Jo relieved her dry throat, then went without resistance back against his chest. She closed her eyes, thinking it had been a very long time since she had been held in anyone's lap and soothed. "Keane," she murmured. She felt his lips brush over the top of her head.

"Hmm?"

"Nothing." Her voice thickened as she drifted toward sleep. "Just Keane."

Chapter 8

Jo felt the sun on her closed lids. There was the summer morning sound of excited birds. Her mind, levitating slowly toward the surface, told her it must be Monday. Only on Monday would she sleep past sunrise. That was the enroute day, the only day in seven the circus held no show. She thought lazily of getting up. She would set aside two hours for reading. Maybe I'll drive into town and see a movie. What town are we in? With a sleepy sigh she rolled onto her stomach.

I'll give the cats a good going over, maybe hose them down if it gets hot enough. Memory flooded back and snapped her awake. *Ari.* Opening her eyes, Jo rolled onto her back and stared at the ceiling. Now she recalled vividly how the old cat had died with his eyes trusting on her face. She sighed again. The sadness was still there, but not the sharp, desperate grief of the night before. Acceptance was settling in. She realized that Keane's insistence on staying with her during the peak of her mourning had helped her. He had given her someone to rail at, then someone to hold on to. She remembered the incredible comfort of being cradled in his lap, the solid dependability of his chest against her cheek. She had fallen asleep with the sound of his heart in her ear.

Turning her head, Jo looked out the window, then at the patch of white light the sun tossed on the floor. But it isn't Monday, she remembered suddenly. It's Thursday. Jo sat up, pushing at her hair, which seemed to tumble everywhere at once. What was she doing in bed on a Thursday when the sun was up? Without giving herself time to work out the answer, she scrambled out of bed and hurried from the room. She gave a soft gasp as she ran headlong into Keane.

His hand ran down the length of her hair before he took her shoulder. "I heard you stirring," he said easily, looking down into her stunned face.

"What are you doing here?"

"Making coffee," he answered as he gave her a critical study. "Or I was a moment ago. How are you?"

"I'm all right." Jo lifted her hand to her temple

as if to gain her bearings. "I'm a bit disoriented, I suppose. I overslept. It's never happened before."

"I gave you a sleeping pill," Keane told her matter-of-factly. He slipped an arm around her shoulder as he turned back to the kitchen.

"A pill?" Jo's eyes flew to his. "I don't remember taking a pill."

"It was in the water you drank." On the stove the kettle began its piercing whistle. Moving to it, Keane finished making the coffee. "I had my doubts as to whether you'd take it voluntarily."

"No, I wouldn't have," Jo agreed with some annoyance. "I've never taken a sleeping pill in my life."

"Well, you did last night." He held out a mug of coffee. "I sent Gerry for it while you were in the cage with Ari." Again he gave her a quick, intense study. "It didn't seem to do you any harm. You went out like a light. I carried you to bed, changed your clothes—"

"Changed my..." All at once Jo became aware that she wore only a thin white nightshirt. Her hand reached instinctively for the top button that nestled just above her bosom. Thinking hard, she found she could recall nothing beyond falling asleep in his arms.

"I don't think you'd have spent a very comfortable night in your costume," Keane pointed out. Enjoying his coffee, he smiled at the nervous hand she held between her breasts. "I've had a certain amount of experience undressing women in the dark." Jo dropped her hand. It was an unmistakable movement of pride. Keane's eyes softened. "You needed a good night's sleep, Jo. You were worn out."

Without speaking, Jo lifted her coffee to her lips and turned away. Walking to the window, she could see that the back yard was deserted. Her sleep must indeed have been deep to have kept her unaware of camp breaking.

"Everyone's gone but a couple of roustabouts and a generator truck. They'll take off when you don't need power anymore."

The vulnerability Jo felt was overwhelming. Several times in the course of the evening before, she had lost control, which had always been an essential part of her. Each time, it had been Keane who had been there. She wanted to be angry with him for intruding on her privacy but found it impossible. She had needed him, and he had known it.

"You didn't have to stay behind," she said, watching a crow swoop low over the ground outside.

"I wasn't certain you'd be in any shape to drive fifty miles this morning. Pete's driving my trailer."

Her shoulders lifted and fell before she turned around. Sunlight streamed through the window at her back and poured through the thin folds of her nightshirt. Her body was a slender shadow. When she spoke, her voice was low with regret. "I was horribly rude to you last night."

Keane shrugged and lifted his coffee. "You were upset."

"Yes." Her eyes were an open reflection of her sorrow. "Ari was very important to me. I suppose he was an ongoing link with my father, with my childhood. I'd known for some time he wouldn't make it through the season, but I didn't want to face it." She looked down at the mug she held gripped in both hands. A faint wisp of steam rose from it and vanished. "Last night was a relief for him. It was selfish of me to wish it otherwise. And I was wrong to strike out at you the way I did. I'm sorry."

"I don't want your apology, Jo." Because he sounded annoyed, she looked up quickly.

"I'd feel better if you'd take it, Keane. You've been very kind."

To her astonishment, he swore under his breath and turned back to the stove. "I don't care for your gratitude any more than your apology." He set down his mug and poured in more coffee. "Neither of them is necessary."

"They are to me," Jo replied, then took a step toward him. "Keane..." She set down her coffee and touched his arm. When he turned, she let impulse guide her. She rested her head on his shoulder and slipped her arms around his waist. He stiffened, putting his hands to her shoulders as if to draw her away. Then she heard his breath come out in a long sigh as he relaxed. For an instant he brought her closer.

"I never know precisely what to expect from you," he murmured. He lifted her chin with his finger. In automatic response, Jo closed her eyes and offered her mouth. She felt his fingers tighten on her skin before his lips brushed hers lightly. "You'd better go change." His manner was friendly but cool as he stepped away. "We'll stop off in town, and I'll buy you some breakfast."

Puzzled by his attitude but satisfied he was no longer annoyed, Jo nodded. "All right."

Spring became summer as the circus wound its way north. The sun stayed longer, peeking into the Big Top until well after the evening show began. Heavy rain came infrequently, but there were quick summer storms with thunder and lightning. Through June, Prescott's Circus Colossus snaked through North Carolina and into western Tennessee.

During the long weeks while spring tripped over into summer, Jo found Keane's attitude a paradox. His friendliness toward her was offhand. He laughed if she said something amusing, listened if she had a complaint and to her confusion, slipped a thin barrier between them. At times she wondered if the passion that had flared between them the night he had returned from Chicago had truly existed. Had the desire she had tasted on his lips been a fantasy? The closeness she had felt blooming between them had withered and blown away. They were only owner and trouper now.

Keane flew back to Chicago twice more during this period, but he brought no surprise presents back with him. Not once during those long weeks did he come by her trailer. Initially, his altered manner confused her. He was not angry. His mood was neither heated nor icy with temper but fell into an odd middle ground she could not understand. Jo ached with love. As days passed into weeks, she was forced to admit that Keane did not seem to be interested in a close relationship.

On the eve of the July Fourth show, Jo sat sleepless in her bed. In her hand she held the volume of Dante, but the book was only a reminder of the emptiness she felt. She closed it, then stared at the ceiling. It's time to snap out of it, she lectured herself. It's time to stop pretending he was ever really part of my life. Loving someone only makes him a part of your wishes. He never talked about love, he never promised anything, never offered anything but what he gave to me. He's done nothing to hurt me. Jo

squeezed her eyes shut and pressed the book between her fingers. How I wish I could hate him for
showing me what life could be like and then turning
away, she thought.

But I can't. Jo let out a shaky breath and relaxed
her grip on the book. Gently, she ran a finger down
its smooth, leather binding. I can't hate him, but I
can't love him openly, either. How do I stop? I
should be grateful he stopped wanting me. I would
have made love with him. Then I'd hurt a hundred
times more. Could I hurt a hundred times more? For
several moments she lay still, trying to quiet her
thoughts.

It's best not to know, she told herself sternly. It's
best to remember he was kind to me when I needed
him and that I haven't a right to make demands.
Summer doesn't last forever. I may never see him
again when it's over. At least I can keep the time
we have pleasant.

The words sounded hollow in her heart.

Chapter 9

The Fourth of July was a full day with a run to a new lot, the tent raising, a street parade and two shows. But it was a holiday. Elephants wore red, white and blue plumes atop their massive heads. The evening performance would be held an hour earlier to allow for the addition of a fireworks display. Traditionally, Prescott's circus arranged to spend the holiday in the same small town in Tennessee. The license and paperwork for the display were seen to in advance, and the fireworks were shipped ahead to be stored in a warehouse. The procedure had been precisely the same for years. It was one of the circus's most profitable nights. Concessions thrived.

Jo moved through the day with determined cheerfulness. She refused to permit the distance between her and Keane to spoil one of the highlights of the summer. Brooding, she decided, would not change things. The mood of the crowd helped to keep her spirits light.

Between shows came the inevitable lull. Some troupers sat outside their trailers exchanging small talk and enjoying the sun. Others got in a bit more practice or worked out a few kinks. Bull hands washed down the elephants, causing a minor flood in the pen area.

Jo watched the bathing process with amusement. She never ceased to enjoy this particular aspect of circus life, especially if there were one or two inexperienced bull hands involved. Invariably, Maggie or one of the other veteran bulls would spray a trunkful of water over the new hands to initiate them. Though Jo knew the other hands encouraged it, they always displayed remarkable innocence.

Spotting Duffy, Jo moved away from the elephant area and wandered toward him. She could see he was deep in discussion with a towner. He was as short as Duffy but wider, with what she had once heard Frank call a successful frame. His stomach started high and barreled out to below his waist. He had a ruddy complexion and pale eyes that squinted hard against the sun. Jo had seen his type before. She wondered what he was selling and how much he wanted for it. Since Duffy was puffing with annoyance, Jo assumed it was quite a lot.

"I'm telling you, Carlson, we've already paid for storage. I've got a signed receipt. And we pay fifteen bucks delivery, not twenty."

Carlson was smoking a small, unfiltered cigarette and dropped it to the ground. "You paid Myers for storage, not me. I bought the place six weeks ago." He shrugged his wide shoulders. "Not my problem you paid in advance."

Looking over, Jo saw Keane approaching with Pete. Pete was talking rapidly, Keane nodding. As Jo watched, Keane glanced up and gave Carlson a quick study. She had seen that look before and knew the older man had been assessed. Keane caught her eye, smiled and began to move past her. "Hello, Jo."

Unashamedly curious, Jo fell into step beside him. "What's going on?"

"Why don't we find out?" he suggested as they stopped in front of Duffy and Carlson. "Gentlemen," Keane said in an easy tone. "Is there a problem?"

"This character," Duffy spouted, jerking a scornful thumb at Carlson's face, "wants us to pay twice for storage on the fireworks. Then he wants twenty for delivery when we agreed on fifteen."

"Myers agreed on fifteen," Carlson pointed out.

He smiled without humor. "I didn't agree on any-thing. You want your fireworks, you gotta pay for them first—cash," he added, then spared Keane a glance. "Who's this guy?"

Duffy began to wheeze with indignation, but Keane laid a restraining hand on his shoulder. "I'm Prescott," he told him in untroubled tones. "Perhaps you'd like to fill me in."

"Prescott, huh?" Carlson stroked both his chins as he studied Keane. Seeing youth and amiable eyes, he felt closer to success. "Well, now we're getting somewhere," he said jovially and stuck out his hand. Keane accepted it without hesitation. "Jim Carl-son," he continued as he gave Keane's hand a brisk pump. "Nice circus you got here, Prescott. Me and the missus see it every year. Well, now," he said again and hitched up his belt. "Seeing as you're a businessman, too, I'm sure we can straighten all this out. Problem is, your fireworks've been stored in my warehouse. Now, I gotta make a living, they can't just sit there for free. I bought the place off Myers six weeks ago. I can't be held responsible for a deal you made with him, can I?" Carlson gave a stretched-lip smile, pleased that Keane listened so politely. "And as for delivery, well…" He made a helpless gesture and patted Keane's shoulder. "You know about gas prices these days, son. But we can work that out after we settle this other little problem.''

Keane nodded agreeably. ''That sounds reasonable.'' He ignored Duffy's huffing and puffing. ''You do seem to have a problem, Mr. Carlson.''

''I don't have a problem,'' Carlson countered. His smile suffered a fractional slip. ''You've got the problem, unless you don't want the fireworks.''

''Oh, we'll have the fireworks, Mr. Carlson,'' Keane corrected with a smile Jo thought more wolfish than friendly. ''According to paragraph three, section five, of the small business code, the lessor is legally bound by all contracts, agreements, liens and mortgages of the previous lessor until such time as all aforesaid contracts, agreements, liens and mortgages are expired or transferred.''

''What the…'' Carlson began with no smile at all, but Keane continued blandly.

''Of course, we won't pursue the matter in court as long as we get our merchandise. But that doesn't solve your problem.''

''My problem?'' Carlson sputtered while Jo looked on in frank admiration. ''I haven't got a problem. If you think…''

''Oh, but you do, Mr. Carlson, though I'm sure there was no intent to break the law on your part.''

''Break the law?'' Carlson wiped damp hands on his slacks.

"Storing explosives without a license," Keane pointed out. "Unless, of course, you obtained one after your purchase of the warehouse."

"Well, no, I..."

"I was afraid of that." Keane lifted his brow in pity. "You see, in paragraph six of section five of the small business code it states that all licenses, permits and warrants shall be nontransferable. Authorization for new licenses, permits or warrants must be requested in writing by the current owner. Notarized, naturally." Keane waited a bit to allow Carlson to wrestle with the idea. "If I'm not mistaken," he continued conversationally, "the fine's pretty hefty in this state. Of course, sentencing depends on—"

"Sentencing?" Carlson paled and mopped the back of his neck with a handkerchief.

"Look, tell you what." Keane gave Carlson a sympathetic smile. "You get the fireworks over here and off your property. We don't have to bring the law in on something like this. Just an oversight, after all. We're both businessmen, aren't we?"

Too overwrought to detect sarcasm, Carlson nodded.

"That was fifteen on delivery, right?"

Carlson didn't hesitate but stuck the damp handkerchief back in his pocket and nodded again.

"Good enough. I'll have the cash for you on delivery. Glad to help you out."

Relieved, Carlson turned and headed for his pickup. Jo managed to keep her features grave until he pulled off the lot. Simultaneously, Pete and Duffy began to hoot with laughter.

"Was it true?" Jo demanded and took Keane's arm.

"Was what true?" Keane countered, merely lifting a brow over the hysterics that surrounded him.

"'Paragraph three, section five, of the small business code,'" Jo quoted.

"Never heard of it," Keane answered mildly, nearly sending Pete into orbit.

"You made it up," Jo said in wonder. "You made it all up!"

"Probably," Keane agreed.

"Smoothest con job I've seen in years," Duffy stated and gave Keane a parental slap on the back. "Son, you could go into business."

"I did," Keane told him and grinned.

"I ever need a lawyer," Pete put in, pushing his cap further back on his head, "I know where to go. You come on by the cookhouse tonight, Captain. We're having ourselves a poker game. Come on, Duffy, Buck's gotta hear about this."

As they moved off, Jo realized that Keane had been officially accepted. Before, he had been the legal owner but an outsider, a towner. Now he was one of them. Turning, she lifted her face to his. "Welcome aboard."

"Thank you." She saw he understood precisely what had been left unsaid.

"I'll see you at the game," she said before her smile became a grin. "Don't forget your money."

She turned away, but Keane touched her arm, bringing her back to him. "Jo," he began, puzzling her by the sudden seriousness of his eyes.

"Yes?"

There was a brief hesitation, then he shook his head. "Nothing, never mind. I'll see you later." He rubbed his knuckles over her cheek, then walked away.

Jo studied her hand impassively. On the deal, she had missed a heart flush by one card and now waited for someone to open. Casually, she moved her glance around the table. Duffy was puffing on a cigar, apparently unconcerned with the dwindling chips in front of him. Pete chewed his gum with equal nonchalance. Amy, the wife of the sword swallower, sat beside him, then Jamie, then Raoul. Directly beside Jo was Keane, who, like Pete, was winning consistently.

The pot grew. Chips clinked on the table. Jo discarded and was pleased to exchange a club for the fifth heart. She slipped it into her hand without blinking. Frank had taught her the game. Before the second round of betting, Jamie folded in disgust. "Should never have taken Buck's seat," he muttered and frowned when Pete raised the bet.

"You got out cheap, kiddo," Duffy told him dolefully as he tossed in chips. "I'm only staying in so I don't change my standard of living. Money'll do that to you," he mumbled obscurely.

"Three kings," Pete announced when called, then spread his cards. Amid a flutter of complaints cards were tossed down.

"Heart flush," Jo said mildly before Pete could rake in the pot. Duffy leaned back and gave a hoot of laughter.

"Atta, girl, Jo. I hate to see him win all my money."

During the next two hours the cookhouse tent grew hot and ripe with the scents of coffee and tobacco and beer. Jamie's luck proved so consistently poor that he called for Buck to relieve him.

Jo found herself with an indifferent pair of fives. Almost immediately the betting grew heavy as Keane raised Raoul's opening. Curiosity kept Jo in one round, but practicality had her folding after the draw. Divorced from the game, she watched it with interest. Leaning on her elbows, she studied each participant. Keane played a good game, she mused.

His eyes gave nothing away. They never did. Casually, he nursed the beer beside him while Duffy, Buck and Amy folded. Studying him closely, Pete chewed his gum. Keane returned the look, keeping the stub of his cigar clamped between his teeth. Raoul muttered in French and scowled at his cards.

"Could be bluffing," Pete considered, seeing Keane's raise. "Let's raise it five more and see what's cooking." Raoul swore in French, then again in English, before he tossed in his hand. Taking his time, Keane counted out the necessary chips and tossed them into the pot. It was a plastic mountain of red, white and blue. Then, he counted out more.

"I'll see your five," he said evenly, "and raise it ten."

There was mumbling around the table. Pete looked into his hand and considered. Shifting his eyes, he took in the generous pile of chips in front of him. He could afford to risk another ten. Glancing up, he studied Keane's face while he fondled his chips. Abruptly, he broke into a grin.

"Nope," he said simply, turning his cards face down. "This one's all yours."

Setting down his cards, Keane raked in a very sweet pot. "Gonna show 'em?" Pete asked. His grin was affable.

Keane pushed a stray chip into the pile and

shrugged. With his free hand he turned over the cards. The reaction ranged from oaths to laughter.

"Trash," Pete mumbled with a shake of his head. "Nothing but trash. You've got nerve, Captain." His grin grew wide as he turned over his own cards. "Even I had a pair of sevens."

Raoul gnashed his teeth and swore elegantly in two languages. Jo grinned at his imaginative choice of words. She rose on a laugh and snatched off the soft felt hat Jamie wore. Deftly, she scooped her chips into it. "Cash me in later," she requested, then gave him a smacking kiss on the mouth. "But don't play with them."

Duffy scowled over at her. "Aren't you cashing in early?"

"You've always told me to leave 'em wanting more," she reminded him. With a grin and a wave, she swung through the door.

"That Jo," said Raoul, chuckling as he shuffled the cards. "She's one smart cracker."

"Cookie," Pete corrected, opening a fresh stick of gum. He noticed that Keane's gaze had drifted to the door she had closed behind her. "Some looker, too," he commented and watched Keane's eyes wander back to his. "Don't you think, Captain?"

Keane slipped his cards into a pile as they were dealt to him. "Jo's lovely."

"Like her mother," Buck put in, frowning at his

cards. "She was a beaut, huh, Duffy?" Duffy grunted in agreement and wondered why Lady Luck refused to smile on him. "Always thought it was a crime for her to die that way. Wilder, too," he added with a shake of his head.

"A fire, wasn't it?" Keane asked as he picked up his cards and spread them.

"Electrical fire." Buck nodded and lifted his beer. "A short in their trailer's wiring. What a waste. If they hadn't been in bed asleep, they'd probably still be alive. The trailer was halfway gone before anybody set up an alarm. Just plain couldn't get to the Wilders. Their side of the trailer was like a furnace. Jo's bedroom was on the other side, and we nearly lost her. Frank busted in the window and pulled her out. Poor little tyke. She was holding onto this old doll like it was the last thing she had left. Kept it with her for I don't know how long. Remember, Duffy?" He glanced into his hand and opened for two. "It only had one arm." Duffy grunted again and folded. "Frank sure knew how to handle that little girl."

"She knew how to handle him, more likely," Duffy mumbled. Raoul bumped the pot five, and Keane folded.

"Deal me out the next hand," he said as he rose and moved to the door. One of the Gribalti brothers took the chair Jo had vacated, and Jamie slipped into

Keane's. Curious, he lifted the tip of the cards. He saw a jack-high straight. With a thoughtful frown, he watched the door swing shut.

Outside, Jo moved through the warm night. With a glance at the sky, she thought of the fireworks. They had been wonderful, she mused, stirring up the stars with exploding color. Though it was over and a new day hovered, she felt some magic remained in the night. Far from sleepy, she wandered toward the Big Top.

"Hello, pretty lady."

Jo looked into the shadows and narrowed her eyes. She could just barely make out a form. "Oh, you're Bob, aren't you?" She stopped and gave him a friendly smile. "You're new."

He stepped toward her. "I've been on for nearly three weeks." He was young, Jo guessed about her own age, with a solid build and sharp-featured face. Just that afternoon she had watched Maggie give him a shower.

Jo pushed her hands into the pockets of her cut-offs and continued to smile. It appeared he thought his tenure made him a veteran. "How do you like working with the elephants?"

"It's okay. I like putting up the tent."

Jo understood his feeling. "So do I. There's a

game in the cookhouse,'' she told him with a gesture of her arm. ''You might like to sit in.''

''I'd rather be with you.'' As he moved closer, Jo caught the faint whiff of beer. He's been celebrating, she thought and shook her head.

''It's a good thing tomorrow's Monday,'' she commented. ''No one's going to be in any shape to pitch a tent. You should go to bed,'' she suggested. ''Or get some coffee.''

''Let's go to your trailer.'' Bob weaved a little, then took her arm.

''No.'' Firmly, Jo turned in the opposite direction. ''Let's go to the cookhouse.'' His advances did not trouble her. She was close enough to the cookhouse tent that if she called out, a dozen able-bodied men would come charging. But that was precisely what Jo wanted to avoid.

''I want to go with you,'' he said, stumbling over the words as he veered away from the cookhouse again. ''You look so pretty in that cage with those lions.'' He put both arms around her, but Jo felt it was as much for balance as romance. ''A fella needs a pretty lady once in a while.''

''I'm going to feed you to my lions if you don't let me go,'' Jo warned.

''Bet you can be a real wildcat,'' he mumbled and made a fumbling dive for her mouth.

Though her patience was wearing thin, Jo endured

the kiss that landed slightly to the left of bull's-eye. His hands, however, had better aim and grabbed the firm roundness of her bottom. Losing her temper, Jo pushed away but found his hold had taken root. In a quick move, she brought up her fist and caught him square on the jaw. With only a faint sound of surprise, Bob sat down hard on the ground.

"Well, so much for rescuing you," Keane commented from behind her.

Turning quickly, Jo pushed at her hair and gave an annoyed sigh. She would have preferred no witnesses. Even in the dim light, she could see he was furious. Instinctively, she stepped between him and the man who sat on the ground fingering his jaw and shaking the buzzing from his ears.

"He—Bob just got a bit overenthusiastic," she said hastily and put a restraining hand on Keane's arm. "He's been celebrating."

"I'm feeling a bit enthusiastic myself," Keane stated. As he made to brush her aside, Jo clung with more fervor.

"No, Keane, please."

Looking down, he fired a glare. "Jo, would you let go so that I can deal with this?"

"Not until you listen." The faint hint of laughter in her eyes only enraged him further, and Jo fought to suppress it. "Keane, please, don't be hard on him. He didn't hurt me."

"He was attacking you," Keane interrupted. He barely resisted the urge to shake her off and drag the still seated Bob by the scruff of the neck.

"No, he was really more just leaning on me. His balance is a trifle impaired. He only tried to kiss me," she pointed out, wisely deleting the wandering hands. "And I hit him much harder than I should have. He's new, Keane, don't fire him."

Exasperated, he stared at her. "Firing was the least of what I had in mind for him."

Jo smiled, unable to keep the gleam from her eyes. "If you were going to avenge my honor, he really didn't do much more than breathe on it. I don't think you should run him through for that. Maybe you could just put him in the stocks for a couple of days."

Keane swore under his breath, but a reluctant smile tugged at his mouth. Seeing it, Jo loosened her hold. "Miss Wilder wants to give you a break," he told the dazed Bob in a tough, no-nonsense voice that Jo decided he used for intimidating witnesses. "She has a softer heart than I do. Therefore, I won't knock you down several more times or kick you off the lot, as I had entertained doing." He paused, allowing Bob time to consider this possibility. "Instead, I'll let you sleep off your—enthusiasm." In one quick jerk, he pulled Bob to his feet. "But if I ever hear of you breathing uninvited on Miss Wilder or any other of my female employees, we'll go back to the first choice. And before I kick you out,'' he added with low menace, ''I'll let it be known that you were decked by one punch from a hundred-pound woman.''

''Yes, sir, Mr. Prescott,'' said Bob as clearly as possible.

''Go to bed,'' Jo said kindly, seeing him pale. ''You'll feel better in the morning.''

''Obviously,'' Keane commented as Bob lurched away, ''you haven't done much drinking.'' He turned to Jo and grinned. ''The one thing he's not going to feel in the morning is better.'' Jo smiled, pleased to have Keane talk to her without the thin shield of politeness. ''And where,'' he asked and took her hand for examination, ''did you learn that right jab?''

Jo laughed, allowing Keane's fingers to interlock with hers. ''It would hardly have knocked him down if he hadn't already been tilting in that direction.'' Her face turned up to his and sparkled with starlight. In his eyes an expression she couldn't comprehend came and went. ''Is something wrong?''

For a moment he said nothing. In her breast her heart began to hammer as she waited to be kissed. ''No, nothing,'' he said. The moment was shattered. ''Come on, I'll walk you back to your trailer.''

''I wasn't going there.'' Wanting to put him back

into an easy mood, she linked her arm with his. "If you come with me, I'll show you some magic." Her smile slanted invitingly. "You like magic, don't you, Keane? Even a sober, dedicated lawyer must like magic."

"Is that how I strike you?" Jo almost laughed at the trace of annoyance in his voice. "As a sober, dedicated lawyer?"

"Oh, not entirely, though that's part of you." She enjoyed feeling that for the moment she had him to herself. "You've also got a streak of adventure and a rather nice sense of humor. And," she added with generous emphasis, "there's your temper."

"You seem to have me all figured out."

"Oh, no." Jo stopped and turned to him. "Not at all. I only know how you are here. I can only speculate on how you are in Chicago."

His brow lifted as she caught his attention. "Would I be different there?"

"I don't know." Jo's forehead wrinkled in thought. "Wouldn't you be? Circumstances would. You probably have a house or a big apartment, and there's a housekeeper who comes in once—no, twice—a week." Caught up in the picture, she gazed off into the distance and built it further. "You have an office with a view of the city, a very efficient secretary and a brilliant law clerk. You go to business lunches at the club. In court you're deadly and very successful. You have your own tailor and work out at the gym three times a week. There's the theater on the weekends, along with something physical. Tennis maybe, not golf. No, handball.''

Keane shook his head. "Is this the magic?"

"No." Jo shrugged and began to walk again. "Just guesswork. You don't have to have a great deal of money to know how people who do behave. And I know you take the law seriously. You wouldn't choose a career that wasn't very important to you.''

Keane walked in silence. When he spoke, his voice was quiet. "I'm not certain I'm comfortable with your little outline of my life.''

"It's very sketchy," Jo told him. "I'd have to understand you better to fill in the gaps.''

"Don't you?"

"What?" Jo asked, pausing. "Understand you?" She laughed, tickled at the absurdity of his question. "No, I don't understand you. How could I? You live in a different world." With this, she tossed aside the flap of the Big Top and stepped into its darkness. When she hit the switch, two rows of overhead lights flashed on. Shadows haunted the corners and fell over the arena seats.

"It's wonderful, isn't it?" Her clear voice ran the length of the tent and echoed back. "It's not empty, you know. They're always here—the troupers, the audience, the animals.'' She walked forward until she stood beside the third ring. ''Do you know what this is?'' she asked Keane, tossing out her arms and turning a full circle. ''It's an ageless wonder in a changing world. No matter what happens on the outside, this is here. We're the most fragile of circuses, at the mercy of the elephants, of emotions, of mechanics, of public whims. But six days a week for twenty-nine weeks we perform miracles. We build a world at dawn, then disappear into the dark. That's part of it—the mystery.'' She waited until Keane moved forward to join her.

''Tents pop up on an empty lot, elephants and lions walk down Main Street. And we never grow old, because each new generation discovers us all over again.'' She stood slender and exquisite in a circle of light. ''Life here's crazy. And it's hard. Muddy lots, insane hours, sore muscles, but when you've finished your act and you get that feeling that tells you it was special, there's nothing else like it in the world.''

''Is that why you do it?'' Keane asked.

Jo shook her head and moved out of the circle of light into the dark and into another ring. ''It's all part of the same thing. We all have our own reasons, I suppose. You've asked me that before; I'm not certain I can explain. Maybe it's that we all believe in miracles.'' She turned under the light, and it shimmered around her. "I've been here all my life. I know every trick, every illusion. I know how Jamie's dad gets twenty clowns into a two-seater car. But each time I see it, I laugh and I believe it. It's not just the excitement, Keane, it's the anticipation of the excitement. It's knowing you're going to see the biggest or the smallest or the fastest or the highest." Jo ran to the center ring and threw up her arms.

"Ladies and gentlemen," she announced with a toss of her head. "For your amazement and astonishment, for the first time in America, a superabundance of mountainous, mighty pachyderms led in a stupendous exhibition of choreography by the Great Serena." Jo laughed and shifted her hair to her back with a quick movement of her hand. "Dancing elephants!" she said to Keane, pleased that he was smiling. "Or you listen to the talker in the sideshow when he starts his spiel. Step right up. Come a little closer." She curled her fingers in invitation. "See the Amazing Serpentina and her monstrous, slithering vipers. Watch the beautiful young girl charm a deadly cobra. Watch her accept the reptilian embrace of the gargantuan boa. Don't miss the chance to see the enchantress of the evil serpent!"

"I suppose Baby might sue for slander."

Jo laughed and stepped up on the ring. "But when the crowds see little Rose with a boa constrictor wrapped around her shoulders, they've gotten their money's worth. We give them what they come for: color, fantasy, the unique. Thrills. You've seen the audience when Vito does his high wire act without a net.''

"A net seems little enough protection when he's balancing on a wire at two hundred feet." Keane stuck his hands in his pockets and frowned. "He risks his life every day."

"So does a police officer or a fire fighter." Jo spoke quietly and rested her hands on his shoulders. It seemed more necessary than ever that she make him understand his father's dream. "I know what you're saying, Keane, but you have to understand us. The element of danger is essential to many of the acts. You can hear the whole audience suck in their breath when Vito does his back somersault on the wire. They'd be impressed if he used a net, but they wouldn't be terrified."

"Do they need to be?"

Jo's sober expression lightened. "Oh, yes! They need to be terrified and fascinated and mesmerized. It's all included in the price of a ticket. This is a world of superlatives. We test the limit of human daring, and every day it changes. Do you know how long it took before the first man accomplished the triple on the trapeze? Now it's nearly a standard." A light of anticipation flared in her eyes. "One day someone will do a quadruple. If a man stands in this ring and juggles three torches today, tomorrow someone will juggle them on horseback and after that there'll be a team tossing them back and forth while swinging on a trap. It's our job to do the incredible, then, when it's done, to do the impossible. It's that simple.''

"Simple," Keane murmured, then lifted a hand to caress her hair. "I wonder if you'd think so if you could see it from the outside.''

"I don't know." Her fingers tightened on his shoulders as he buried his other hand in her hair. "I never have.''

As if his thoughts centered on it, Keane combed his fingers through her hair. Gradually, he pushed it back until only his hands framed her face. They stood in a pool of light that threw their shadows long behind them. "You are so lovely," he murmured.

Jo neither spoke nor moved. There was something different this time in the way he touched her. There was a gentleness and a hesitation she had not felt before. Though they looked directly into hers, she could not read his eyes. Their faces were close, and his breath fluttered against her mouth. Jo slid her arms around his neck and pressed her mouth to his.

Not until that moment had she realized how empty she had felt, how desperately she had needed to hold him. Her lips were hungry for his. She clung while all gentleness fled from his touch. His hands were greedy. The weeks that he had not touched her were forgotten as her skin warmed and hummed with quickening blood. Passion stripped her of inhibitions, and her tongue sought his, taking the kiss into wilder and darker depths. Their lips parted, only to meet again with sharp new demands. She understood that all needs and all desires were ultimately only one—Keane.

His mouth left hers, and for an instant he rested his cheek against her hair. For that moment Jo felt a contentment more complete than she had ever known. Abruptly, he drew away.

Puzzled, she watched as he drew out a cigar. She lifted a hand to run it through the hair he had just disturbed. He flicked on his lighter. "Keane?" She looked at him, knowing her eyes offered everything.

"You've had a long day," he began in an oddly polite tone. Jo winced as if he had struck her. "I'll walk you back to your trailer."

She stepped off the ring and away from him. Pain seared along her skin. "Why are you doing this?" To her humiliation, tears welled in her eyes and lodged in her throat. The tears acted as a prism, refracting the light and clouding her vision. She blinked them back. Keane's brows drew together at the gesture.

"I'll take you back," he said again. The detached tone of his voice accelerated all Jo's fury and grief.

"How dare you!" she demanded. "How dare you make me…" The word *love* nearly slipped through her lips, and she swallowed it. "How dare you make me want you, then turn away! I was right about you from the beginning. I thought I'd been wrong. You're cold and unfeeling." Her breath came quickly and unevenly, but she refused to retreat until she had said it all. Her face was pale with the passion of her emotions. "I don't know why I thought you'd ever understand what Frank had given you. You need a heart to see the intangible. I'll be glad when the season's over and you do whatever it is you're going to do. I'll be glad when I never have to see you again. I won't let you do this to me anymore!" Her voice wavered, but she made no attempt to steady it. "I don't want you to ever touch me again."

Keane studied her for a long moment, then took a careful drag on his cigar. "All right, Jo."

The very calmness of his answer tore a sob from her before she turned and ran from the Big Top.

Chapter 10

In July the troupe circled through Virginia, touched the tip of West Virginia on their way into Kentucky, then moved into Ohio. Audiences fanned themselves as the temperatures in the Big Top rose, but they still came.

Since the evening of the Fourth, Jo had avoided Keane. It was not as difficult as it might have been, as he spent half the month in Chicago dealing with his business. Jo functioned. She ate because eating was necessary in order to maintain her strength. She slept because rest was essential to remaining alert in the cage. She did not find any enjoyment in food nor was her sleep restful. Because so many in the troupe knew her well, Jo struggled to keep on a mask of normalcy. Above all, she needed to avoid any questions, any advice, any sympathy. It was necessary, because of her profession, to put her emotions on hold a great deal of the time. After some struggle and some failure, Jo achieved a reasonable success.

Her training of Gerry continued, as did his progress. The additional duty of working with him helped fill her small snatches of spare time. On afternoons when no matinee was scheduled, Jo took him into the big cage. As he grew more proficient, she brought other cats in to join Merlin. By the first week in August they were working together with her full complement of lions.

The only others who were rehearsing in the Big Top were the equestrian act. They ran through the Thread the Needle routine in the first ring. Hooves echoed dully on tanbark. Jo supervised while Gerry sent the cats into a pyramid. At his urging, Lazarus climbed up the wide, arched ladder that topped the grouping. Twice he balked, and twice Gerry was forced to reissue the command.

"Good," Jo commented when the pyramid was complete.

"He wouldn't go." Gerry began to complain, but she cut him off.

"Don't be in too much of a hurry. Bring them down." Her tone was brisk and professional. "Make certain they dismount and take their seats in the right order. It's important to stick to routine.''

Hands resting on hips, Jo watched. In her opinion, Gerry had true potential. His nerves were good, he had a feeling for the animals, and he was slowly developing patience. Still she balked at the next step in his training: leaving him alone in the arena. Even with only Merlin, she felt it too risky. He was still too casual. Not yet did he possess enough respect for the lion's guile.

Jo moved around the arena, and the lions, used to her, were not disturbed. As the cats settled onto their pedestals, she once more moved to stand beside Gerry. ''Now we'll walk down the line. You make each do a sit-up before we send them out.''

One by one the cats rose on their haunches and pawed the air. Jo and Gerry moved down their ranks. The heat was becoming oppressive, and Jo shifted her shoulders, longing for a cool shower and a change of clothes. When they came to Hamlet, he ignored the command with a rebellious snarl.

Bad-tempered brute, thought Jo absently as she waited for Gerry to reissue the command. He did so but moved forward as if to emphasize the words.

''No, not so close!'' Jo warned quickly. Even as she spoke, she saw the change in Hamlet's eyes.

Instinctively, she stepped over, nudging Gerry back and shielding his body with hers. Hamlet struck out, claws extended. There was a moment of blind heat in her shoulder as the skin ripped. Swiftly, she was facing the cat, holding tightly onto Gerry's arm as they stood just out of range.

"Don't run," she ordered, feeling his jerk of panic. Her arm was on fire as the blood began to flow freely. Keeping her movements quick but smooth, she took the whip from Gerry's nerveless hand and cracked it hard, using her left arm. She knew that if Hamlet continued his defiance and attacked, it was hopeless. The other cats were certain to join in a melee. It would be over before anything could be done. Already, Abra shifted restlessly and bared her teeth.

"Open the chute," Jo called out. Her voice was cool as ice. "Back toward the safety cage," she instructed Gerry as she gave the cats their signal to leave the arena. "I've got to get them out one at a time. Move slow, and if I tell you to stop, you stop dead. Understand?"

She heard him swallow as she watched the cats begin to leap off their pedestals and file into the chute. "He got you. Is it bad?" The words were barely a whisper and drenched in terror.

"I said go." Half the cats were gone, and still Hamlet's eyes were locked on hers. There was no time to waste. One part of her brain heard shouting outside the cage, but she blocked it out and focused

all her concentration on the cat. "Go now," she repeated to Gerry. "Do as you're told."

He swallowed again and began to back away.
Long seconds dragged until she heard the rattle of
the safety cage door. When his turn came, Hamlet
made no move to leave his seat. Jo was alone with
him. She could smell the heat, the scent of the wild
and the fragrance of her own blood. Her arm was
alive with pain. Slowly, she tested him by backing
up. The safety cage seemed hundreds of miles away.
The cat tensed immediately, and she stopped. She
knew he would not let her cross the arena. Outrun-
ning him was impossible, as the distance between
them could be covered in one spring. She had to
outbluff him instead.

"Out," she ordered firmly. "Out, Hamlet." As
he continued to watch her, Jo felt a trickle of sweat
slide down between her shoulder blades. Her skin
was clammy with it in contrast to the warmth of the
blood that ran down her arm. There was a sudden,
vivid picture inside her head of her father being
dragged around the cage. Fear tripped inside her
throat. There was a lightness fluttering in the top of
her head, and she knew that a moment's terror would
cause her to faint. She stiffened her spine and pushed
it away.

Speed was important. The longer she allowed the
cat to remain in the arena after his cue, the more

defiant he would become. And the more dangerous. As yet he was unaware that he held her at such a sharp disadvantage. "Out, Hamlet." Jo repeated the command with a crack of the whip. He leaped from the pedestal. Jo's stomach trembled. She locked every muscle, and as the cat hesitated, she repeated the command. He was confused, and she knew this could work as an advantage or a curse. Confused, he might spring or retreat. Her fingers tightened on the stock of the whip and trembled. The cat paced nervously and watched her.

"Hamlet!" She raised her voice and bit off each syllable. "Go out." To the words she added the hand signal she had used before he was fully trained to voice command.

As if rebuffed, Hamlet relaxed his tail and padded into the chute. Before the door slid completely closed, Jo sank to her knees. Her body began to quake fiercely with the aftershock. No more than five minutes had passed since Hamlet had defied Gerry's command, but her muscles bore the strain of hours. For an instant her vision blurred. Even as she shook her head to clear it, Keane was on the ground beside her.

She heard him swear, ripping the tattered sleeve of her blouse from her arm. He fired questions at her, but she could do no more than shake her head and gulp in air. Focusing on him, she noticed his eyes were unusually dark against his face.

"What?" She followed his voice but not the words. He swore again, sharply enough to penetrate the first layer of her shock. He pulled her to her feet, then continuing the motion smoothly, lifted her into his arms. "Don't." Her mind struggled to break through the fog and function. "I'm all right."

"Shut up," he said harshly as he carried her from the cage. "Just shut up."

Because speaking cost her some effort, Jo obeyed. Closing her eyes, she let the mixture of excited voices whirl around her. Her arm screamed with pain, but the throbbing reassured her. Numbness would have terrified her. Still she kept her eyes shut, not yet having the courage to look at the damage. Being alive was enough.

When she opened her eyes again, Keane was carrying her into the administration wagon. At the sound of the chaos that followed them, Duffy strode through from his office. "What the…" he began, then stopped and paled beneath his freckles. He moved quickly forward as Keane set Jo in a chair. "How bad?"

"I don't know yet," Keane muttered. "Get a towel and the first-aid kit."

Buck had come in behind them and, already having secured the items, handed them to Keane. Then he moved to a cabinet and located a bottle of brandy.

"It's not too bad," Jo managed. Because her voice was tolerably steady, she screwed up her courage and looked down. Keane had fastened a rough bandage from the remains of her sleeve. Though the flow of blood had slowed, there were streaks of it down her arm, and too much spreading from the wound to be certain how extensive the cuts were. Nausea rocked in her stomach.

"How do you know?" Keane demanded between his teeth as he began to clean the wound. He wrung out the towel in the basin Buck set beside him.

"It's not bleeding that badly." Jo swallowed the queasiness. As her mind began to clear, she frowned at the tone of Keane's voice. Feeling her stare, he glanced up. In his eyes was such fury, she pulled away.

"Be still," he ordered roughly and gave his attention back to her arm.

The cat had delivered only a glancing blow, but even so, there were four long slices in her upper arm. Jo set her jaw as pain ripped through her. Keane's brusqueness brought more hurt, and she fought to show no reaction to either. The aftermath of fear was bubbling through her. She longed to be held, to be soothed by the hands that tended to her wound.

"She's going to need stitches," Keane said without looking at her.

"And an antitoxin shot," Buck added, handing Jo a generous glass of brandy. "Drink this, honey. It'll help settle you."

The gentleness in his voice nearly undid her. He laid his big hand against her cheek, and for a moment she pressed against it.

"Drink now," Buck ordered again. Obediently, Jo lifted the glass and swallowed. The room whirled, then snapped into focus. She made a small sound and pressed the glass to her forehead. "Tell me what happened in there." Buck crouched down beside her as Keane began to apply a temporary bandage.

Jo took a moment to draw air in and out of her lungs. She lowered the glass and spoke steadily. "Hamlet didn't respond, and Gerry repeated a command, but he stepped forward. Too close. I saw Hamlet's eyes, and I knew. I should have moved faster. I should have been watching him more carefully. It was a stupid mistake." She stared into the brandy as she berated herself.

"She stepped between the boy and the cat." Keane bit off the words as he completed the bandaging. Rising, he moved to the brandy and poured. Not once did he turn to look at Jo. Hurt, she stared at his back before looking back at Buck.

"How's Gerry?"

Buck urged the glass back to her lips. A faint tint of pink was creeping into her cheeks. "Pete's with him. Got his head between his knees. He'll be fine."

Jo nodded. "I guess I'll have to go to town and have this seen to." She handed the glass to Buck and wondered if she dare attempt to rise yet. With another deep breath, she glanced at Duffy. "Make sure he's ready to go in when I get back."

Keane turned from the window. "Go in where?" His face was set in hard lines.

In response, Jo's voice was chilled. "In the cage." She turned her eyes to Buck. "We should be able to have a short run-through before the evening show."

"No." Jo's head snapped up as Keane spoke. For a long moment they stared at each other with odd, unreasonable antagonism. "You're not going back in there today." His voice held curt authority.

"Of course I am," Jo countered, managing to keep the combination of pain and anger from her words. "And if Gerry wants to be a cat man, he's going in, too."

"Jo's right," Buck put in, trying to soothe what he sensed was an explosive situation. "It's like falling off a horse. You can't wait too long before you get back up, or you won't ride again."

Keane never took his eyes from Jo. He continued as if Buck hadn't spoken. "I won't permit it."

"You can't stop me." Indignation forced her to

her feet. The brisk movement caused her arm to protest, and her struggle against it showed momentarily in her eyes.

"Yes, I can." Keane took a long swallow of brandy. "I own this circus."

Jo's fists tightened at his tone, at his careless use of his authority. Not once since he had knelt beside her in the cage had he given her any sign of comfort or reassurance. She had needed it from him. To masquerade its trembling, she kept her voice low. "But you don't own me, Mr. Prescott. And if you'll check your papers and the legalities, you'll see you don't own the lions or my equipment. I bought them, and I maintain them out of my salary. My contract doesn't give you the right to tell me when I can or can't rehearse my cats."

Keane's face was granite hard. "Neither does it give you the right to set up in the Big Top without my permission."

"Then I'll set up some place else," she tossed back. "But I *will* set up. That cat will be worked again today. I won't take the risk of losing months of training."

"But you will risk being killed," Keane shot back and slammed down his glass.

"What do you care?" Jo shouted. All control deserted her. The cuts were deep on her emotions as well as her flesh. She had passed through a terror more acute than she had known since the night of her parents' death. More than anything else, she wanted to feel Keane's arms around her. She wanted to know the security she had felt when he had let her weep out her grief for Ari in his arms. "I'm nothing to you!" Her head shook quickly, tossing her hair. There was a bubble of hysteria in her voice, and Buck reached out to lay a hand on her shoulder.

"Jo," he warned in his soft, rumbling voice.

"No!" She shook her head and spoke rapidly. "He hasn't the right. You haven't the right to interfere with my life." She flared at Keane again with eyes vivid with emotion. "I know what I have to do. I know what I *will* do. Why should it matter to you? You aren't legally responsible if I get mauled. No one's going to sue you."

"Hold on, Jo." This time Buck spoke firmly. As he took her uninjured arm, he felt the tremors shooting through her. "She's too upset to know what she's saying," he told Keane.

There was a mask over Keane's face which concealed all emotion. "Oh, I think she knows what she's saying," he disagreed quietly. For a moment there was only the sound of Jo shuddering and the splash of brandy being poured into a glass. "You do what you have to do, Jo," he said after drinking again. "You're perfectly correct that I haven't any rights where you're concerned. Take her into town,'' he told Buck, then turned back to the window.

''Come on, Jo.'' Buck urged her to the door, slipping a supportive arm around her waist. Even as they stepped outside, Rose came running from the direction of the midway.

''Jo!'' Her face was white with concern. ''Jo, I just heard.'' She glanced at the bandage with wide, terrified eyes. ''How bad is it?''

''Just scratches, really,'' Jo assured her. She added the best smile she could muster. ''Buck's going to take me into town for a couple of stitches.''

''Are you sure?'' She looked up at the tall man for reassurance. ''Buck?''

''Several stitches,'' he corrected but patted Rose's hand. ''But it's not too bad.''

''Do you want me to come with you?'' She fell into step beside them as Buck began to lead Jo again.

''No. Thank you, Rose.'' Jo smiled with more feeling. ''I'll be fine.''

Because of the smile, Rose was able to relax. ''I thought when I heard…well, I imagined all sorts of terrible things. I'm glad you're not badly hurt.'' They had reached Buck's truck, and Rose leaned over to kiss Jo's cheek. ''We all love you so.''

''I know.'' Squeezing her hand, Jo let Buck help her into the cab of his truck. As he maneuvered from the lot, Jo rested her head against the back of the seat and shut her eyes. Never could she remember feeling more spent, more battered.

"Hurt bad?" Buck asked as they switched to an asphalt road.

"Yes," she answered simply, thinking of her heart as much as her arm.

"You'll feel better when you're patched up."

Jo kept her eyes shut, knowing some wounds never heal. Or if they did, they left scars that ached at unexpected times.

"You shouldn't have gone off on him that way, Jo." There was light censure in Buck's voice.

"He shouldn't have interfered," Jo retorted. "It's none of his business. *I'm* none of his business."

"Jo, it's not like you to be so hard."

"Hard?" She opened her eyes and turned to Buck. "What about him? Couldn't he have been kinder, shown even the barest trace of compassion? Did he have to speak to me as if I were a criminal?"

"Jo, the man was terrified. You're only looking at this from one side." He scratched his beard and gave a gusty sigh. "You can't know what it's like to be outside that cage, helpless when someone you care about is facing down death. I had to all but knock him unconscious to keep him out of there until we got it through his head that he'd just get you killed for sure. He was scared, Jo. We were all scared."

Jo shook her head, certain Buck exaggerated because of his affection for her. Keane's voice had been hard, his eyes angry. "He doesn't care," she corrected quietly. "Not like the rest of you. You didn't swear at me. You weren't cold."

"Jo, people have different ways—" Buck began, but she interrupted.

"I know he wouldn't want to see me hurt, Buck. He's not heartless or cruel." She sighed as all the force of anger and fear washed out of her body and left her empty. "Please, I don't want to talk about him."

Buck heard the weariness in her voice and patted her hand. "Okay, honey, just relax. We'll have you all fixed up in no time."

Not all fixed up, Jo thought. Far from all fixed up.

Chapter 11

As the weeks passed, Jo's arm lost its stiffness. She healed cleanly. The only traces were thin scars that promised to fade but not disappear. She found, however, that some spark had gone out of her life. Constantly, she fought against a vague dissatisfaction. Nothing—not her work, not her friends, not her books—brought about the contentment she had grown up with. She had become a woman, and her needs had shifted. Jo knew the root of her problem was Keane, but the knowledge was not a solution. He had left the circus again on the very night of her accident. Nearly four weeks later he had not returned.

Three times Jo had sat down to write him, needing

to assuage her guilt for the harsh things she had said to him. Three times she had torn up the paper in frustration. No matter how she rearranged the words, they were wrong. Instead, she clung to the hope that he would come back one last time. If, she felt, they could part as friends, without bitterness or hard words, she could accept the separation. Willing this to happen, she was able to return to her routine with some tranquility. She rehearsed, performed, joined in the daily duties of circus life. She waited. The caravan moved closer to Chicago.

Jo stood in the steaming Big Top on a late August afternoon. Dressed in a leotard, she worked on ground exercises with the Beirot Brothers. It was this daily regimentation that had aided in keeping her arm limber. She could now move into a back walk-over without feeling any protest in her injured arm.

"I feel good," Jo told Raoul as they worked out. "I feel really good." She did a quick series of pir-ouettes.

"You don't keep your shoulder in shape by dancing on your feet," Raoul challenged.

"My shoulder's fine," she tossed back, then proved her point by bending into a handstand. Slowly, she lowered her legs to a forty-five degree angle, bringing one foot to rest on the knee of the opposite leg. "It's perfect." She executed a forward roll and sprang to her feet. "I'm strong as an ox," she claimed and did a quick back handspring followed by a back flip.

She landed at Keane's feet.

The cascade of emotions that raced through her reflected briefly in her eyes before she regained her balance. "I didn't—I didn't know you were back." Instantly, she regretted the inanity of the words but could find no others. The longing was raw in her to hurl herself into his arms. She wondered that he could not feel her need through the pores of her skin.

"I just got in." His eyes continued to search her face after his hands dropped to his sides. "This is my mother," he added. "Rachael Loring, Jovilette Wilder."

At his words, Jo's gaze moved from his face. She saw the woman beside him. If she had seen Rachael Loring in a crowd of two thousand, she would have known her for Keane's mother. The bone structure was the same, though hers was more elegant. Her brows were golden wings, flaring out at the end, as Keane's did. Her hair was smooth, brushed up and away from her face with no gray to mar its tawny perfection. But it was the eyes that sent a jolt through Jo. She had not thought to see them in anyone's face but Keane's. The woman was dressed simply in an unpretentiously tailored suit that bespoke taste and wealth. There was, however, none of the cool, distant polish that Jo had always attributed to the woman who had taken her son and left Frank. There was a charm to the smile that curved in greeting.

"Jovilette, such a lovely name. Keane's told me of you." She extended her hand, and Jo accepted, intending a quick, impersonal shake. Rachael Loring, however, laid her other hand atop their joined ones and added warmth. "Keane tells me you were very close to Frank. Perhaps we could talk."

The affection in her voice confused Jo into a stumbling reply. "I—Yes. I—if you'd like."

"I should like very much." She squeezed Jo's hand again before releasing it. "Perhaps you have time to show me around?" She smiled with the question, and Jo found it increasingly difficult to remain aloof. "I'm sure there've been some changes since I was here last. You must have some business to attend to," she said, looking up at Keane. "I'm sure Jovilette will take good care of me. Won't you, dear?" Without waiting for either to respond, Rachael tucked her arm through Jo's and began to walk. "I knew your parents," she said as Keane watched them move away. "Not terribly well, I'm afraid. They came here the same year I left. But I recall they were both thrilling performers. Keane tells me you've followed your father's profession."

"Yes, I…" She hesitated, feeling oddly at a disadvantage. "I did," she finished lamely.

"You're so young." Rachael gave her a gentle smile. "How terribly brave you must be."

"No...no, not really. It's my job."

"Yes, of course." Rachael laughed at some private memory. "I've heard that before."

They were outside now, and she paused to look thoughtfully around her. "I think perhaps I was wrong. It hasn't really changed, not in thirty years. It's a wonderful place, isn't it?"

"Why did you leave?" As soon as the words were spoken, Jo regretted them. "I'm sorry," she said quickly. "I shouldn't have asked."

"Of course you should." Rachael sighed and patted Jo's hand. "It's only natural. Duffy's still here, Keane tells me." At the change in subject, Jo imagined her question had been evaded.

"Yes, I suppose he always will be."

"Could we have some coffee, or some tea, perhaps?" Rachael smiled again. "It's such a long drive from town. Is your trailer nearby?"

"It's just over in the back yard."

"Oh, yes." Rachael laughed and began to walk again. "The neighborhood that never changes over thousands of miles. Do you know the story of the dog and the bones?" she asked. Though Jo knew it well, she said nothing. "One version is that a roustabout gave his dog a bone every night after dinner. The dog would bury the bone under the trailer, then the next day try to dig it back up. Of course, it was fifty miles behind in an empty lot. He never figured it out." Quietly, she laughed to herself.

Feeling awkward, Jo opened the door to her trailer. How could this woman be the one she had resented all of her life? How could this be the cold, heartless woman who had left Frank? Oddly, Rachael seemed totally at ease in the narrow confines of the trailer.

"How efficient these are." She looked around with interest and approval. "You must barely realize you're on wheels." Casually, she picked up the volume of Thoreau which lay on Jo's counter. "Keane told me you have an avid interest in literature. In language, too," she added, glancing up from the book. Her eyes were golden and direct like her son's. Jo was tossed back suddenly to the first morning of the season when she had looked down and found Keane's eyes on her.

It made her uncomfortable to learn Keane had discussed her with his mother. "I have some tea," Jo told her as she moved toward the kitchen. "It's a better gamble than my coffee."

"That's fine," Rachael said agreeably and followed her. "I'll just sit here while you fix it." She settled herself with apparent ease at the tiny table across from the kitchen.

"I'm afraid I haven't anything else to offer you."

Jo kept her back turned as she routed through her cupboard.

"Tea and conversation," Rachael answered in mild tones, "will be fine."

Jo sighed and turned. "I'm sorry." She shook her head. "I'm being rude. I just don't know what to say to you, Mrs. Loring. I've resented you for as long as I can remember. Now you're here and not at all as I imagined." She managed to smile, albeit ruefully. "You're not cold and hateful, and you look so much like…" She stopped, horrified that she had nearly blurted out Keane's name. For a moment her eyes were utterly naked.

Rachael smoothed over the awkwardness. "I don't wonder you resented me if you were as close to Frank as Keane tells me. Jovilette," she said softly, "did Frank resent me, too?"

Helpless, Jo responded to the hint of sadness. "No. Not while I knew him. I don't think Frank was capable of resentments."

"You understood him well, didn't you?" Rachael watched as Jo poured boiling water into mugs. "I understood him, too," she continued as Jo brought the mugs to the table. "He was a dreamer, a marvelous free spirit." Absently, she stirred her tea.

Consumed with curiosity, Jo sat across from her and waited for the story she sensed was coming.

"I was eighteen when I met him. I had come to

the circus with a cousin. The Colossus was a bit smaller in those days," she added with a reminiscent smile, "but it was all the same. Oh, the magic!" She shook her head and sighed. "We tumbled into love so fast, married against all my family's objections and went on the road. It was exciting. I learned the web routine and helped out in wardrobe."

Jo's eyes widened. "You performed?"

"Oh, yes." Rachael's cheeks tinted a bit with pride. "I was quite good. Then I became pregnant. We were both like children waiting for Christmas. I wasn't quite nineteen when I had Keane, and I'd been with the circus for nearly a year. Things became difficult over the next season. I was young and a bit frightened of Keane. I panicked if he sneezed and was constantly dragging Frank into town to see doctors. How patient he was."

Rachael leaned forward and took Jo's hand. "Can you understand how hard this life is for one not meant for it? Can you see that through the magic of it, the excitement and wonder, there are hardships and fears and impossible demands? I was little more than a child myself, with an infant to care for, without the endurance or vocation of a trouper, without the experience or confidence of a mother. I lived on nerves for an entire season." She let out a little rush of breath. "When it was over, I went home to Chicago."

For the first time, Jo imagined the flight from Rachael's point of view. She could see a girl, younger than herself, in a strange, demanding world with a baby to care for. Over the years Jo had seen scores of people try the life she'd led and last only weeks. Still she shook her head in confusion.

"I think I understand how difficult it must have been for you. But if you and Frank loved each other, couldn't you have worked it out somehow?"

"How?" Rachael countered. "Should I have taken a house somewhere and lived with him half a year? I would have hated him. Should he have given up his life here and settled down with me and Keane? It would have destroyed everything I loved about him." Rachael shook her head, giving Jo a soft smile. "We did love each other, Jovilette, but not enough. Compromise isn't always possible, and neither of us were capable of adjusting to the needs of the other. I tried, and Frank would have tried had I asked him. But it was lost before it had really begun. We did the wisest thing under the circumstances." Looking into Jo's eyes, she saw youth and confidence. "It seems cold and hard to you, but it was no use dragging out a painful situation. He gave me Keane and two years I've always treasured. I gave him his freedom without bitterness. Ten years after Frank, I found happiness again." She smiled softly with the memory. "I loved Frank, and that love remains as young and sweet as the day I met him.''

Jo swallowed. She searched for some way to apologize for a grudge held for a lifetime. ''He—Frank kept a scrapbook on Keane. He followed the Chicago papers.''

''Did he?'' Rachael beamed, then leaned back in her chair and lifted her mug. ''How like him. Was he happy, Jovilette? Did he have what he wanted?''

''Yes,'' Jo answered without hesitation. ''Did you?''

Rachael's eyes came back to Jo's. For a moment the look was speculative, then it grew warm. ''What a good heart you have, generous and understanding. Yes, I had what I wanted. And you, Jovilette, what do you want?''

At ease now, Jo shook her head and smiled. ''More than I can have.''

''You're too smart for that,'' Rachael observed, studying her. ''I think you're a fighter, not a dreamer. When the time comes to make your choice, you won't settle for anything less than all.'' She smiled at Jo's intent look, then rose. ''Will you show me your lions? I can't tell you how I'm looking forward to seeing you perform.''

''Yes, of course.'' Jo stood, then hesitated. She held out her hand. ''I'm glad you came.''

Rachael accepted the gesture. ''So am I.''

* * *

Throughout the rest of the day Jo looked for Keane without success. After meeting and talking with his mother, it had become even more imperative that she speak with him. Her conscience would have no rest until she made amends. By showtime she had not yet found him.

Each act seemed to run on and on as she fretted for the finish. He would be with his mother in the audience, and undoubtedly she would find him after the show. She strained with impatience as the acts dragged.

After the finale she stood at the back door, unsure whether to wait or to go to his trailer. She was struck with both relief and alarm when she saw him approaching.

"Jovilette." Rachael spoke first, taking Jo's hands in hers. "How marvelous you were, and how stunning. I see why Keane said you had an untamed beauty."

Surprised, Jo glanced up at Keane but met impassive amber eyes. "I'm glad you enjoyed it."

"Oh, I can't tell you how much. The day has brought me some very precious memories. Our talk this afternoon meant a great deal to me." To Jo's surprise, Rachael leaned over and kissed her. "I hope to see you again. I'm going to say goodbye to Duffy before you drive me back, Keane," she con-

tinued. "I'll meet you in the car. Goodbye, Jovilette."

"Goodbye, Mrs. Loring." Jo watched her go before she turned to Keane. "She's a wonderful person. She makes me ashamed."

"There's no need for that." He tucked his hands
into his pockets and watched her. "We both had our
reasons for resentments, and we were both wrong.
How's your arm?"

"Oh." Jo's fingers traveled to the wound automatically. "It's fine. There's barely any scarring."

"Good." The word was short and followed by
silence. For a moment Jo felt her courage fail her.

"Keane," she began, then forced herself to meet
his eyes directly. "I want to apologize for the horrible way I behaved after the accident."

"I told you once before," he said coolly, "I don't
care for apologies."

"Please." Jo swallowed her pride and touched his
arm. "I've been saving this one for a very long time.
I didn't mean those things I said," she added
quickly. "I hope you'll forgive me." It wasn't the
eloquent apology she had planned, but it was all she
could manage. His expression never altered.

"There's nothing to forgive."

"Keane, please." Jo grabbed his arm again as he
turned to go. "Don't leave me feeling as if you don't
forgive me. I know I said dreadful things. You have

every right to be furious, but couldn't you—can't we be friends again?''

Something flickered over his face. Lifting his hand, he touched the back of it to her cheek. ''You have a habit of disconcerting me, Jovilette.'' He dropped his hand, then thrust it into his pocket. ''I've left something for you with Duffy. Be happy.'' He walked away from her while she dealt with the finality of his tone. He was walking out of her life. She watched him until he disappeared.

Jo had thought she would feel something, but there was nothing; no pain, no tears, no desperation. She had not known a human being could be so empty and still live.

''Jo.'' Duffy lumbered up to her, then held out a thick envelope. ''Keane left this for you.'' Then he moved past her, anxious to see that all straggling towners were nudged on their way.

Jo felt all emotions had been stripped away. Absently, she glanced at the envelope as she walked to her trailer. Without enthusiasm, she stepped inside, then tore it open. She remained standing as she pulled out the contents. It took her several moments to decipher the legal jargon. She read the group of papers through twice before sitting down.

He's given it to me, she thought. Still she could not comprehend the magnitude of it. *He's given me the circus.*

Chapter 12

O'Hare Airport was an army of people and a cacophony of sound. Nearly losing herself in the chaos of it, Jo struggled through the masses and competed for a cab. At first she had merely gawked at the snow like a towner seeing his first sword swallower. Then, though she shivered inside the corduroy coat she had bought for the trip, she began to enjoy it. It was beautiful as it lay over the city, and it helped to turn her mind from the purpose of her journey. Never had she been north so late in the year. Chicago in November was a sensational sight.

She had learned, after the initial shock had worn off, that Keane had not only given her the circus but a responsibility as well. Almost immediately there had been contracts to negotiate. She had been tossed into a sea of paperwork, forced to rely heavily on Duffy's experience as she tried to regain her balance. As the season had come to a close, Jo had attempted a dozen times to call Chicago. Each time, she had hung up before Keane's number could be dialed. It would be, she had decided, more appropriate to see him in person. Her trip had been postponed a few weeks due to Jamie and Rose's wedding.

It was there, as she had stood as maid of honor, that Jo had realized what she must do. There was only one thing she truly wanted, and that was to be with Keane. Watching Rose's face as their vows had been exchanged, Jo had recalled her unflagging determination to win the man she loved.

And will I stay here? Jo had demanded of herself thousands of miles away from him. No. Her heart had begun to thud as she had mapped out a plan. She would go to Chicago to see him. She would not be turned away. He had wanted her once; she would make him want her again. She would not live out her life without at least some small portion of it being part of his. He didn't have to love her. It was enough that she loved him.

And so, shivering against the unfamiliar cold, Jo scrambled into a cab and headed across town. She brushed her hair free of snow with chilled fingers, thinking how idiotic she had been to forget to buy a

hat and gloves. What if he isn't home? she thought
suddenly. What if he's gone to Europe or Japan or
California? Panic made her giddy, and she pushed it
down. He has to be home. It's Sunday, and he's
sitting at home reading or going over a brief—or
entertaining a woman, she thought, appalled. I
should stop and call. I should tell the driver to take
me back to the airport. Closing her eyes, Jo fought
to regain her calm. She took long, deep breaths and
stared at the buildings and sidewalks. Gradually, she
felt the tiny gurgle of hysteria dissipate.

I won't be afraid, she told herself and tried to
believe it. I won't be afraid. But Jovilette, the
woman who reclined on a living rug of lions, was
very much afraid. What if he rejected her? I won't
let him reject me, she told herself with a confident
lift of her chin. *I'll seduce him.* She pressed her fingers to her temples. *I wouldn't know how to begin.*
I've got to tell the driver to turn around.

But before she could form the words, the cab
pulled up to a curb. With the precision of a robot,
Jo paid the fare, overtipping in her agitation, and
climbed out.

Long after the cab had pulled away, she stood
staring up at the massive glass-girdled building.
Snow waltzed around her, sprinkling her hair and
shoulders. A jostle from a rushing pedestrian broke

the spell. She picked up her suitcases and hurried through the front door of the apartment buildings.

The lobby was enormous, with smoked glass walls and a deep shag carpet. Not knowing she should give her name at the desk, Jo wandered toward the elevators, innocently avoiding detection by merging with a group of tenants. Once inside the car, Jo pushed the button for the penthouse with a nerveless forefinger. The chatter of those in the elevator with her registered only as a distant humming. She never noticed when the car stopped for their departure.

When it stopped a second time and the doors slid open, she stared at the empty space for ten full seconds. Only as the automatic doors began to close did she snap out of her daze. Pushing them open again, she stepped through and into the hall. Her legs were wobbly, but she forced them to move forward in the direction of the penthouse. Panic sped up and down her spine until she set down her bags and leaned her brow against Keane's door. She urged air in and out of her lungs. She remembered that Rachael Loring had called her a fighter. Jo swallowed, lifted her chin and knocked. The wait was mercifully brief before Keane opened the door. She saw surprise light his eyes as he stared at her.

Her hair was dusted with snow as it lay over the shoulders of her coat. Her face glowed with the cold, and her eyes were bright, nearly feverish with her struggle for calm. Only once did her mouth tremble before she spoke.

"Hello, Keane."

He only stared, his eyes running over her in disbelief. He was leaner, she thought as she studied his face. As she filled herself with the sight of him, she saw he wore a sweatshirt and jeans. His feet were bare. He hadn't shaved, and her hand itched to test the roughness of his beard.

"What are you doing here?" Jo felt a resurgence of panic. His tone was harsh, and he had not answered her smile. She strained for poise.

"May I come in?" she asked, her smile cracking.

"What?" He seemed distracted by the question. His brows lowered into a frown.

"May I come in?" she repeated, barely defeating the urge to turn tail and run.

"Oh, yes, of course. I'm sorry." Running a hand through his hair, Keane stepped back and gestured her inside.

Instantly, Jo's shoes sank into the luxurious pile of the buff-colored carpet. For a moment she allowed herself to gaze around the room, using the time for the additional purpose of regaining her composure. It was an open, sweeping room with sharp, contrasting colors. There was a deep brown sectional sofa with a chrome and glass coffee table. There were high-backed chairs in soft creams and vivid slashes of blue in chunky floor pillows. There were paintings, one she thought she recognized as a Picasso, and a sculpture she was certain was a Rodin.

On the far right of the room there was an elevation of two steps. Just beyond was a huge expanse of glass that featured a spreading view of Chicago. Jo moved toward it with undisguised curiosity. Now, unexplicably, fear had lessened. She found that once she had stepped over the threshold she had committed herself. She was no longer afraid.

"It's wonderful," she said, turning back to him. "How marvelous to have a whole city at your feet every day. You must feel like a king."

"I've never thought of it that way." With half the room between them, he studied her. She looked small and fragile with the bustling city at her back.

"I would," she said, and now her smile came easily. "I'd stand at the window and feel regal and pompous."

At last she saw his lips soften and curve. "Jovilette," he said quietly. "What are you doing in my world?"

"I needed to talk to you," she answered simply. "I had to come here to do it."

He moved to her then, but slowly, with his eyes on hers. "It must be important."

"I thought so."

His brow lifted, then he shrugged. "Well, then, we'll talk. But first, let's have your coat."

Jo's cold fingers fumbled with the buttons and caused Keane to frown again. "Good heavens, you're frozen." He captured her hands between his and swore. "Where are your gloves?" he demanded like an irate parent. "It must be all of twelve degrees outside."

"I forgot to buy any," Jo told him as she dealt with the heavenly feeling of his hands restoring warmth to hers.

"Idiot. Don't you know better than to come to Chicago in November without gloves?"

"No." Jo responded to his anger with a cheerful smile. "I've never been to Chicago in November before. It's wonderful."

His eyes lifted from her hands to her face. He watched her for a long moment, then she heard him sigh. "I'd nearly convinced myself I could be cured."

Jo's eyes clouded with concern. "Have you been ill?"

Keane laughed with a shake of his head, then he pushed away the question and became brisk again. "Here, let's have your coat. I'll get you some coffee."

"You needn't bother," she began as he undid the

buttons on the coat himself and drew it from her shoulders.

"I'd feel better if I was certain your circulation was restored." He paused and looked down at her as he laid her coat over his arm. She wore a green angora sweater with pearl buttons and a gray skirt in thin wool. The soft fabric draped softly at her breasts and over her hips and thighs. Her shoes were dainty and impractical sling-back heels.

"Is something wrong?"

"I've never seen you wear anything but a costume or jeans."

"Oh." Jo laughed and combed her fingers through her damp hair. "I expect I look different."

"Yes, you do." His voice was low, and there was a frown in his eyes. "Right now you look as if you've come from college for the holidays." He touched the ends of her hair, then turned away. "Sit down. I'll get the coffee."

A bit puzzled by his mercurial moods, Jo wandered about the room, finally ignoring a chair to kneel beside one of the pillows near the picture window. Though the carpet swallowed Keane's footsteps, she sensed his return.

"How wonderful to have a real winter, if just for the snow." She turned a radiant face his way. "I've always wondered what Christmas is like with snow and icicles." Images of snowflakes danced in her eyes. Seeing he carried two mugs of coffee, she rose and took one. "Thank you."

"Are you warm enough?" he asked after a moment.

Jo nodded and sat in one of the two chairs opposite the sofa. The novelty of the city made her mission seem like a grand adventure. Keane sat beside her, and for a moment they drank in companionable silence.

"What did you want to talk to me about, Jo?"

Jo swallowed, ignoring the faint trembling in her chest. "A couple of things. The circus, for one." She shifted in her chair until she faced him. "I didn't write because I felt it too important. I didn't phone for the same reason. Keane..." All her carefully thought-out speeches deserted her. "You can't just give something like that away. I can't take it from you."

"Why not?" He shrugged and sipped his coffee. "We both know it's always been yours. A piece of paper doesn't change that one way or the other."

"Keane, Frank left it to you."

"And I gave it to you."

Jo made a small sound of frustration. "Perhaps if I could pay you for it..."

"Someone asked me once what was the value of a dream or the price of a human spirit." Jo shifted her eyes to his helplessly. "I didn't have an answer then. Do you have one now?"

She sighed and shook her head. "I don't know what to say to you. 'Thank you' is far from adequate."

"It's not necessary, either," Keane told her. "I simply gave back what was yours in any case. What else was there, Jo? You said there were a couple of things."

This was it, Jo's brain told her. Carefully, she set down the coffee and rose. Waiting for her stomach to settle, she walked a few feet out into the room, then turned. She allowed herself a deep breath before she met Keane's eyes.

"I want to be your mistress," she said with absolute calm.

"*What?*" Both Keane's face and voice registered utter shock.

Jo swallowed and repeated. "I want to be your mistress. That's still the right term, isn't it, or is it antiquated? Is *lover* right? I've never done this before."

Slowly, Keane set his mug beside hers and rose. He did not move toward her but watched her with probing eyes. "Jo, you don't know what you're saying."

"Oh, yes, I do," she cut him off and nodded. "I might not have the terminology exactly right, but I do know what I mean, and I'm sure you do, too. I want to be with you," she continued and took a step toward him. "I want you to make love to me. I want to live with you if you'll let me, or at least close by."

"Jo, you're not talking sensibly." Sharply, Keane broke into her speech. Turning away, he thrust his hands into his pockets and balled them into fists. "You don't know what you're asking."

"Don't I appeal to you anymore?"

Keane whirled, infuriated with the trace of curiosity in her voice. "How can you ask me that?" he demanded. "Of course you appeal to me! I'm not dead or in the throes of senility!"

She moved closer to him. "Then if I want you, and you want me, why can't we be lovers?"

Keane swore violently and grabbed her shoulders. "Do you think I could have you for a winter and then blithely let you go? Do you think I could untangle myself at the start of the season and watch you stroll out of my life? Haven't you the sense to see what you do to me?" He shook her hard with the question, stealing any breath she might have used to answer him.

"You make me crazy!" Abruptly, he dragged her against him. His mouth bruised hers, his fingers dug into her flesh. Jo's head spun with confusion and pain and ecstasy. It seemed centuries since she had tasted his mouth on hers. She heard him groan as he tore himself away. He turned, leaving her to find her own balance as the room swayed. "What do I have to do to be rid of you?" His words came in furious undertones.

Jo blew out a breath. "I don't think kissing me like that is a very good start."

"I'm aware of that," he murmured. She watched the rise and fall of his shoulders. "I've been trying to avoid doing it since I opened the door."

Quietly, Jo walked to him and put a hand on his arm. "You're tense," she discovered and automatically sought to soothe the muscles. "I'm sorry if I'm going about this the wrong way. I thought telling you outright would be better than trying to seduce you. I don't think I'd be very good at that."

Keane made a sound somewhere between a laugh and a moan. "Jovilette," he murmured before he turned and gathered her into his arms. "How do I resist you? How many times must I pull away before I'm free of you? Even the thought of you drives me mad."

"Keane." She sighed and shut her eyes. "I've wanted you to hold me for so long. I want to belong to you, even for just a little while."

"No." He pulled away, then forced her chin up with his thumb and forefinger. "Don't you see that once would be too much and a lifetime wouldn't be enough? I love you too much to let you go and enough to know I have to.'' Shock robbed her of speech. She only stared as he continued. ''It was different when I didn't know, when I thought I was—how did you put it? 'Dazzled.''' He smiled briefly at the word. ''I was certain if I could make love to you, I could get you out of my system. Then, the night Ari died, I held you while you slept. I realized I was in love with you, had been in love with you right from the beginning.''

''But you…'' Jo shook her head as if to clear it. ''You never told me, and you seemed so cold, so distant.''

''I couldn't touch you without wanting more.'' He pulled her close again and for a moment buried his face in her hair. ''But I couldn't stay away. I knew if I wanted to have you, to really have you, one of us had to give up what we did, what we were. I wondered if I could give up the law; it was really all I ever wanted to do. I discovered I wanted you more.''

''Oh, Keane.'' She shook her head, but he put her from him suddenly.

''Then I found out that wouldn't work, either.'' Keane turned, paced to the window and stared out. The snow was falling heavily. ''Every time you walked into that cage, I walked into hell. I thought perhaps I'd get used to it, but it only got worse. I tried leaving, coming back here, but I could never shake you loose. I kept coming back. The day you were hurt…'' Keane paused. Jo heard him draw in his breath, and when he continued, his voice was deeper. ''I watched you step in front of that boy and take the blow. I can't tell you what I felt at that moment; there aren't words for it. All I could think of was getting to you. I wonder if Pete ever told you that I decked him before Buck got to me. He took it very well, considering. Then I had to—to just stand there and watch while that cat stalked you. I've never known that kind of fear before. The kind that empties you out, body and soul.''

He lapsed into silence. ''Then it was over,'' he continued, ''and I got to you. You were so white, and you were bleeding in my arms.'' He muttered an oath, then was silent again. He shook his head. ''I wanted to burn the place down, get you away, strangle the cats with my bare hands. Anything. I wanted to hold you, but I couldn't get past the fear and the unreasonable anger at having been helpless. Before my hands stopped shaking, you were making plans to go back into that damnable cage. I wanted to kill you myself then and be done with it.''

Slowly, Keane turned and walked back to her. ''I saw it happen again every time I closed my eyes for weeks afterward. I can show you exactly where the scars are.'' He lifted a finger and traced four lines on her upper arm precisely where the claws had ripped her skin. He dropped his hand and shook his head. "I can't watch you go in the cage, Jo." He lifted his hand again and let it linger over her hair. "If I let you stay with me now, I wouldn't be able to let you go back to your own life. And I can't ask you to give it up."

"I wish you would." Solemn-eyed, Jo watched him. "I very much wish you would."

"Jo." Shaking his head, he turned away. "I know what it means to you."

"No more than the law means to you, I imagine," she said briskly. "But you said you were willing to give that up."

"Yes, but..."

"Oh, very well." She pushed back her hair. "If you won't ask me, I'll have to ask you. Will you marry me?"

Keane turned back, giving her his lowered brow frown. "Jo, you can't..."

"Of course I can. This is the twentieth century. If I want to ask you to marry me, then I will. I did," she pointed out.

"Jo, I don't..."

"Yes or no, please, counselor. This isn't an easy question." She stepped forward until they stood toe to toe. "I'm in love with you, and I want to marry you and have several babies. Is that agreeable?"

Keane's mouth opened and closed. He gave her an odd smile and lifted his hands to her shoulders. "This is rather sudden."

Jo felt a wild surge of joy. "Perhaps it is," she admitted. "I'll give you a minute to think about it. But I might as well tell you, I won't take no for an answer."

Keane's fingers traced the curve of her neck. "It seems I have little choice."

"None at all," she corrected. Boldly, she locked her arms around him and pulled his mouth down to hers. The kiss was instantly urgent, instantly searching. Joined, they lowered to the rug and clung. For a long, long moment, their lips were united in a language too complex for words. Then, as if to reassure himself she was real, Keane searched the familiar curves of her body, tasted the longed-for flavor of her skin.

"Why did I think I could live without you?" he whispered. His mouth came desperately back to hers. "Be sure, Jo, be sure." Roughened with emotion, his voice was low while the words were spoken against her lips. "I'll never be able to let you go. I'm asking you for everything."

"No. No, it's not like that. Hold me tighter. Kiss me again," she demanded as his lips roamed her face. "Kiss me." She wondered if the sound of pleasure she heard was his or her own. She had not known a kiss could be so intimate, so terrifyingly exciting. No, she thought as she soared with the knowledge that he loved her. He wasn't asking everything, he was giving it.

"I'm leaving something behind," she told him when their lips parted, "and replacing it with something infinitely more important." She buried her face in the curve of his neck. "When you realize how much I love you, you'll understand."

Keane drew away and stared down at her. At last he spoke, but it was only her name. It was a soft sigh of a sound. She smiled at it and lifted a hand to his cheek. "If there's a way to compromise..."

"No." She shook her head, remembering his mother's words. "Sometimes there can't be a compromise. We love each other enough not to need one. Please, don't think I'm making a sacrifice; I'm not." She smiled a little and rubbed her palm experimentally over the stubble of his neglected beard. "I don't regret one minute of my life in the circus, and I don't regret changing it. You've given me the circus, so I'll always be a part of it." Her smile faded, and her eyes grew serious. "Will you belong to me, Keane?"

He took her hand from his cheek and pressed it to his lips. "I already do. I love you, Jovilette. I'll spend a lifetime loving you."

''That's not long enough,'' she said as their lips met again. ''I want more. I want forever.''

With slow, building passion, his hands moved over her. Taking his time, he loosened the buttons on her sweater. ''So beautiful,'' he murmured as his lips trailed down her throat and found the gentle swell. Jo's breath caught at the new intimacy. ''You're trembling. I love knowing I can make your skin tremble under my hands.'' His lips roamed back to hers before he cradled her in his arms. ''I've wanted to be with you, to hold you, just hold you, for so long. I can't remember not wanting it.''

With a sigh washed with contentment, Jo snuggled against him. ''Keane,'' she murmured.

''Hmm?''

''You never answered me.''

''About what?'' He kissed her closed lids, then tangled his fingers in her hair.

Jo opened her eyes. Her brows arched over them. ''Are you going to marry me or not?''

Keane laughed, rolled her onto her back and planted a long, lingering kiss on her mouth. ''Is tomorrow soon enough?''

*   *   *   *   *

Less of a
Stranger

For my friend, Joanne

Chapter 1

He watched her coming. Though she wore jeans and a jacket, with a concealing helmet over her head, Katch recognized her femininity. She rode a small Honda motorcycle. He drew on his thin cigar and appreciated the competent way she swung into the market's parking lot.

Settling the bike, she dismounted. She was tall, Katch noted, perhaps five feet eight, and slender. He leaned back on the soda machine and continued to watch her out of idle curiosity. Then she removed the helmet. Instantly, his curiosity was intensified. She was a stunner.

Her hair was loose and straight, swinging nearly to her shoulders, with a fringe of bangs sweeping over her forehead. It was a deep, rich brunette that showed glints of red and gold from the sun. Her face was narrow, the features sharp and distinct. He'd known models who'd starved themselves to get the angles and shadows that were in this woman's face. Her mouth, however, was full and generous.

Katch recognized the subtleties of cosmetics and knew that none had been used to add interest to the woman's features. She didn't need them. Her eyes were large, and even with the distance of the parking lot between them, he caught the depth of dark brown. They reminded him of a colt's eyes—deep and wide and aware. Her movements were unaffected. They had an unrefined grace that was as coltish as her eyes. She was young, he decided, barely twenty. He drew on the cigar again. She was definitely a stunner.

"Hey, Megan!"

Megan turned at the call, brushing the bangs from her eyes as she moved. Seeing the Bailey twins pull to the curb in their Jeep, she smiled.

"Hi." Clipping the helmet onto a strap on her bike, Megan walked to the Jeep. She was very fond of the Bailey twins.

Like herself, they were twenty-three and had golden, beach-town complexions, but they were petite, blue-eyed and pertly blond. The long, baby-fine hair they shared had been tossed into confusion by the wind. Both pairs of blue eyes drifted past

Megan to focus on the man who leaned against the soda machine. In reflex, both women straightened and tucked strands of hair behind their ears. Tacitly, they agreed their right profile was the most comely.

"We haven't seen you in a while." Teri Bailey kept one eye cocked on Katch as she spoke to Megan.

"I've been trying to get some things finished before the season starts." Megan's voice was low, with the gentle flow of coastal South Carolina. "How've you been?"

"Terrific!" Jeri answered, shifting in the driver's seat. "We've got the afternoon off. Why don't you come shopping with us?" She, too, kept Katch in her peripheral vision.

"I'd like to—" Megan was already shaking her head "—but I've got to pick up a few things here."

"Like the guy over there with terrific gray eyes?" Jeri demanded.

"What?" Megan laughed.

"And shoulders," Teri remarked.

"He hasn't taken those eyes off her, has he, Teri?" Jeri remarked. "And we spent twelve-fifty for this blouse." She fingered the thin strap of the pink camisole top which matched her twin's.

"What," Megan asked, totally bewildered, "are you talking about?"

"Behind you," Teri said with a faint inclination

of her fair head. "The hunk by the soda machine. Absolutely gorgeous." But as Megan began to turn her head, Teri continued in a desperate whisper, "Don't turn around, for goodness sake!"

"How can I see if I don't look?" Megan pointed out reasonably as she turned.

His hair was blond, not pale like the twins', but dusky and sun-streaked. It was thick and curled loosely and carelessly around his face. He was lean, and the jeans he wore were well faded from wear. His stance was negligent, completely relaxed as he leaned back against the machine and drank from a can. But his face wasn't lazy, Megan thought as he met her stare without a blink. It was sharply aware. He needed a shave, certainly, but his bone structure was superb. There was the faintest of clefts in his chin, and his mouth was long and thin.

Normally, Megan would have found the face fascinating—strongly sculpted, even handsome in a rough-and-ready fashion. But the eyes were insolent. They were gray, as the twins had stated, dark and smoky. And, Megan decided with a frown, rude. She'd seen his type before—drifters, loners, looking for the sun and some fleeting female companionship. Under her bangs, her eyebrows drew together. He was openly staring at her. As the can touched his lips, he sent Megan a slow wink.

Hearing one of the twins giggle, Megan whipped her head back around.

''He's adorable,'' Jeri decided.

''Don't be an idiot.'' Megan swung her hair back with a toss of her head. ''He's typical.''

The twins exchanged a look as Jeri started the Jeep's engine. ''Too choosy,'' she stated. They gave Megan mirror smiles as they pulled away from the curb. ''Bye!''

Megan wrinkled her nose at them, but waved before she turned away. Purposefully ignoring the man who loitered beside the concessions, Megan walked into the market.

She acknowledged the salute from the clerk behind the counter. Megan had grown up in Myrtle Beach. She knew all the small merchants in the five-mile radius around her grandfather's amusement park.

After choosing a basket, she began to push it down the first aisle. Just a few things, she decided, plucking a quart of milk from a shelf. She had only the saddlebags on the bike for transporting. If the truck hadn't been acting up... She let her thoughts drift away from that particular problem. Nothing could be done about it at the moment.

Megan paused in the cookie section. She'd missed lunch and the bags and boxes looked tempting. Maybe the oatmeal...

"These are better."

Megan started as a hand reached in front of her to choose a bag of cookies promising a double dose of chocolate chips. Twisting her head, she looked up into the insolent gray eyes.

"Want the cookies?" He grinned much as he had outside.

"No," she said, giving a meaningful glance at his hand on her basket. Shrugging, he took his hand away but, to Megan's irritation, he strolled along beside her.

"What's on the list, Meg?" he asked companionably as he tore open the bag of cookies.

"I can handle it alone, thanks." She started down the next aisle, grabbing a can of tuna. He walked, Megan noted, like a gunslinger—long, lanky strides with just a hint of swagger.

"You've got a nice bike." He bit into a cookie as he strolled along beside her. "Live around here?"

Megan chose a box of tea bags. She gave it a critical glance before tossing it into the basket. "It lives with me," she told him as she moved on.

"Cute," he decided and offered her a cookie. Megan ignored him and moved down the next aisle. When she reached for a loaf of bread, however, he laid a hand on top of hers. "Whole wheat's better for you." His palm was hard and firm on the back of her hand. Megan met his eyes indignantly and tried to pull away.

"Listen, I have…"

"No rings," he commented, lacing his fingers through hers and lifting her hand for a closer study. "No entanglements. How about dinner?"

"No way." She shook her hand but found it firmly locked in his.

"Don't be unfriendly, Meg. You have fantastic eyes." He smiled into them, looking at her as though they were the only two people on earth. Someone reached around her, with an annoyed mutter, to get a loaf of rye.

"Will you go away?" she demanded in an undertone. It amazed her that his smile was having an effect on her even though she knew what was behind it. "I'll make a scene if you don't."

"That's all right," he said genially, "I don't mind scenes."

He wouldn't, she thought, eyeing him. He'd thrive on them. "Look," she began angrily, "I don't know who you are, but…"

"David Katcherton," he volunteered with another easy smile. "Katch. What time should I pick you up?"

"You're not going to pick me up," she said distinctly. "Not now, not later." Megan cast a quick look around. The market was all but empty. She couldn't cause a decent scene if she'd wanted to. "Let go of my hand," she ordered firmly.

"The Chamber of Commerce claims Myrtle Beach is a friendly town, Meg." Katch released her hand. "You're going to give them a bad name."

"And stop calling me Meg," she said furiously. "I don't know you."

She stomped off, wheeling the basket in front of her.

"You will." He made the claim quietly, but she heard him.

Their eyes met again, hers dark with temper, his assured. Turning away, she quickened her pace to the check-out counter.

"You wouldn't believe what happened at the market." Megan set the bag on the kitchen table with a thump.

Her grandfather sat at the table, on one of the four matching maple chairs, earnestly tying a fly. He grunted in acknowledgment but didn't glance up. Wires and feathers and weights were neatly piled in front of him.

"This man," she began, pulling the bread from the top bag. "This incredibly rude man tried to pick me up. Right in the cookie section." Megan frowned as she stored tea bags in a canister. "He wanted me to go to dinner with him."

"Hmm." Her grandfather meticulously attached a yellow feather to the fly. "Have a nice time."

"Pop!" Megan shook her head in frustration, but a smile tugged at her mouth.

Timothy Miller was a small, spare man in his mid-sixties. His round, lined face was tanned, surrounded by a shock of white hair and a full beard. The beard was soft as a cloud and carefully tended. His blue eyes, unfaded by the years, were settled deeply into the folds and lines of his face. They missed little. Megan could see he was focused on his lures. That he had heard her at all was a tribute to his affection for his granddaughter.

Moving over, she dropped a kiss on the crown of his head. "Going fishing tomorrow?"

"Yessiree, bright and early." Pop counted out his assortment of lures and mentally reviewed his strategy. Fishing was a serious business. "The truck should be fixed this evening. I'll be back before supper."

Megan nodded, giving him a second kiss. He needed his fishing days. The amusement parks opened for business on weekends in the spring and fall. In the three summer months they worked seven days a week. The summer kept the town alive; it drew tourists, and tourists meant business. For one-fourth of the year, the town swelled from a population of thirteen or fourteen thousand to three hundred thousand. The bulk of those three hundred thousand people had come to the small coastal town to have fun.

To provide it, and make his living, her grandfather worked hard. He always had, Megan mused. It would have been a trial if he hadn't loved the park so much. It had been part of her life for as long as she could remember.

Megan had been barely five when she had lost her parents. Over the years, Pop had been mother, father and friend to her. And Joyland was home to her as much as the beach-side cottage they lived in. Years before, they had turned to each other in grief. Now, their love was bedrock firm. With the exclusion of her grandfather, Megan was careful with her emotions, for once involved, they were intense. When she loved, she loved totally.

"Trout would be nice," she murmured, as she gave him a last, quick hug. "We'll have to settle for tuna casserole tonight."

"Thought you were going out."

"Pop!" Megan leaned back against the stove and pushed her hair from her face with both hands. "Do you think I'd spend the evening with a man who tried to pick me up with a bag of chocolate chip cookies?" With a jerk of her wrist, she flicked on the burner under the teakettle.

"Depends on the man." She saw the twinkle in

his eye as he glanced up at her. Megan knew she finally had his full attention. "What'd he look like?"

"A beach bum," she retorted, although she knew the answer wasn't precisely true. "With a bit of cowboy thrown in." She smiled then in response to Pop's grin. "Actually, he had a great face. Lean and strong, very attractive in an unscrupulous sort of way. He'd do well in bronze."

"Sounds interesting. Where'd you meet him again?"

"In the cookie section."

"And you're going to fix tuna casserole instead of having dinner out?" Pop gave a heavy sigh and shook his head. "I don't know what's the matter with this girl," he addressed a favored lure.

"He was cocky," Megan claimed and folded her arms. "And he *leered* at me. Aren't grandfathers supposed to tote shotguns around for the purpose of discouraging leerers?"

"Want to borrow one and go hunting for him?"

The shrill whistling of the kettle drowned out her response. Pop watched Megan as she rose to fix the tea.

She was a good girl, he mused. A bit too serious about things at times, but a good girl. And a beauty, too. It didn't surprise him that a stranger had tried to make a date with her. He was more surprised that it hadn't happened more often. But Megan could discourage a man without opening her mouth, he re-called. All she had to do was aim one of her ''I beg your pardon'' looks and most of them backed off. That seemed to be the way she wanted it.

Between the amusement park and her art, she never seemed to have time for much socializing. Or didn't make time, Pop amended thoughtfully. Still, he wasn't certain that he didn't detect more than just annoyance in her attitude toward the man in the mar-ket. Unless he missed his guess, she had been amused and perhaps a touch attracted. Because he knew his granddaughter well, he decided to let the subject ride for the time being.

''The weather's supposed to hold all weekend,'' he commented as he carefully placed his lures in his fishing box. ''There should be a good crowd in the park. Are you going to work in the arcade?''

''Of course.'' Megan set two cups of tea on the table and sat again. ''Have those seats been adjusted on the Ferris wheel?''

''Saw to it myself this morning.'' Pop blew on his tea to cool it, then sipped.

He was relaxed, Megan saw. Pop was a simple man. She'd always admired his unassuming manner, his quiet humor, his lack of pretensions. He loved to watch people enjoy. More, she added with a sigh, than he liked to charge them for doing so. Joyland never made more than a modest profit. He was, Megan concluded, a much better grandfather than businessman.

To a large extent, it was she who handled the profit-and-loss aspect of the park. Though the responsibility took time away from her art, she knew it was the park that supported them. And, more important, it was the park that Pop loved.

At the moment, the books were teetering a bit too steeply into the red for comfort. Neither of them spoke of it at any length with the other. They mentioned improvements during the busy season, talked vaguely about promoting business during the Easter break and over Memorial Day weekend.

Megan sipped at her tea and half listened to Pop's rambling about hiring summer help. She would see to it when the time came. Pop was a whiz in dealing with cranky machines and sunburned tourists, but he tended to overpay and underwork his employees. Megan was more practical. She had to be.

I'll have to work full-time myself this summer, she reflected. She thought fleetingly of the half-completed sculpture in her studio over the garage. It'll just have to wait for December, she told herself and tried not to sigh. There's no other way until things are on a more even keel again. Maybe next year…it was always next year. There were things to do, always things to do. With a small shrug, she turned back to Pop's monologue.

"So, I figure we'll get some of the usual college kids and drifters to run the rides."

"I don't imagine that'll be a problem," Megan murmured. Pop's mention of drifters had led her thoughts back to David Katcherton.

Katch, she mused, letting his face form in her mind again. Ordinarily, she'd have cast his type as a drifter, but there had been something more than that. Megan prided herself on her observations, her characterizations of people. It annoyed her that she wasn't able to make a conclusive profile on this man. It annoyed her further that she was again thinking of a silly encounter with a rude stranger.

"Want some more tea?" Pop was already making his way to the stove when Megan shook herself back.

"Ah…yeah, sure." She scolded herself for dwelling on the insignificant when there were things to do. "I guess I'd better start dinner. You'll want an early night if you're going fishing in the morning."

"That's my girl." Pop turned the flame back on under the kettle as he glanced out the window. He cast a quick look at his unsuspecting granddaughter. "I hope you've got enough for three," he said casually. "It looks like your beach-cowboy found his way to the ranch."

"What?" Megan's brows drew together as she stood up.

"A perfect description, as usual, Megan," Pop complimented her as he watched the man approach, loose-limbed with a touch of a swashbuckler, a strong, good-looking face. Pop liked his looks. He turned with a grin as Megan walked to the window to stare out. Pop suppressed a chuckle at her expression.

"It *is* him," she whispered, hardly believing her eyes as she watched Katch approach her kitchen door.

"I thought it might be," Pop said mildly.

"Of all the nerve," she muttered darkly. "Of all the *incredible* nerve!"

Chapter 2

Before her grandfather could comment, Megan took the few strides necessary to bring her to the kitchen door. She swung it open just as Katch stepped up on the stoop. There was a flicker, only a flicker, of surprise in the gray eyes.

"You have a nerve," she said coolly.

"So I've been told," he agreed easily. "You're prettier than you were an hour ago." He ran a finger down her cheek. "There's a bit of rose under the honey now. Very becoming." He traced the line of her chin before dropping his hand. "Do you live here?"

"You know very well I do," she retorted. "You followed me."

Katch grinned. "Sorry to disappoint you, Meg. Finding you here's just a bonus. I'm looking for Timothy Miller. Friend of yours?"

"He's my grandfather." She moved, almost imperceptibly, positioning herself between Katch and the doorway. "What do you want with him?"

Katch recognized the protective move, but before he could comment, Pop spoke from behind her.

"Why don't you let the man in, Megan? He can tell me himself."

"I'm basically human, Meg," Katch said quietly. The tone of his voice had her looking at him more closely.

She glanced briefly over her shoulder, then turned back to Katch. The look she gave him was a warning. Don't do anything to upset him.

She noticed something in his eyes she hadn't expected—gentleness. It was more disconcerting than his earlier arrogance. Megan backed into the kitchen, holding open the door in silent invitation.

Katch smiled at her, casually brushing a strand of hair from her cheek as he walked by and into the kitchen. Megan stood for a moment, wondering why she should be so moved by a stranger's touch.

"Mr. Miller?" She heard the unaffected friendliness in Katch's voice and glanced over as he held out a hand to her grandfather. "I'm David Katcherton."

Pop nodded in approval. "You're the fellow who called me a couple of hours ago." He shot a look past Katch's shoulder to Megan. "I see you've already met my granddaughter."

His eyes smiled in response. "Yes. Charming."

Pop chuckled and moved toward the stove. "I was just about to make some more tea. How about a cup?"

Megan noticed the faint lift of his brow. Tea, she thought, was probably not his first choice.

"That'd be nice. Thanks." He walked to the table and sat, Megan decided, as if his acquaintance were long-standing and personal. Half reluctant, half defiant, she sat next to him. Her eyes asked him questions behind Pop's back.

"Did I tell you before that you have fabulous eyes?" he murmured. Without waiting for her answer, he turned his attention to Pop's tackle box. "You've got some great lures here," he observed to Pop, picking up a bone squid, then a wood plug painted to simulate a small frog. "Do you make any of your own?"

"That's half the sport," Pop stated, bringing a fresh cup to the table. "Have you done much fishing?"

"Here and there. I'd guess you'd know the best spots along the Grand Strand."

"A few of them," Pop said modestly.

Megan scowled into her tea. Once the subject of fishing had been brought up, Pop could go on for hours. And hours.

"I thought I'd do some surf casting while I'm here," Katch mentioned offhandedly. Megan was surprised to catch a shrewdly measuring expression in his eyes.

"Well now—" Pop warmed to the theme "—I might just be able to show you a spot or two. Do you have your own gear?"

"Not with me, no."

Pop brushed this off as inconsequential. "Where are you from, Mr. Katcherton?"

"Katch," he corrected, leaning back in his chair. "California originally."

That, Megan decided, explained the beachboy look. She drank her cooling tea with a casual air while studying him over the rim.

"You're a long way from home," Pop commented. He shifted comfortably, then brought out a pipe he saved for interesting conversations. "Do you plan to be in Myrtle Beach long?"

"Depends. I'd like to talk with you about your amusement park."

Pop puffed rapidly on his pipe while holding a match to the bowl. The tobacco caught, sending out cherry-scented smoke. "So you said on the phone. Funny, Megan and I were just talking about hiring on help for the summer. Only about six weeks before the season starts.'' He puffed and let the smoke waft lazily. ''Less than three until Easter. Ever worked rides or a booth?''

''No.'' Katch sampled his tea.

''Well...'' Pop shrugged his inexperience away. ''It's simple enough to learn. You look smart.'' Again, Megan caught the flash of Katch's grin. She set down her cup.

''We can't pay more than minimum to a novice,'' she said dampeningly.

He made her nervous, she was forced to admit. With any luck, she could discourage him from Joyland so that he'd try his luck elsewhere. But something nagged at her. He didn't look the type to take a job running a roller coaster or hawking a pitch-and-toss for a summer. There were hints of authority in his face, touches of casual power in his stance. Yet there was something not altogether respectable in his raffish charm.

He met her stare with a complete lack of self-consciousness. ''That seems reasonable. Do you work in the park, Meg?''

She bit back a retort to his familiarity. ''Often,'' she said succinctly.

''Megan's got a good business head,'' Pop interjected. ''She keeps me straight.''

''Funny,'' Katch said speculatively. ''Somehow I

thought you might be a model. You've the face for it." There was no flirtatiousness in his tone.

"Megan's an artist," Pop said, puffing contentedly at his pipe.

"Oh?"

She watched Katch's eyes narrow and focus on her. Uncomfortable, she shifted in her chair. "We seem to be drifting away from the subject," she said crisply. "If you've come about a job—"

"No."

"But...didn't you say—"

"I don't think so," he cut her off again and added a smile. He turned to Pop now, and Megan recognized a subtle change in his manner. "I don't want a job in your park, Mr. Miller. I want to buy it."

Both men were intent on each other. Pop was surprised, unmistakably so, but there was also a look of consideration in his eyes. Neither of them noticed Megan. She stared at Katch, her face open and young, and just a little frightened. She wanted to laugh and say he was making a foolish joke, but she knew better. Katch said exactly what he meant.

She'd recognized the understated authority and power beneath the glib exterior. This was business, pure and simple. She could see it on his face. There was a flutter of panic in her stomach as she looked at her grandfather.

"Pop?" Her voice was very small, and he made no sign that he heard her.

"You're a surprise," the old man said eventually. Then he began to puff on his pipe again. "Why my park?"

"I've done some research on the amusements here." Katch shrugged off the details. "I like yours."

Pop sighed and blew smoke at the ceiling. "I can't say I'm interested in selling out, son. A man gets used to a certain way of life."

"With the offer I'm prepared to make, you might find it easy to get used to another."

Pop gave a quiet laugh. "How old are you, Katch?"

"Thirty-one."

"That's just about how long I've been in this business. How much do you know about running a park?"

"Not as much as you do." Katch grinned and leaned back again. "But I could learn fast with the right teacher."

Megan saw that her grandfather was studying Katch carefully. She felt excluded from the conversation and resented it. Her grandfather was capable of doing this very subtly. She recognized that David Katcherton had the same talent. Megan sat silently;

natural courtesy forbade her interrupting private conversation.

"Why do you want to own an amusement park?" Pop asked suddenly. Megan could tell he was interested in David Katcherton. A warning bell began to ring in her head. The last thing she wanted was for her grandfather to become too involved with Katch. He was trouble, Megan was sure of it.

"It's good business," Katch answered Pop's question after a moment. "And fun." He smiled. "I like things that put fun into life."

He knows how to say the right thing, Megan acknowledged grudgingly, noting Pop's expression.

"I'd appreciate it if you'd think about it, Mr. Miller," Katch continued. "We could talk about it again in a few days."

And how to advance and retreat, she thought.

"I can't refuse to think about it," Pop agreed, but shook his head. "Still, you might take another look around. Megan and I've run Joyland for a good many years. It's home to us." He looked to his granddaughter teasingly. "Weren't you two going out to dinner?"

"No!" She flashed him a scowl.

"Exactly what I had in mind," Katch said smoothly. "Come on, Meg, I'll buy you a hamburger." As he rose, he took her hand, pulling her to her feet. Feeling her temper rise with her, Megan attempted to control it.

"I can't tell you how I hate to refuse such a charming invitation," she began.

"Then don't," Katch cut her off before turning to Pop. "Would you like to join us?"

Pop chuckled and motioned them away with the back of his hand. "Go on. I've got to get my gear together for the morning."

"Want company?"

Pop studied Katch over the bowl of his pipe. "I'm leaving at five-thirty," he said after a moment. "I have extra gear."

"I'll be here."

Megan was so astonished that she allowed Katch to lead her outside without making another protest. Pop never invited anyone along on his fishing mornings. They were his relaxation, and he enjoyed his solitude too much to share it.

"He never takes anyone with him," she murmured, thinking aloud.

"Then I'm flattered."

Megan noticed that Katch still had her hand, his fingers comfortably laced with hers.

"I'm not going out with you," she said positively and stopped walking. "You might be able to charm Pop into taking you fishing, but—"

"So you think I'm charming?" His smile was audacious as he took her other hand.

"Not in the least," she said firmly, repressing an answering smile.

"Why won't you have dinner with me?"

"Because," she said, meeting his eyes directly, "I don't like you."

His smile broadened. "I'd like the chance to change your mind."

"You couldn't." Megan started to draw her hands away, but he tightened his fingers.

"Wanna bet?" Again, she squashed the desire to smile. "If I change your mind, you'll go to the park with me Friday night."

"And if I don't change my mind?" she asked. "What then?"

"I won't bother you anymore." He grinned, as persuasive, she noted, as he was confident.

Her brow lifted in speculation. It might, she reflected, it just might be worth it.

"All you have to do is have dinner with me tonight," Katch continued, watching Megan's face. "Just a couple of hours."

"All right," she agreed impulsively. "It's a deal." She wriggled her fingers, but he didn't release them. "We could shake on it," she said, "but you still have my hands."

"So I do," he agreed. "We'll seal it my way then."

With a quick tug, he had her colliding against his chest. She felt a strength there which wasn't apparent in the lean, somewhat lanky frame. Before she could express annoyance, his mouth had taken hers.

He was skillful and thorough. She never knew whether she had parted her lips instinctively or if he had urged her to do so with the gently probing tip of his tongue.

From the instant of contact, Megan's mind had emptied, to be filled only with thoughts she couldn't center on. Her body dominated, taking command in simple surrender. She was melted against him, aware of his chest hard against her breasts...aware of his mouth quietly savaging hers. There was nothing else. She found there was nothing to hold on to. No anchor to keep her from veering off into wild water. Megan gave a small, protesting moan and drew away.

His eyes were darker than she'd thought, and too smoky to read clearly. Why had she thought them so decipherable? Why had she thought him so manageable? Nothing was as she had thought it had been minutes before. Her breath trembled as she fought to collect herself.

"You're very warm," Katch said softly. "It's a pity you struggle so hard to be remote."

"I'm not. I don't..." Megan shook her head, wishing desperately for her heartbeat to slow.

"You are," he corrected, "and you do." Katch gave her hands a companionable squeeze before releasing one of them. The other he kept snugly in his as he turned toward his car.

Panic was welling up inside Megan, and she tried to suppress it. *You've been kissed before,* she reminded herself. This was just unexpected. It just caught you off guard. Even as the excuse ran through her mind, she knew it for a lie. She'd never been kissed like that before. And the situation was no longer under her control.

"I don't think I'll go after all," she told him in calmer tones.

Katch turned, smiling at her as he opened the car door. "A bet's a bet, Meg."

Chapter 3

Katch drove a black Porsche. Megan wasn't surprised. She wouldn't have expected him to drive anything ordinary. It wasn't difficult to deduce that David Katcherton could afford the best of everything.

He'd probably inherited his money, she decided as she settled back against the silver gray seat cushion. He'd probably never worked a day in his life. She remembered the hard, unpampered feel of his palm. Probably a whiz at sports, she thought. Plays tennis, squash, sails his own yacht. Never does anything worthwhile. Only looks for pleasure. *And finds it,* she thought.

Megan turned to him, pushing her swinging hair

back behind her shoulders. His profile was sharply attractive, with the dusky blond hair curling negligently over his ear.

"See something you like?"

Megan flushed in annoyance, aware that she'd been caught staring.

"You need a shave," she said primly.

Katch turned the rearview mirror toward him as if to check her analysis. "Guess I do." He smiled as they merged into the traffic. "On our next date I'll be sure to remember. Don't say anything," he added, feeling her stiffen at his side. "Didn't your mother ever tell you not to say anything if you couldn't say something pleasant?"

Megan stifled a retort.

Katch smiled as he merged into traffic. "How long have you lived here?"

"Always." With the windows down, Megan could hear the outdoor noises. The music from a variety of car radios competed against each other and merged into a strange sort of harmony. Megan liked the cluttered, indefinable sound. She felt herself relaxing and straightened her shoulders and faced Katch again.

"And what do you do?"

He caught the thread of disdain in the question, but merely lifted a brow. "I own things."

"Really? What sort of things?"

Katch stopped at a red light, then turned, giving her a long, direct look. "Anything I want." The light changed and he deftly slid the car into the parking lot.

"We can't go in there," Megan told him with a glance at the exclusive restaurant.

"Why not?" Katch switched off the ignition. "The food's good here."

"I know, but we're not dressed properly, and—"

"Do you like doing things properly all the time, Meg?"

The question stopped her. She searched his face carefully, wondering if he was laughing at her, and unsure of the answer.

"Tell you what." He eased himself out of the car, then leaned back in the window. "Think about it for a few minutes. I'll be back."

Megan watched him slide through the elegant doors of the restaurant and shook her head. They'll boot him out, she thought. Still, she couldn't help admiring his confidence. There was something rather elusive about it. She crossed her arms over. "Still, I don't really *like* him," she muttered.

Fifteen minutes later, she decided she liked him even less. How impossibly rude! she fumed as she slammed out of his car. Keeping me waiting out here all this time!

She decided to find the nearest phone booth and

call her grandfather to ask him to come pick her up. She searched the pockets in her jeans and her jacket. Not a dime, she thought furiously. Not one thin dime to my name. Taking a deep breath, she stared at the doors of the restaurant. She'd have to borrow change, or beg their permission to use the house phone. Anything was better than waiting in the car. Just as she pulled open the door of the restaurant, Katch strolled out.

"Thanks," he said casually and moved past her.

Megan stared after him. He was carrying the biggest picnic basket she'd ever seen. After he'd opened the trunk and settled it inside, he glanced back up at her.

"Well come on." He slammed the lid. "I'm starving."

"What's in there?" she asked suspiciously.

"Dinner." He motioned for her to get in the car. Megan stood beside the closed door on the passenger side.

"How did you get them to do that?"

"I asked. Are you hungry?"

"Well, yes… But how—"

"Then let's go." Katch dropped into the driver's seat and started the engine. The moment she sat beside him, he swung out of the parking lot. "Where's your favorite place?" he demanded.

"My favorite place?" she repeated dumbly.

"You can't tell me you've lived here all your life and don't have a favorite place." Katch turned the car toward the ocean. "Where is it?"

"Toward the north end of the beach," she said. "Not many people go there, except at the height of the season."

"Good. I want to be alone with you."

The simple directness had butterflies dancing in her stomach. Slowly, she turned to look at him again.

"Anything wrong with that?" The smile was back, irreverent and engaging. Megan sighed, feeling like she was just climbing the first hill of a roller coaster.

"Probably," she murmured.

The beach was deserted but for the crying gulls. She stood for a moment facing west, enjoying the rich glow of the dying sun.

"I love this time of day," she said softly. "Everything seems so still. As if the day's holding its breath." She jumped when Katch's hands came to her shoulders.

"Easy," he murmured, kneading the suddenly tense muscles as he stood behind her. He looked over her head to the sunset. "I like it just before dawn, when the birds first start to sing and the light's still soft.

"You should relax more often," he told her. He

slid his fingers lazily up her neck and down again. The pleasure became less quiet and more demanding. When she would have slipped away, Katch turned her to face him.

"No," she said immediately, "don't." Megan placed both her hands on his chest. "Don't."

"All right." He relaxed his hold, but didn't release her for a moment. Then he stooped for the picnic basket and pulled out a white tablecloth saying briskly, "Besides, it's time to eat." Megan took it from him, marveling that the restaurant had given him their best linen.

"Here you go." With his head still bent over the basket, he handed her the glasses.

And they're crystal, she thought, dazed as she accepted the elegant wineglasses. There was china next, then silver.

"Why did they give you all this?"

"They were low on paper plates."

"Champagne?" She glanced at the label as he poured. "You must be crazy!"

"What's the matter?" he returned mildly. "Don't you like champagne?"

"Actually I do, though I've only had American."

"Here's to the French." Katch held out a glass to her.

Megan sipped. "It's wonderful," she said before

experimenting with another sip. "But you didn't have to…" she gestured expansively.

"I decided I wasn't in the mood for a hamburger." Katch screwed the bottle down into the sand. He placed a small container on the cloth, then dived back into the basket.

"What's this?" Megan demanded as she opened it. She frowned at the shiny black mass inside. He placed toast points on a plate. "Is it…" She paused in disbelief and glanced at him. "Is this caviar?"

"Yeah. Let me have some, will you? I'm starving." Katch took it from her and spread a generous amount on a piece of toast. "Don't you want any?" he asked her as he took a bite.

"I don't know." Megan examined it critically. "I've never tasted it before."

"No?" He offered her his piece. "Taste it." When she hesitated, Katch grinned and held it closer to her mouth. "Go on, Meg, have a bite."

"It's salty," she said with surprise. She plucked the toast from his hand and took another bite. "And it's good," she decided, swallowing.

"You might've left me some," he complained when Megan finished off the toast. She laughed and, heaping caviar onto another piece, handed it to him. "I wondered how it would sound." Katch took the offering, but his attention was on Megan.

"What?" Still smiling, she licked a bit of caviar from her thumb.

"Your laugh. I wondered if it would be as appealing as your face." He took a bite now, still watching her. "It is."

Megan tried to calm her fluttering pulse. "You didn't have to feed me caviar and champagne to hear me laugh." With a casual shrug, she moved out of his reach. "I laugh quite a bit."

"Not often enough."

She looked back at him in surprise. "Why do you say that?"

"Your eyes are so serious. So's your mouth." His glance swept over her face. "Perhaps that's why I feel compelled to make you smile."

"How extraordinary." Megan sat back on her heels and stared at him. "You barely know me."

"Does it matter?"

"I always thought it should," she murmured as he reached into the hamper again. Megan watched, no longer surprised as he drew out lobster tails and fresh strawberries. She laughed again and, pushing back her hair, moved closer to him.

"Here," she said. "Let me help."

The sun sank as they ate. The moon rose. It shot a shimmering white line across the sea. Megan thought it was like a dream—the china and silver gleaming in the moonlight, the exotic tastes on her tongue, the familiar sound of surf and the stranger beside her, who was becoming less of a stranger every minute.

Already Megan knew the exact movement of his face when he smiled, the precise tonal quality of his voice. She knew the exact pattern of the curls over his ear. More than once, bewitched by moonlight and champagne, she had to restrain her fingers from reaching for them, experimenting with them.

"Aren't you going to eat any cheesecake?" Katch gestured with a forkful, then slid it into his mouth.

"I can't." Megan brought her knees up to her chest and rested her chin on them. She watched his obvious enjoyment with dessert. "How do you do it?"

"Dedication." Katch took the last bite. "I try to see every project through to the finish."

"I've never had a picnic like this," she told him with a contented sigh. Leaning back on her elbows, she stretched out her legs and looked up at the stars. "I've never tasted anything so wonderful."

"I'll give Ricardo your compliments." Katch moved to sit beside her. His eyes moved from the crown of her head down the slender arch of her neck. Her face was thrown up to the stars.

"Who's Ricardo?" she asked absently. There was no thought of objection when Katch tucked her hair behind her ear with his fingertip.

''The chef. He loves compliments.''

Megan smiled, liking the way the sound of his voice mixed with the sound of the sea. ''How do you know?''

''That's how I lured him away from Chicago.''

''Lured him away? What do you mean?'' It took only an instant for the answer to come to her. ''You own that restaurant?''

''Yes.'' He smiled at the incredulity in her face. ''I bought it a couple of years ago.''

Megan glanced at the white linen cloth scattered with fine china and heavy silver. She recalled that a little more than two years before, the restaurant had been ready to go under. The food had been over-priced and the service slack. Then it had received a face-lift. The interior had been redesigned, boasting, she was told, a mirrored ceiling. Since its reopening, it had maintained the highest of reputations in a town which prided itself on its quality and variety of res-taurants.

She shifted her attention back to him. ''*You* bought it?''

''That's right.'' Katch smiled at her. He sat In-dian-style, facing her as she leaned back on her el-bows. ''Does that surprise you?''

Megan looked at him carefully: the careless toss of curls, the white knees of his jeans, the frayed sneakers. He was not her conception of a successful businessman. Where was the three-piece suit, the careful hairstyling? And yet…she had to admit there was something in his face.

"No," she said at length. "No, I suppose it doesn't." Megan frowned as he shifted his position. In a moment he was close, facing the sea as she did. "You bought it the same way you want to buy Joyland."

"I told you, that's what I do."

"But it's more than owning things, isn't it?" she insisted, not satisfied with his offhand answers. "It's making a success of them."

"That's the idea," he agreed. "There's a certain satisfaction in succeeding, don't you think?"

Megan sat up and turned to him. "But you can't have Joyland, it's Pop's whole life. You don't understand…"

"Maybe not," he said easily. "You can explain it to me later. Not tonight." He covered her hand with his. "This isn't a night for business."

"Katch, you have to—"

"Look at the stars, Meg," he suggested as he did so himself. "Have you ever tried to count them?"

Her eyes were irresistibly drawn upward. "When I was little. But—"

"Star counting isn't just for kids," he instructed in a voice warm and laced with humor. "Do you come here at night?"

The stars were brilliant and low over the sea. "Sometimes," she murmured. "When a project isn't going well and I need to clear my head, or just be alone."

"What sort of artist are you?" His fingers trailed over her knuckles. "Do you paint seascapes? Portraits?"

She smiled and shook her head. "No, I sculpt."

"Ah." He lifted her hand, then examined it—one side, then the other—while she watched him. "Yes, I can see that. Your hands are strong and capable." When he pressed his lips to the center of her palm, she felt the jolt shoot through her entire body.

Carefully, Megan drew her hand away; then, bringing her knees up to her chest, wrapped her arms around them. She could feel Katch smile without seeing it.

"What do you work in? Clay, wood, stone?"

"All three." Turning her head, she smiled again. "Where did you study?"

"I took courses in college." With a shrug, she passed this off. "There hasn't been much time for it." She looked up at the sky again. "The moon's so white tonight. I like to come here when it's full like this, so that the light's silvery."

When his lips brushed her ear, she would have jerked away, but he slipped an arm around her shoulders. "Relax, Meg." His voice was a whisper at her cheek. "There's a moon and the ocean. That's all there is besides us."

With his lips tingling on her skin, she could almost believe him. Her limbs were heavy, drugged with wine and the magic of his touch. Katch trailed his mouth down to her throat so that she moaned with the leap of her pulse.

"Katch, I'd better go." He was tracing her jaw with light kisses. "Please," she said weakly.

"Later," he murmured, going back to nuzzle her ear. "Much, much later."

"No, I..." Megan turned her head, and the words died.

Her lips were no more than a breath from his. She stared at him, eyes wide and aware as he bent closer. Still his mouth didn't touch hers. It hovered, offering, promising. She moaned again, lids lowering as he teased the corners of her lips. His hands never touched her. He had moved his arm so that their only contact was his mouth and tongue on her skin and the mingling of their breath.

Megan felt her resistance peel away, layer by layer until there was only need. She forgot to question the dangers, the consequences. She could only feel. Her mouth sought his. There was no hesitation or shyness now but demand, impatient demand, as she hungered to feel what she had felt before—the delicious confusion, the dark awareness.

When he still didn't touch her, Megan slipped her arms around him. She pulled him close, enjoying his soft sound of pleasure as the kiss deepened. Still, he let her lead, touching her now, but lightly, his fingers in her hair. She could barely hear the hissing of the surf over the pounding of her heart. Finally, she drew away, pulling in a deep breath as their lips separated.

But he wouldn't let her go. "Again?" The question was quiet and seemed to shout through the still night.

Refusal trembled on Megan's tongue. She knew the ground beneath her was far from solid. His hand on the back of her neck brought her a whisper closer.

"Yes," she said, and went into his arms.

This time he was less passive. He showed her there were many ways to kiss. Short and light, long and deep. Tongue and teeth and lips could all bring pleasure. Together, they lowered themselves to the sand.

It was a rough blanket, but she felt only the excitement of his lips on her skin as they wandered to her throat. She ran her fingers through his hair. His mouth returned to hers, harder now, more insistent. She was ready for it, answering it. Craving it.

When his hand took the naked skin of her breast, she murmured in resistance. She hadn't felt him release the zipper of her jacket or the buttons of her shirt. But his hand was gentle, persuasive. He let his fingers trail over her, a whispering touch. Resistance melted into surrender, then heated into passion. It was smoldering just under her skin, threatening to explode into something out of her control. She moved under him and his hands became less gentle.

There was a hunger in the kiss now. She could taste it, a flavor sharper than any she'd known. It was more seductive than soft words or champagne, and more frightening.

"I want you." Katch spoke against her mouth, but the words were not in his easygoing tone. "I want to make love with you."

Megan felt control slipping from her grasp. Her need for him was overpowering, her appetite ravenous. She struggled to climb back to reality, to remember who they were. Names, places, responsibilities. There was more than the moon and the sea. And he was a stranger, a man she barely knew.

"No." Megan managed to free her mouth from his. She struggled to her feet. "No." The repetition was shaky. Quickly, she began to fumble with the buttons of her shirt.

Katch stood and gathered the shirttail in his hands. Surprised, Megan looked up at him. His eyes were no longer calm, but his voice was deadly so. "Why not?"

Megan swallowed. There wasn't lazy arrogance here, but a hint of ruthlessness. She had sensed it, but seeing it was much more potent. "I don't want to."

"Liar," he said simply.

"All right." She nodded, conceding his point. "I don't know you."

Katch inclined his head in agreement but tugged on the tails of her shirt to bring her closer. "You will," he assured her. He kissed her then, searingly. "But we'll wait until you do."

She fought to steady her breathing and stabilize her pulse. "Do you think you should always get what you want?" she demanded. The defiance was back, calming her.

"Yes," he said and grinned. "Of course."

"You're going to be disappointed." She smacked his hands from her shirt and began doing the buttons. Her fingers were unfaltering. "You can't have Joyland and you can't have me. Neither of us is for sale."

The roughness with which he took her arm had her eyes flying back to his face. "I don't buy women." He was angry, his eyes dark with it. The appealing voice had hardened like flint. The artist in her was fascinated by the planes of his face, the woman was uneasy with his harsh tone. "I don't have to. We're both aware that with a bit more persuasion I'd have had you tonight."

Megan pulled out of his hold. "What happened

tonight doesn't mean I find you irresistible, you know." She zipped up her jacket with one quick jerk. "I can only repeat, you can't have Joyland and you can't have me."

Katch watched her a moment as she stood in the moonlight, her back to the sea. The smile came again, slowly, arrogantly. "I'll have you both, Meg," he promised quietly. "Before the season begins."

Chapter 4

The afternoon sun poured into Megan's studio. She was oblivious to it, and to the birdsong outside the windows. Her mind was focused on the clay her hands worked with, or, more precisely, on what she saw in the partially formed mound.

She had put her current project aside, something she rarely did, to begin a new one. The new subject had haunted her throughout the night. She would exorcise David Katcherton by doing a bust of him.

Megan could see it clearly, knew precisely what she wanted to capture: strength and determination behind a surface affability.

Though she had yet to admit it, Katch had frightened her the night before. Not physically—he was too intelligent to use brute force, she acknowledged—but by the force of his personality. Angrily, she stabbed at the clay. Obviously, this was a man who got what he wanted. But she was determined that this time he would not have his way. He would soon find out that she couldn't be pushed around any more than Pop could. Slowly and meticulously, her fingers worked to mold the planes of his face. It gave her a certain satisfaction to have control over him—if only vicariously with the clay.

Almost without thinking, she shaped a careless curl over the high brow. She stepped back to survey it. Somehow, she had caught a facet of his nature. He was a rogue, she decided. The old-fashioned word suited him. She could picture him with boots and six-guns, dealing cards for stud poker in a Tucson saloon; with a saber, captaining a ship into the Barbary Coast. Her fingers absently caressed the clay curls. He would laugh in the face of the wind, take treasure and women where he found them. *Women.* Megan's thoughts zeroed in on the night before.... On the feel of his lips on hers, the touch of his hand on her skin. She could remember the texture of the sand as they had lain together, the scent and sounds of the sea. And she remembered how the moonlight had fallen on his hair, how her hands had sought it while his lips had wandered over her. How thick and soft it had felt. How...

Megan stopped, appalled. She glanced down to see her fingers in the clay replica of Katch's hair. She swore, and nearly, very nearly, reduced the clay to a formless mass. Controlling herself, she rose, backing away from the forming bust. I should never allow myself to be distracted from my work by petty annoyances, she thought. Her evening with Katch belonged in that category. Just a petty annoyance. Not important.

But it was difficult for Megan to convince herself this was true. Both her intuition and her emotions told her that Katch was important, far more important than a stranger should be to a sensible woman.

And I *am* sensible, she reminded herself. Taking a long breath, she moved to the basin to rinse the clay from her hands. She had to be sensible. Pop needed someone around to remind him that bills had to be paid. A smile crept across her mouth as she dried her hands. Megan thought, as she did from time to time, that she had been almost as much of a savior to her grandfather as he had been to her.

In the beginning, she'd been so young, so dependent upon him. And he hadn't let her down. Then, as she had grown older, Megan had helped by assuming the duties her grandfather had found tiresome: accounts and bank reconciliations. Often, Megan suppressed her own desires in order to fulfill what she thought of as her duty. She dealt with fig-

ures, the unromantic process of adding and subtract-
ing. But she also dealt with the illusionary world of
art. There were times, when she was deep in her
work, that she forgot the rules she had set up for
day-to-day living. Often she felt pulled in two directions. She had enough to think about without David
Katcherton.

Why a man virtually unknown to her should so
successfully upset the delicate balance of her world,
she didn't know. She shook her head. Instead of
dwelling on it, she decided, she would work out her
frustration by finishing the bust. When it was done,
perhaps she would be able to see more clearly exactly how she perceived him. She returned to her
work.

The next hour passed quickly. She forgot her irritation with Katch for going fishing with her grandfather. How annoying to have seen him so eager and
well rested when she had peeked through her bedroom curtain at five-thirty that morning! She'd fallen
back into her rumpled bed to spend another hour
staring, heavy-eyed, at the ceiling. She refused to
remember how appealing his laugh had sounded in
the hush of dawn.

The planes of his face were just taking shape under her hands when she heard a car drive up. Katch's
laugh was followed by the more gravelly tones of
her grandfather's.

Because her studio was above the garage, Megan had a bird's-eye view of the house and drive. She watched as Katch lifted their fishing cooler from the back of the pickup. A grin was on his face, but whatever he said was too low for Megan to hear. Pop threw back his head, his dramatic mane of white flying back as he roared his appreciation. He gave Katch a companionable slap on the back. Unaccountably, Megan was miffed. They seemed to be getting along entirely too well.

She continued to watch the man as they unloaded tackle boxes and gear. Katch was dressed much as he had been the day before. The pale blue T-shirt had lettering across the chest, but the words were faded and the distance was too great for Megan to read them. He wore Pop's fishing cap, another source of annoyance for Megan. She was forced to admit the two of them looked good together. There was the contrast between their ages and their builds, but both seemed to her to be extraordinarily masculine men. Their looks were neither smooth nor pampered. She became engrossed with the similarities and differences between them. When Katch looked up, spotting her at the window, Megan continued to stare down, oblivious, absorbed with what she saw in them.

Katch grinned, pushing the fishing cap back so that he had a clearer view. The window was long, the sill coming low at her knees. It had the effect of making Megan seem to be standing in a full-size picture frame. As was her habit when working, she had pulled her hair back in a ribbon. Her face seemed younger and more vulnerable, her eyes wider. The ancient shirt of Pop's she used as a smock dwarfed her.

Her eyes locked on Katch's, and for a moment she thought she saw something flash in them—something she'd seen briefly the night before in the moonlight. A response trembled along her skin. Then his grin was arrogant again, his eyes amused.

"Come on down, Meg." He gestured before he bent to lift the cooler again. "We brought you a present." He turned to carry the cooler around the side of the house.

"I'd rather have emeralds," she called back.

"Next time," Katch promised carelessly, before turning to carry the cooler around the side of the house.

She found Katch alone, setting up for the cleaning of the catch. He smiled when he saw her and set down the knife he held, then pulled her into his arms and kissed her thoroughly, to her utter astonishment. It was a kiss of casual ownership rather than passion, but it elicited a response that surprised her with its force. More than a little shaken, Megan pushed away.

"You can't just…"

"I already did," he pointed out. "You've been working," Katch stated as if the searing kiss had never taken place. "I'd like to see your studio."

It was better, Megan decided, to follow his lead and keep the conversation light. "Where's my grandfather?" she asked as she moved to the cooler and prepared to lift the lid.

"Pop's inside stowing the gear."

Though it was the habit of everyone who knew him to refer to Timothy Miller as Pop, Megan frowned at Katch.

"You work fast, don't you?"

"Yes, I do. I like your grandfather, Meg. You of all people should understand how easy that is to do."

Megan regarded him steadily. She took a step closer, as if testing the air between them. "I don't know if I should trust you."

"You shouldn't." Katch grinned again and ran a finger down the bridge of her nose. "Not for a second." He tossed open the lid of the cooler, then gestured to the fish inside. "Hungry?"

Megan smiled, letting herself be charmed despite the warnings of her sensible self. "I wasn't. But I could be. Especially if I don't have to clean them."

"Pop told me you were squeamish."

"Oh, he *did,* did he?" Megan cast a long, baleful look over her shoulder toward the house. "What else did he tell you?"

"That you like daffodils and used to have a stuffed elephant named Henry."

Megan's mouth dropped open. "He told you that?"

"And that you watch horror movies, then sleep with the blankets over your head."

Megan narrowed her eyes as Katch's grin widened. "Excuse me," she said crossly, pushing Katch aside before racing through the kitchen door. She could hear Katch's laughter behind her.

"Pop!" She found him in the narrow room off the kitchen where he stored his fishing paraphernalia. He gave her an affectionate smile as she stood, hands on hips, in the doorway.

"Hi, Megan. Let me tell you, that boy knows how to fish. Yessiree, he knows how to fish."

His obvious delight with Katch caused Megan to clench her teeth. "That's the best news I've had all day," she said, stepping into the room. "But exactly why did you feel it necessary to tell *that boy* that I had a stuffed elephant and slept with the covers over my head?"

Pop lifted a hand, ostensibly to scratch his head. It wasn't in time, however, to conceal the grin. Megan's brows drew together.

"Pop, really," she said in exasperation. "Must you babble about me as if I were a little girl?"

"You'll always be my little girl," he said maddeningly, and kissed her cheek. "Did you see those trout? We'll have a heck of a fish fry tonight."

"I suppose," Megan began and folded her arms, "*he's* going to eat with us."

"Well, of course." Pop blinked his eyes. "After all, Meg, he caught half the fish."

"That's just peachy."

"We thought you might whip up some of your special blueberry tarts." He smiled ingenuously.

Megan sighed, recognizing defeat.

Within minutes, Pop heard the thumping and banging of pans. He grinned, then slipped out of the room, moving noiselessly through the house and out the front door.

"Whip up some tarts," Megan muttered later as she cut shortening into the flour. *"Men."*

She was bending over to slip the pastry shells into the oven when the screen door slammed shut behind her. Turning, she brushed at the seat of her pants and met the predictable grin.

"I've heard about your tarts," Katch commented, setting the cleaned, filleted fish on the counter. "Pop said he had a few things to see to in the garage and to call him when dinner's ready."

Megan glared through the screen door at the ad-

joining building. "Oh, he did, did he?" She turned
back to Katch. "Well, if you think you can just sit
back and be waited on, then you're in for a disappointment."

"You didn't think I'd allow you to cook my fish,
did you?" he interrupted.

She stared at his unperturbed face.

"I always cook my own fish. Where's the frying
pan?"

Silently, still eyeing him, Megan pointed out the
cabinet. She watched as he squatted down to rum-
mage for it.

"It's not that I don't think you're a good cook,"
he went on as he stood again with the cast-iron skil-
let in his hand. "It's that I know I am."

"Are you implying I couldn't cook those pathetic
little sardines properly?"

"Let's just say I just don't like to take chances
with my dinner." He began poking into cupboards.
"Why don't you make a salad," he suggested
mildly, "and leave the fish to me?" There was a
grunt of approval as he located the cracker meal.

Megan watched him casually going through her
kitchen cupboards. "Why don't you," she began,
"take your trout and…"

Her suggestion was interrupted by the rude buzz
of the oven timer.

"Your tarts." Katch walked to the refrigerator for eggs and milk.

With supreme effort, Megan controlled herself enough to deal with the pastry shells. Setting them on the rack to cool, she decided to create the salad of the decade. It would put his pan-fried trout to shame.

For a time there were no words. The hot oil hissed as Katch added his coated trout. Megan tore the lettuce. She sliced raw vegetables. The scent from the pan was enticing. Megan peeled a carrot and sighed. Hearing her, Katch raised a questioning eyebrow.

"You had to be good at it, didn't you?" Megan's smile was reluctant. "You had to do it right."

He shrugged, then snatched the peeled carrot from her hand. "You'd like it better if I didn't?" Katch took a bite of the carrot before Megan could retrieve it. Shaking her head, she selected another.

"It would have been more gratifying if you'd fumbled around and made a mess of things."

Katch tilted his head as he poked at the sizzling fish with a spatula. "Is that a compliment?"

Megan diced the carrot, frowning at it thoughtfully. "I don't know. It might be easier to deal with you if you didn't seem so capable."

He caught her off guard by taking her shoulders and turning her around to face him. "Is that what you want to do?" His fingers gently massaged her flesh. "Deal with me?" When she felt herself being drawn closer, she placed her hands on his chest. "Do I make you nervous?"

"No." Megan shook her head with the denial. "No, of course not." Katch only lifted a brow and drew her closer. "Yes," she admitted in a rush, and pulled away. "Yes, blast it, you do." Stalking to the refrigerator, she yanked out the blueberry filling she had prepared. "You needn't look so pleased about it," she told him, wishing she could work up the annoyance she thought she should feel.

"Several things make me nervous." Megan moved to the pastry shells and began to spoon in the filling. "Snakes, tooth decay, large unfriendly dogs." When she heard him chuckle, Megan turned her head and found herself grinning at him. "It's difficult to actively dislike you when you make me laugh."

"Do you have to actively dislike me?" Katch flipped the fish expertly and sent oil sizzling.

"That was my plan," Megan admitted. "It seemed like a good idea."

"Why don't we work on a different plan?" Katch suggested, searching through a cupboard again for a platter. "What do you like? Besides daffodils?"

"Soft ice cream," Megan responded spontaneously. "Oscar Wilde, walking barefoot."

"How about baseball?" Katch demanded.

Megan paused in the act of filling the shells. "What about it?"

"Do you like it?"

"Yes," she considered, smiling. "As a matter of fact, I do."

"I knew we had something in common." Katch grinned. He turned the flame off under the pan. "Why don't you call Pop? The fish is done."

There was something altogether too cozy about the three of them sitting around the kitchen table eating a meal each of them had a part in providing, Megan thought. She could sense the growing affection between the two men and it worried her. She was sure that Katch was still as determined as ever to buy Joyland. Yet Pop was so obviously happy in his company. Megan decided that, while she couldn't trust Katch unreservedly, neither could she maintain her original plan. She couldn't dislike him or keep him from touching their lives. She thought it best not to dwell on precisely how he was touching hers.

"Tell you what." Pop sighed over his empty plate and leaned back in his chair. "Since the pair of you cooked dinner, I'll do the dishes." His eyes passed over Megan to Katch. "Why don't you two go for a walk? Megan likes to walk on the beach."

"Pop!"

"I know you young people like to be alone," he continued shamelessly.

Megan opened her mouth to protest, but Katch spoke first. "I'm always willing to take a walk with a beautiful woman, especially if it means getting out of KP," he said.

"You have such a gracious way of putting things," Megan began.

"Actually, I'd really like to see your studio."

"Take Katch up, Megan," Pop insisted. "I've been bragging about your pieces all day. Let him see for himself."

After a moment's hesitation, Megan decided it was simpler to agree. Certainly she didn't mind showing Katch her work. And, there was little doubt that it was safer to let him putter around her studio than to walk with him on the beach.

"All right." She rose. "I'll take you up."

As they passed through the screen door, Katch slipped his arm over her shoulders. "This is a nice place," he commented. He looked around the small trim yard lined with azalea shrubs. "Very quiet and settled."

The weight of his arm was pleasant. Megan allowed it to remain as they walked toward the garage. "I wouldn't think you'd find something quiet and settled terribly appealing."

"There's a time for porch swings and a time for

roller coasters.'' Katch glanced down at her as she paused at the foot of the steps. ''I'd think you'd know that.''

''I do,'' she said, knowing her involvement with him was beginning to slip beyond her control. ''I wasn't aware you did.'' Thoughtfully, Megan climbed the stairs. ''It's rather a small-scale studio, I suppose, and not very impressive. It's really just a place to work where I won't disturb Pop and he won't disturb me.''

Megan opened the door, flicking on the light as the sun was growing dim.

There was much less order here than she permitted herself in other areas of her life. The room was hers, personally, more exclusively than her bedroom in the house next door. There were tools—calipers, chisels, gouges, and an assortment of knives and files. There was the smock she'd carelessly thrown over a chair when Katch had called her downstairs. Future projects sat waiting inside, untouched slabs of limestone and chunks of wood. There was a precious piece of marble she hoarded like a miser. Everywhere, on shelves, tables and even the floor, were samples of her work.

Katch moved past her into the room. Strangely, Megan felt a flutter of nerves. She found herself wondering how to react if he spoke critically, or worse, offered some trite compliment. Her work was important to her and very personal. To her surprise she realized that she cared about his opinion. Quietly, she closed the door behind her, then stood with her back against it.

Katch had gone directly to a small walnut study of a young girl building a sand castle. She was particularly pleased with the piece, as she had achieved exactly the mood she had sought. There was more than youth and innocence in the child's face. The girl saw herself as the princess in the castle tower. The half-smile on her face made the onlooker believe in happy endings.

It was painstakingly detailed, the beginnings of a crenellated roof and the turrets of the castle, the slender fingers of the girl as she sculpted the sand. Her hair was long, falling over her shoulders and wisping into her face as though a breeze teased it. Megan had felt successful when the study had been complete, but now, watching Katch turn it over in his hands, his mouth oddly grave, his eyes intent, she felt a twinge of doubt.

"This is your work?" Because the silence had seemed so permanent, Megan jerked when Katch spoke.

"Well, yes." While she was still searching for something more to say, Katch turned away to prowl the room.

He picked up piece after piece, examining, saying

nothing. As the silence dragged on, minute upon minute, Megan became more and more tense. If he'd just say something, she thought. She picked up the discarded smock and folded it, nervously smoothing creases as she listened to the soft sound of his tennis shoes on the wood floor.

"What are you doing here?"

She whirled, eyes wide. Whatever reaction she had expected, it certainly hadn't been anger. And there was anger on his face, a sharp, penetrating anger which caused her to grip the worn material of the smock tighter.

"I don't know what you mean." Megan's voice was calm, but her heart had begun to beat faster.

"Why are you hiding?" he demanded. "What are you afraid of?"

She shook her head in bewilderment. "I'm not hiding, Katch. You're not making any sense."

"I'm not making sense?" He took a step toward her, then stopped, turning away to pace again. She watched in fascination. "Do you think it makes sense to create things like this and lock them up in a room over a garage?" He lifted polished limestone which had been formed into a head-and-shoulders study of a man and a woman in each other's arms. "When you've been given talent like this, you have an obligation. What are you going to do, continue to stack them in here until there isn't any more room?"

His reaction had thrown Megan completely off-balance. She looked around the room. "No, I...I take pieces into an art gallery downtown now and then. They sell fairly well, especially during the season, and—"

Katch's pungent oath cut her off. Megan gave her full attention back to him. Was this furious, disapproving man the same one who had amiably prepared trout in her kitchen a short time ago?

"I don't understand why you're so mad." Annoyed with herself for nervously pleating the material of the smock, Megan tossed it down.

"Waste," he said tersely, placing the limestone back on the shelf. "Waste infuriates me." He came to her, taking her deliberately by the shoulders. "Why haven't you done anything with your work?" His eyes were direct on hers, demanding answers, not evasions.

"It's not as simple as that," she began. "I have responsibilities."

"Your responsibilities are to yourself, to your talent."

"You make it sound as though I've done something wrong." Confused, Megan searched his face. "I've done what I know how to do. I don't understand why you're angry. There are things, like time and money, to be considered," she went on. "A business to run. And reality to face." Megan shook her head. "I can hardly cart my work to a Charleston art gallery and demand a showing."

"That would make more sense than cloistering it up here." He released her abruptly, then paced again.

He was, Megan discovered, much more volatile than her first impression had allowed. She glanced at the clay wrapped in the damp towel. Her fingertips itched to work while fresh impressions were streaming through her brain.

"When's the last time you've been to New York?" Katch demanded, facing her again. "Chicago, L.A.?"

"We can't all be globetrotters," she told him. "Some are born to other things."

He picked up the sand-castle girl again, then strode over to the limestone couple. "I want these two," he stated. "Will you sell them to me?"

They were two of her favorites, though totally opposite in tone. "Yes, I suppose. If you want them."

"I'll give you five hundred." Megan's eyes widened. "Apiece."

"Oh, no, they're not worth—"

"They're worth a lot more, I imagine." Katch lifted the limestone. "Have you got a box I can carry them in?"

"Yes, but, Katch." Megan paused and pushed the bangs from her eyes. "A thousand dollars?"

He set down both pieces and came back to her. He was still angry; she could feel it vibrating from him. "Do you think it's safer to underestimate yourself than to face up to your own worth?"

Megan started to make a furious denial, then stopped. Uncertain, she made a helpless gesture with her hands. Katch turned away again to search for a box himself. She watched him as he wrapped the sculptures in old newspapers. The frown was still on his face, the temper in his eyes.

"I'll bring you a check," he stated, and was gone without another word.

Chapter 5

There was a long, high-pitched scream. The roller coaster rumbled along the track as it whipped around another curve and tilted its passengers. Lights along the midway were twinkling, and there was noise. Such noise. There was the whirl and whine of machinery, the electronic buzz and beeps from video games, the pop of arcade rifles and the call of concessionaires.

Tinny music floated all over, but for the most part, there was the sound of people. They were laughing, calling, talking, shouting. There were smells: popcorn, peanuts, grilled hot dogs, machine oil.

Megan loaded another clip into the scaled-down rifle and handed it to a would-be Wyatt Earp. "Rabbits are five points, ducks ten, deer twenty-five and the bears fifty.''

The sixteen-year-old sharpshooter aimed and managed to bag a duck and a rabbit. He chose a rubber snake as his prize, to the ensuing screams and disgust of his girl.

Shaking her head, Megan watched them walk away. The boy slipped his arm around the girl's shoulders, then pursued the romance by dangling the snake in front of her face. He earned a quick jab in the ribs.

The crowd was thin tonight, but that was to be expected in the off-season. Particularly, Megan knew, when there were so many other parks with more rides, live entertainment and a more sophisticated selection of video games. She didn't mind the slack. Megan was preoccupied, as she had been since the evening Katch had seen her studio. In three days, she hadn't heard a word from him. At first, she had wanted badly to see him, to talk about the things he'd said to her. He had made her think, made her consider a part of herself she had ignored or submerged most of her life.

Her desire to speak with Katch had faded as the days had passed, however. After all, what right did he have to criticize her life-style? What right did he have to make her feel as if she'd committed a crime?

He'd accused, tried and condemned her in the space of minutes. Then, he'd disappeared.

Three days, Megan mused, handing another hopeful deadeye a rifle. Three days without a word. And she'd watched for him—much to her self-disgust. She'd waited for him. As the days had passed, Megan had taken refuge in anger. Not only had he criticized and scolded her, she remembered, but he'd walked out with two of her favorite sculptures. A thousand dollars my foot, she mused, frowning fiercely as she slid a fresh clip into an empty rifle. Just talk, that's all. Talk. He does that very well. It was probably all a line, owning that restaurant. *But why?* Men like that don't need logical reasons, she decided. It's all ego.

"Men," she muttered as she handed a rifle to a new customer.

"I know what you mean, honey." The plump blond woman took the rifle from Megan with a wink.

Megan pushed her bangs back and frowned deeper. "Who needs them?" she demanded.

The woman shouldered the rifle. "We do, honey. That's the problem."

Megan let out a long sigh as the woman earned 125 points. "Nice shooting," she congratulated. "Your choice on the second row."

"Let me have the hippo, sweetie. It looks a little like my second husband."

Laughing, Megan plucked it from the shelf and handed it over. "Here you go." With another wink, the woman tucked the hippo under her arm and waddled off.

Megan settled back while two kids tried their luck. The exchange had been typical of the informality enjoyed by people in amusement parks. She smiled, feeling less grim, if not entirely mollified by the woman's remarks. But she doesn't know Katch, Megan reflected, again exchanging a rifle for a quarter. And neither, she reminded herself, do I.

Automatically, Megan made change when a dollar bill was placed on the counter. "Ten shots for a quarter," she began the spiel. "Rabbits are five, ducks ten…" Megan pushed three quarters back as she reached for a rifle. The moment the fingers pushed the change back to her, she recognized them.

"I'll take a dollar's worth," Katch told her as she looked up in surprise. He grinned, then leaned over to press a quick kiss to her lips. "For luck," he claimed when she jerked away.

Before Megan had pocketed the quarters, Katch had bull's-eyed every one of the bears.

"Wow!" The two boys standing next to Katch were suitably impressed. "Hey, mister, can you do it again?" one asked.

"Maybe." Katch turned to Megan. "Let's have a reload." Without speaking, she handed him the rifle.

"I like the perfume you're wearing," he commented as he sighed. "What is it?"

"Gun oil."

He laughed, then blasted the hapless bears one by one. The two boys gave simultaneous yelps of appreciation. A crowd began to gather.

"Hey, Megan." She glanced up to see the Bailey twins leaning over the counter. Both pairs of eyes drifted meaningfully to Katch. "Isn't he the…"

"Yes," Megan said shortly, not wanting to explain.

"Delicious," Teri decided quietly, giving Katch a flirtatious smile when he straightened.

"Mmm-hmm," Jeri agreed with a twin smile.

Katch gave them a long, appreciative look.

"Here." Megan shoved the rifle at him. "This is your last quarter."

Katch accepted the rifle. "Thanks." He hefted it again. "Going to wish me luck?"

Megan met his eyes levelly. "Why not?"

"Meg, I'm crazy about you."

She dealt with the surge his careless words brought her as he picked off his fourth set of bears. Bystanders broke into raucous applause. Katch set the rifle on the counter, then gave his full attention to Meg.

"What'd I win?"

"Anything you want."

His grin was a flash, and his eyes never left her face. She blushed instantly, hating herself. Deliberately, she stepped to the side and gestured toward the prizes.

"I'll take Henry," he told her. When she gave him a puzzled look, he pointed. "The elephant." Glancing up, Megan spotted the three-foot lavender elephant. She lifted it down from its perch. Even as she set it on the counter for him, Katch took her hands. "And you."

She made her voice prim. "Only the items on display are eligible prizes."

"I love it when you talk that way," he commented.

"Stop it!" she hissed, flushing as she heard the Bailey twins giggle.

"We had a bet, remember?" Katch smiled at her. "It's Friday night."

Megan tried to tug her hands away, but his fingers interlocked with hers. "Who says I lost the bet?" she demanded. The crowd was still milling around the stand so she spoke in an undertone, but Katch didn't bother.

"Come on, Meg, I won fair and square. You're not going to welch, are you?"

"Shh!" She glanced behind him at the curious crowd. "I never welch," she whispered furiously. "And even if I did lose, which I never said I did, I

can't leave the stand. I'm sure you can find somebody else to keep you company.''

"I want you."

She struggled to keep her eyes steady on his.
"Well, I can't leave. Someone has to run the
booth."

"Megan." One of the part-timers slipped under
the counter. "Pop sent me to relieve you." He
smiled innocently when she gave him a disgusted
look.

"Perfect timing," she mumbled, then stripped off
the change apron and stuffed it in his hands.
"Thanks a lot."

"Sure, Megan."

"Hey, keep this back there for me, will you?"
Katch dumped the elephant into his arms and captured Megan's hands again as she ducked under the
counter. As she straightened, he tugged, tumbling
her into his arms.

The kiss was long and demanding. When Katch
drew her away, her arms were around his neck. She
left them there, staring up into his face with eyes
newly aware and darkened.

"I've wanted to do that for three days," he murmured, and rubbed her nose lightly with his.

"Why didn't you?"

He lifted a brow at that, then grinned when her
blush betrayed the impetuousness of her words.

"I didn't mean that the way it sounded," Megan began, dropping her arms and trying to wriggle away.

"Yes you did," he countered. Katch released her but dropped a friendly arm over her shoulder. "It was nice, don't spoil it." He took a sweeping glance of the park. "How about a tour?"

"I don't know why you want one. We're not selling."

"We'll see about that," he said, as maddeningly confident as ever. "But in any case, I'm interested. Do you know why people come here? To a place like this?" He gestured with his free arm to encompass the park.

"To be entertained," Megan told him as she followed the movement of his arm.

"You left out two of the most important reasons," he added. "To fantasize and to show off."

They stopped to watch a middle-aged man strip out of his jacket and attempt to ring the bell. The hammer came down with a loud thump, but the ball rose only halfway up the pole. He rubbed his hands together and prepared to try again.

"Yes, you're right." Megan tossed her hair back with a move of her head, then smiled at Katch. "You ought to know."

He tilted his head and shot her a grin. "Want me to ring the bell?"

"Muscles don't impress me," she said firmly.

"No?" He guided her away with his arm still around her. "What does?"

"Poetry," Megan decided all at once.

"Hmm." Katch rubbed his chin and avoided a trio of teenagers. "How about a limerick? I know some great limericks."

"I bet you do." Megan shook her head. "I think I'll pass."

"Coward."

"Oh? Let's ride the roller coaster, then we'll see who's a coward."

"You're on." Taking her hand, he set off in a sprint. He stopped at the ticket booth, and gratefully she caught her breath.

I might as well face it, she reflected as she studied his face. I enjoy him. There isn't any use in pretending I don't.

"What are you thinking?" Katch demanded as he paid for their ride.

"That I could learn to like you—in three or four years. For short periods of time," she added, still smiling.

Katch took both her hands and kissed them, surprising Megan with the shock that raced up her arms. "Flatterer," he murmured, and his eyes laughed at her over their joined hands.

Distressed by the power she felt rushing through

her system, Megan tried to tug her hands from his. It was imperative, for reasons only half-formed in her brain, that she keep their relationship casual.

"You have to hold my hand." Katch jerked his head toward the roller coaster. "I'm afraid of heights."

Megan laughed. She let herself forget the tempestuous instant and the hint of danger. She kept her hand in his.

Katch wasn't satisfied with only the roller coaster. He pulled Megan to ride after ride. They were scrambled on the Mind Maze, spooked in the Haunted Castle and spun lazily on the Ferris wheel.

From the top of the wheel, they watched the colored lights of the park, and the sea stretching out to the right. The wind tossed her hair into her face. Katch took it in his hand as they rose toward the top again. When he kissed her, it felt natural and right...a shared thing, a moment which belonged only to them. The noise and people below were of another world. Theirs was only the gentle movement of the wheel and the dance of the breeze. And the touch of mouth on mouth. There was no demand, only an offering of pleasure.

Megan relaxed against him, finding her head fit naturally in the curve of his shoulder. Held close beside him, she watched the world revolve. Above, the stars were scattered and few. A waning moon shifted in and out of the clouds. The air was cool with a hint of the sea. She sighed, utterly content.

"When's the last time you did this?"

"Did what?" Megan tilted her head to look at him. Their faces were close, but she felt no danger now, only satisfaction.

"Enjoyed this park." Katch had caught the confusion on her face. "Just enjoyed it, Megan, for the fun."

"I..." The Ferris wheel slowed, then stopped. The carts rocked gently as old passengers were exchanged for new. She remembered times when she had been very young. When had they stopped? "I don't know." Megan rose when the attendant lifted the safety bar.

This time, as she walked with Katch, she looked around thoughtfully. She saw several people she knew; locals out for an evening's entertainment mixed with tourists taking a preseason vacation.

"You need to do this more often," Katch commented, steering her toward the east end of the park. "Laugh," he continued as she turned her head to him. "Unbend, relax those restrictions you put on yourself."

Megan's spine stiffened. "For somebody who barely knows me, you seem remarkably certain of what's good for me."

"It isn't difficult." He stopped at a concession

wagon and ordered two ice-cream cones. "You haven't any mysteries, Meg."

"Thank you very much."

With a laugh, Katch handed her a cone. "Don't get huffy, I meant that as a compliment."

"I suppose you've known a lot of sophisticated women."

Katch smiled, then his arm came around her as they began to walk again. "There's one, her name's Jessica. She's one of the most beautiful women I know."

"Really?" Megan licked at the soft swirl of vanilla.

"That blond, classical look. You know, fair skin, finely chiseled features, blue eyes. Terrific blue eyes."

"How interesting."

"Oh, she's all of that," he continued. "And more: intelligent, a sense of humor."

"You sound very fond of her." Megan gave the ice cream her undivided attention.

"A bit more than that actually. Jessica and I lived together for a number of years." He dropped the bomb matter-of-factly. "She's married now and has a couple of kids, but we still manage to see each other now and again. Maybe she can make it down for a few days, then you can meet her."

"Oh, really!" Megan stopped, incensed. "Flaunt

your relationship somewhere else. If you think I want to meet your—your…''

''Sister,'' Katch supplied, then crunched into his cone. ''You'd like her. Your ice cream's dripping, Meg.''

They walked to the entrance gates of the park.

''It's a very nice park,'' Katch murmured. ''Small but well set up. No bored-faced attendants.'' He reached absently in his pocket and pulled out a slip of paper.

''I forgot to give you your check.''

Megan stuffed it into her pocket without even glancing at it. Her eyes were on Katch's face. She was all too aware of the direction his thoughts had taken. ''My grandfather's devoted his life to this park,'' she reminded him.

''So have you,'' Katch said.

''Why do you want to buy it?'' she asked. ''To make money?''

Katch was silent for a long moment. By mutual consent, they cut across the boardwalk and moved down the sloping sand toward the water. ''Is that such a bad reason, Megan? Do you object to making money?''

''No, of course not. That would be ridiculous.''

''I wondered if that was why you haven't done anything with your sculpting.''

"No. I do what I'm capable of doing, and what I have time for. There are priorities."

"Perhaps you have them wrong." Before she could comment, he spoke again. "How would it affect the park's business if it had some updated rides and an expanded arcade?"

"We can't afford…"

"That wasn't my question." He took her by the shoulders and his eyes were serious.

"Business would improve, naturally," Megan answered. "People come here to be entertained. The more entertainment provided, the slicker, the faster the entertainment, the happier they are. And the more money they spend."

Katch nodded as he searched her face. "Those were my thoughts."

"It's academic because we simply haven't the sort of money necessary for an overhaul."

"Hmm?" Though he was looking directly at her, Megan saw that his attention had wandered. She watched it refocus.

"What are you thinking?" she demanded.

The grip on her shoulder altered to a caress. "That you're extraordinarily beautiful."

Megan pulled away. "No, you weren't."

"It's what I'm thinking now." The gleam was back in his eyes as he put his hands to her waist. "It's what I was thinking the first time I saw you."

"You're ridiculous." She made an attempt to pull away, but he caught her closer.

"I've never denied that. But you can't call me ridiculous for finding you beautiful." The wind blew her hair back, leaving her face unframed. He laid a soft, unexpected kiss on her forehead. Megan felt her knees turn to water. She placed her hands on his chest both for support and in protest. "You're an artist." He drew her fractionally closer, and his voice lowered. "You recognize beauty when you see it."

"Don't!" The protest was feeble as she made no attempt to struggle out of his gentle hold.

"Don't what? Don't kiss you?" Slowly, luxuriously, his mouth journeyed over her skin. "But I have to, Meg." His lips touched hers softly, then withdrew, and her heart seemed to stop. The flavor of his lips as they brushed against hers overwhelmed her. They tempted, then ruled. With a moan of pleasure, Megan drew him close against her.

Something seemed to explode inside her as the kiss deepened. She clung to him a moment, dazed, then terrified by the power of it. Needs, emotions and new sensations tumbled together too quickly for her to control them. As panic swamped her, Megan struggled in his arms. She would have run, blindly, without direction, but Katch took her arms and held her still.

"What is it? You're trembling." Gently, he tilted her chin until their eyes met. Hers were wide, his serious. "I didn't mean to frighten you. I'm sorry."

The gentleness was nearly her undoing. Love, so newly discovered, hammered for release. She shook her head, knowing her voice would be thick with tears if she spoke. Swallowing, Megan prayed she could steady it.

"No, it's...I have to get back. They're closing." Behind him, she could see the lights flickering off.

"Meg." The tone halted her. It was not a demand this time, but a request. "Have dinner with me."

"No—"

"I haven't even suggested an evening," he pointed out mildly. "How about Monday?"

Megan stood firm. "No."

"Please."

Her resolution dissolved on a sigh. "You don't play fair," she murmured.

"Never. How about seven?"

"No picnics on the beach," she compromised.

"We'll eat inside, I promise."

"All right, but just dinner." She stepped away from him. "Now, I have to go."

"I'll walk you back." Katch took her hand and kissed it before she could stop him. "I have to get my elephant."

Chapter 6

Megan held Katch's face in her hands. With totally focused absorption, she formed his cheekbones. She had thought when she had first begun to work on this bust that morning that it would be good therapy. To an extent, she'd been right. The hours had passed peacefully, without the restless worry of the past two nights. Her mind was centered on her work, leaving no spaces for the disturbing thoughts that had plagued her all weekend.

She opened and closed her hands slowly, using the muscles until the cramping was a dull ache. A glance at her watch told her she had worked for longer than she'd intended. Late afternoon sun poured through the windows. Critically, as she pulled on each finger to soothe it, Megan studied her work.

The model was good, she decided, with just the proper touches of roughness and intelligence she had aimed for. The mouth was strong and sensuous, the eyes perceptive and far too aware. The mobility of the face which Megan found fascinating could only be suggested. It was a face that urged one to trust against better judgment and common sense.

Narrowing her eyes, she studied the clay replica of Katch's face. There are certain men, she thought, who make a career out of women—winning them, making love to them, leaving them. There are other men who settle down and marry, raise families. How could she doubt what category Katch fell into?

Megan rose to wash her hands. Infatuation, she reflected. It's simply infatuation. He's different, and I can't deny he's exciting. I wouldn't be human if I weren't flattered that he's attracted to me. I've over-reacted, that's all. She dried her hands on a towel and tried to convince herself. A person doesn't fall in love this quickly. And if they do, it's just a surface thing, nothing lasting. Megan's eyes were drawn to the clay model. Katch's smile seemed to mock all her sensible arguments. She hurled the towel to the floor.

"It can't happen this fast!" she told him furiously.

"Not this way. Not to me." She swung away from his assured expression. "I won't let it."

It's only the park he wants, she reminded herself. Once he's finally convinced he can't have it, he'll go away. The ache was unexpected, and unwelcome. That's what I want, she thought. For him to go away and leave us alone. She tried not to remember the new frontiers she had glimpsed while being held in his arms.

With a brisk shake of her head, Megan pulled the tie from her hair so that it tumbled back to brush her shoulders. I'll start in wood tomorrow, she decided, and covered the clay model. Tonight, I'll simply enjoy a dinner date with an attractive man. It's that simple.

With a great deal more ease than she was feeling, Megan took off her work smock and left her studio.

"Hi, sweetheart." Pop pulled the truck into the driveway just as Megan reached the bottom step.

She noticed the weariness the moment he climbed from the cab. Knowing he hated fussing, she said nothing, but walked over and slipped an arm around his waist.

"Hi, yourself. You've been gone a long time."

"A problem or two at the park," he told her as they moved together toward the house.

That explained the weariness, Megan thought as

she pushed open the back door. "What sort of problem?" Megan waited for him to settle himself at the kitchen table before she walked to the stove to brew tea.

"Repairs, Megan, just repairs. The coaster and the Octopus and a few of the smaller rides." He leaned back in his chair as Megan turned to face him.

"How bad?"

Pop sighed, knowing it was better to tell her outright than to hedge. "Ten thousand, maybe fifteen."

Megan let out a long, steady breath. "Ten thousand dollars." She ran a hand under her bangs to rub her brow. There was no purpose in asking if he was sure. If he'd had any doubt, he'd have kept the matter to himself.

"Well, we can come up with five," she began, lumping the check she had just received from Katch into their savings. "We'll have to have a more exact amount so we can decide how big a loan we'll need."

"Banks take a dim view of lending great lumps of money to people my age," Pop murmured.

Because she saw he was tired and discouraged, she spoke briskly. "Don't be silly." She walked back to the stove to set on the kettle. "In any case, they'd be lending it to the park, wouldn't they?" She tried not to think of tight money and high interest rates.

"I'll go see a few people tomorrow," he promised, reaching for his pipe as if to indicate their business talk was over. "You're having dinner with Katch tonight?"

"Yes." Megan took out cups and saucers.

"Fine young man." He puffed pleasantly on his pipe. "I like him. Has style."

"He has style all right," she grumbled as the kettle began to sing. Carefully, she poured boiling water into cups.

"Knows how to fish," Pop pointed out.

"Which, of course, makes him a paragon of virtue."

"Well, it doesn't make me think any less of him." He spoke genially, smiling into Megan's face. "I couldn't help noticing the two of you on the wheel the other night. You looked real pretty together."

"Pop, really." Feeling her cheeks warm, Megan walked back to fiddle with the dishes in the sink.

"You seemed to like him well enough then," he pointed out before he tested his tea. "I didn't notice any objections when he kissed you." Pop sipped, enjoying. "In fact, you seemed to like it."

"Pop!" Megan turned back, astonished.

"Now, Meg, I wasn't spying," he said soothingly, and coughed to mask a chuckle. "You were right out in public, you know. I'd wager a lot of people noticed. Like I said, you looked real pretty together.''

Megan came back to sit at the table without any idea of what she should say. ''It was just a kiss,'' she managed at length. ''It didn't mean anything.''

Pop nodded twice and drank his tea.

''It didn't,'' Megan insisted.

He gave her one of his angelic smiles. ''But you do like him, don't you?''

Megan dropped her eyes. ''Sometimes,'' she murmured. ''Sometimes I do.''

Pop covered her hand with his and waited until she looked at him again. ''Caring for someone is the easiest thing in the world if you let it be.''

''I hardly know him,'' she said quickly.

''I trust him,'' Pop said simply.

Megan searched his face. ''Why?''

After a shrug, Pop drew on his pipe again. ''A feeling I have, a look in his eyes. In a people business like mine, you get to be a good judge of character. He has integrity. He wants his way, all right, but he doesn't cheat. That's important.''

Megan sat silently for a moment, not touching her cooling tea. ''He wants the park,'' she said quietly.

Pop looked at her through a nimbus of pipe smoke. ''Yes, I know. He said so up front. He doesn't sneak around either.'' Pop's expression softened a bit as he looked into Megan's eyes. ''Things don't always stay the same in life, Megan. That's what makes it work.''

''I don't know what you mean. Do you…are you thinking of selling him the park?''

Pop heard the underlying hint of panic and patted her hand again. ''Let's not worry about that now. The first problem is getting the rides repaired for the Easter break. Why don't you wear the yellow dress I like tonight, Meg? The one with the little jacket. It makes me think of spring.''

Megan considered questioning him further, then subsided. There was no harder nut to crack than her grandfather when he had made up his mind to close a subject. ''All right. I think I'll go up and have a bath.''

''Megan.'' She turned at the door and looked back at him. ''Enjoy yourself. Sometimes it's best to roll with the punches.''

When she walked away, he looked at the empty doorway and thoughtfully stroked his beard.

An hour later, Megan looked at herself in the yellow dress. The shade hinted at apricot and warmed against her skin. The lines were simple, suiting her willow-slim figure and height. Without the jacket, her arms and shoulders were bare but for wispy straps. She ran a brush through her hair in long, steady strokes. The tiny gold hoops in her ears were her only jewelry.

"Hey, Megan!"

The brush paused in midair as she watched her own eyes widen in the mirror. He wasn't really standing outside shouting for her!

"Meg!"

Shaking her head in disbelief, Megan went to the window. Katch stood two stories down. He lifted a hand in salute when she appeared in the window.

"What are you doing?" she demanded.

"Open the screen."

"Why?"

"Open it," he repeated.

"If you expect me to jump, you can forget it." Out of curiosity, she leaned out the window.

"Catch!"

Her reflexes responded before she could think. Megan reached for the bundle he tossed up to her, and found her hands full of daffodils. She buried her face in the bouquet.

"They're beautiful." Her eyes smiled over the blooms and down at him. "Thank you."

"You're welcome," he returned. "Are you coming down?"

"Yes." She tossed her hair behind her shoulder. "Yes, yes, in a minute."

Katch drove quickly and competently, but not toward Restaurant Row as Megan had anticipated. He turned toward the ocean and headed north. She relaxed, enjoying the quieting light of dusk and his effortless driving.

She recognized the area. The houses there were larger, more elaborate than those in and on the very outskirts of town. There were tall hedges to assure privacy both from other houses and the public beaches. There were neatly trimmed lawns, willows, blossoming crepe myrtle, and asphalt drives. Katch pulled into one set well away from the other homes and bordered by purplish shrubbery.

The house was small by the neighborhood standards, and done in the weathered wood Megan invariably found attractive. It was a split-level building, with an observation deck crowning the upper story.

"What's this?" she asked, liking the house immediately.

"This is where I live." Katch leaned across her to unlatch her door, then slid out his own side.

"You live here?"

Katch smiled at the surprised doubt in her voice. "I have to live somewhere, Meg."

She wandered farther along the stone path that led to the house. "I suppose I really didn't think about you buying a house here. It suggests roots."

"I have them," he told her. "I just transplant them easily."

She looked at the house, the widespread yard. "You've picked the perfect spot."

Katch took her hand, interlocking fingers. "Come inside," he invited.

"When did you buy this?" she asked as they climbed the front steps.

"Oh, a few months ago when I came through. I moved in last week and haven't had a lot of time to look for furniture." The key shot into the lock. "I've picked up a few things here and there, and had others sent down from my apartment in New York."

It was scantily furnished, but with style. There was a low, sectional sofa in biscuit with a hodge-podge of colored pillows and a wicker throne chair coupled with a large hanging ivy in a pottery dish. A pair of étagères in brass and glass held a collection of shells; on the oak planked floor lay a large sisal rug.

The room was open, with stairs to the right leading to the second level, and a stone fireplace on the left wall. The quick survey showed Megan he had not placed her sculptures in the main room. She wondered fleetingly what he had done with them.

"It's wonderful, Katch." She wandered to a window. The lawn sloped downward and ended in tall hedges that gave the house comfortable privacy. "Can you see the ocean from the top level?"

When he didn't answer, she turned back to him.

Her smile faded against the intensity of his gaze. Her heart beat faster. This was the part of him she had to fear, not the amiable gallant who had tossed her daffodils.

She tilted her head back, afraid, but wanting to meet him equally. He brought his hands to her face, and she felt the hardness of his palms on her skin. He brushed her hair back from her face as he brought her closer. He lowered his mouth, pausing only briefly before it claimed hers, as if to ascertain the need mirrored in her eyes. The kiss was instantly deep, instantly seeking.

She had been a fool—a fool to believe she could talk herself out of being in love with him. A fool to think that reason had anything to do with the heart.

When Katch drew her away, Megan pressed her cheek against his chest, letting her arms wind their way around his waist. His hesitation was almost too brief to measure before he gathered her close. She felt his lips in her hair and sighed from the sheer joy of it. His heartbeat was quick and steady in her ear.

"Did you say something?" he murmured.

"Hmm? When?"

"Before." His fingers came up to massage the back of her neck. Megan shivered with pleasure as she tried to remember the world before she had been in his arms.

"I think I asked if I could see the ocean from the top level."

"Yes." Again he took his hands to her face to tilt it back for one long, searing kiss. "You can."

"Will you show me?"

The grip on her skin tightened and her eyes closed in anticipation of the next kiss. But he drew her away until only their hands were touching. "After dinner."

Megan, content with looking at him, smiled. "Are we eating here?"

"I hate restaurants," Katch said, leading her toward the kitchen.

"An odd sentiment from a man who owns one."

"Let's say there are times when I prefer more intimate surroundings."

"I see." He pushed open the door to the kitchen and Megan glanced around at efficiency in wood and stainless steel. "And who's doing the cooking this time?"

"We are," he said easily, and grinned at her. "How do you like your steak?"

There was a rich, red wine to accompany the meal they ate at a smoked-glass table. A dozen candles flickered on a sideboard behind them, held in small brass holders. Megan's mood was as mellow as the wine that waltzed in her head. The man across from her held her in the palm of his hand. When she rose to stack the dishes, he took her hand. "Not now. There's a moon tonight."

Without hesitation, she went with him.

They climbed the stairs together, wide, uncarpeted stairs which were split into two sections by a landing. He led her through the main bedroom, a room dominated by a large bed with brass head- and footboards. There were long glass doors which led to a walkway. From there, stairs ascended to the observation deck.

Megan could hear the breakers before she moved to the rail. Beyond the hedgerow, the surf was turbulent. White water frothed against the dark. The moon's light was thin, but was aided by the power of uncountable stars.

She took a long breath and leaned on the rail. "It's lovely here. I never tire of looking at the ocean." There was a click from his lighter, then tobacco mixed pleasantly with the scent of the sea.

"Do you ever think about traveling?"

Megan moved her shoulders, a sudden, restless gesture. "Of course, sometimes. It isn't possible right now."

Katch drew on the thin cigar. "Where would you go?"

"Where would I go?" she repeated.

"Yes, where would you go if you could?" The

smoke from his cigar wafted upward and vanished. "Pretend, Meg. You like to pretend, don't you?"

She closed her eyes a moment, letting the wine swim with her thoughts. "New Orleans," she murmured. "I've always wanted to see New Orleans. And Paris. When I was young I used to dream about studying in Paris like the great artists." She opened her eyes again. "You've been there, I suppose. To New Orleans and to Paris?"

"Yes, I've been there."

"What are they like?"

Katch traced the line of her jaw with a fingertip before answering. "New Orleans smells of the river and swelters in the summer. There's music at all hours from open nightclubs and street musicians. It moves constantly, like New York, but at a more civilized pace."

"And Paris?" Megan insisted, wanting to see her wishes through his eyes. "Tell me about Paris."

"It's ancient and elegant, like a grand old woman. It's not very clean, but it never seems to matter. It's best in the spring; nothing smells like Paris in the spring. I'd like to take you there." Unexpectedly he took her hair in his hand. His eyes were intense again and direct on hers. "I'd like to see the emotions you control break loose. You'd never restrict them in Paris."

''I don't do that.'' Something more than wine began to swim in her head.

He tossed the cigar over the rail, then his free hand came to her waist to press her body against his. ''Don't you?'' There was a hint of impatience in his voice as he began to slide the jacket from her shoulders. ''You've passion, but you bank it down. It escapes into your work, but even that's kept closed up in a studio. When I kiss you, I can taste it struggling to the surface.''

He freed her arms from the confines of the jacket and laid it over the rail. Slowly, deliberately, he ran his fingers over the naked skin, feeling the warmth of response. ''One day it's going to break loose. I intend to be there when it does.''

Katch pushed the straps from her shoulders and replaced them with his lips. Megan made no protest as the kisses trailed to her throat. His tongue played lightly with the pulse as his hand came up to cup her breast. But when his mouth came to hers, the gentleness fled, and with it her passivity. Hunger incited hunger.

When he nipped her bottom lip, she gasped with pleasure. His tongue was avid, searching while his hands began a quest of their own. He slipped the bodice of her dress to her waist, murmuring with approval as he found her naked breasts taut with desire. Megan allowed him his freedom, riding on the

crest of the wave that rose inside her. She had no
knowledge to guide her, no experience. Desire ruled
and instinct followed.

She trailed her fingers along the back of his neck,
kneading the warm skin, thrilling to the response she
felt to her touch. Here was a power she had never
explored. She slipped her hands under the back of
his sweater. Their journey was slow, exploring. She
felt the muscles of his shoulders tense as her hands
played over them.

The quality of the kiss changed from demanding
to urgent. His passion swamped her, mixing with her
own until the combined power was more than she
could bear. The ache came from nowhere and spread
through her with impossible rapidity. She hurt for
him. Desire was a pain as sharp as it was irresistible.
In surrender, in anticipation, Megan swayed against
him.

"Katch." Her voice was husky. "I want to stay
with you tonight."

She was crushed against him for a moment, held
so tightly, so strongly, there was no room for breath.
Then, slowly, she felt him loosen his hold. Taking
her by the shoulders, Katch looked down at her, his
eyes dark, spearing into hers. Her breath was uneven; shivers raced along her skin. Slowly, with
hands that barely touched her skin, he slipped her
dress back into place.

"I'll take you home now."

The shock of rejection struck her like a blow. Her mouth trembled open, then shut again. Quickly, fighting against the tears that were pressing for release, she fumbled for her jacket.

"Meg." He reached out to touch her shoulders, but she backed away.

"No. No, don't touch me." The tears were thickening her voice. She swallowed. "I won't be patted on the head. It appears I misunderstood."

"You didn't misunderstand anything," he tossed back. "And don't cry, damn it."

"I have no intention of crying," she said. "I'd like to go home." The hurt was in her eyes, shimmering behind the tears she denied.

"We'll talk." Katch took her hand, but she jerked it away.

"Oh, no. No, we won't." Megan straightened her shoulders and looked at him squarely. "We had dinner—things got a bit beyond what they should have. It's as simple as that, and it's over."

"It's not simple or over, Meg." Katch took another long look into her eyes. "But we'll drop it for now."

Megan turned away and walked back down the stairs.

Chapter 7

Amusement parks lose their mystique in the light of day. Dirt, scratched paint and dents show up. What is shiny and bright under artificial light is ordinary in the sunshine. Only the very young or the very young hearted can believe in magic when faced with reality.

Megan knew her grandfather was perennially young. She loved him for it. Fondly, she watched him supervising repairs on the Haunted Castle. His ghosts, she thought with a smile, are important to him. She walked beside the track, avoiding her own ghost along the way. It had been ten days since Pop had told her of the repair problems. Ten days since she had seen Katch. Megan pushed thoughts of him

from her mind and concentrated on her own reality—her grandfather and their park. She was old
enough to know what was real and what was fantasy.

"Hi," she called out from behind him. "How are
things going?"

Pop turned at the sound of her voice, and his grin
was expansive. "Just fine, Megan." The sound of
repairs echoed around his words. "Quicker than I
thought they would. We'll be rolling before the
Easter rush." He swung an arm around her shoulder
and squeezed. "The smaller rides are already back
in order. How about you?"

She made no objection when he began to steer her
outside. The noise made it difficult to hear. "What
about me?" she replied. The sudden flash of sunlight
made her blink. The spring day had all the heat of
midsummer.

"You've that unhappy look in your eyes. Have
had, for more than a week." Pop rubbed his palm
against her shoulder as if to warm her despite the
strength of the sun. "You know you don't hide
things from me, Megan. I know you too well."

She was silent a moment, wanting to choose her
words carefully. "I wasn't trying to hide anything,
Pop." Megan shrugged, turning to watch the crew
working on the roller coaster. "It's just not important enough to talk about, that's all. How long before
the coaster's fixed?"

"Important enough to make you unhappy," he countered, ignoring her evasion. "That's plenty important to me. You haven't gotten too old to talk to me about your problems now, have you?"

She turned dark apologetic eyes on him. "Oh no, Pop, I can always talk to you."

"Well," he said simply, "I'm listening."

"I made a mistake, that's all." She shook her head and would have walked closer to inspect the work crew had he not held her to him with a firm hand.

"Megan." Pop placed both hands on her shoulders and looked into her eyes. As they were nearly the same height, their eyes were level. "I'm going to ask you straight," he continued. "Are you in love with him?"

"No," she denied quickly.

Pop raised an eyebrow. "I didn't have to mention any names, I see."

Megan paused a moment. She had forgotten how shrewd her grandfather could be. "I thought I was," she said more carefully. "I was wrong."

"Then why are you so unhappy?"

"Pop, please." She tried to back away, but again his broad hands held her steady.

"You've always given me straight answers, Meg, even when I've had to drag them out of you."

She sighed, knowing evasions and half-truths were

useless when he was in this mood. "All right. Yes, I'm in love with him, but it doesn't matter."

"Not a very bright statement from a bright girl like you," he said with a gentle hint of disapproval. Megan shrugged. "Why don't you explain why being in love doesn't matter," he invited.

"Well, it certainly doesn't work if you're not loved back," Megan murmured.

"Who says you're not?" Pop wanted to know. His voice was so indignant, she felt some of the ache subside.

"Pop." Her expression softened. "Just because you love me doesn't mean everyone else does."

"What makes you so sure he doesn't?" her grandfather argued. "Did you ask him?"

"No!" Megan was so astonished, she nearly laughed at the thought.

"Why not? Things are simpler that way."

Megan took a deep breath, hoping to make him understand. "David Katcherton isn't a man who falls in love with a woman, not seriously. And certainly not with someone like me." The broad gesture she made was an attempt to enhance an explanation she knew was far from adequate. "He's been to Paris, he lives in New York. He has a sister named Jessica."

"That clears things up," Pop agreed, and Megan made a quick sound of frustration.

"I've never been anywhere." She dragged a hand through her hair. "In the summer I see millions, literally millions of people, but they're all transient. I don't know who they are. The only people I really know are ones who live right here. The farthest I've been away from the beach is Charleston."

Pop brushed a hand over her hair to smooth it. "I've kept you too close," he murmured. "I always told myself there'd be other times."

"Oh no, Pop, I didn't mean it that way." She threw her arms around him, burying her face in his shoulder. "I didn't mean to sound that way. I love you, I love it here. I wouldn't change anything. That was hateful of me."

He laughed and patted her back. The subtle scent of her perfume reminded him forcefully that she was no longer a girl but a woman. The years had been incredibly quick. "You've never done a hateful thing in your life. We both know you've wanted to see a bit of the world, and I know you've stuck close to keep an eye on me. Oh yes," he said, anticipating her objection. "And I was selfish enough to let you."

"You've never done anything selfish," she retorted and drew away. "I only meant that Katch and I have so little common ground. He's bound to see things differently than I do. I'm out of my depth with him."

"You're a strong swimmer, as I recall." Pop shook his head at her expression and sighed. "All right, we'll let it lie awhile. You're also stubborn."

"Adamant," she corrected, smiling again. "It's a nicer word."

"Just a fancy way of saying pigheaded," Pop said bluntly, but his eyes smiled back at her. "Why aren't you back in your studio instead of hanging around an amusement park in the middle of the day?"

"It wasn't going very well," she confessed, thinking of the half-carved face that haunted her. "Besides, I've always had a thing for amusement parks." She tucked her arm in his as they began to walk again.

"Well, this one'll be in apple-pie order in another week," Pop said, looking around in satisfaction. "With luck, we'll have a good season and be able to pay back a healthy chunk of that ten thousand."

"Maybe the bank will send us some customers so they'll get their money faster," Megan suggested, half listening to the sound of hammer against wood as they drew closer to the roller coaster.

"Oh, I didn't get the money from the bank, I got it from—" Pop cut himself off abruptly. With a cough and a wheeze, he bent down to tie his shoe.

"You didn't get the money from the bank?" Megan frowned at the snowy white head in puzzlement. "Well, where in the world did you get it then?"

His answer was an unintelligible grunt.

"You don't know anybody with that kind of money," she began with a half-smile. "Where…" The smile flew away. "No. No, you didn't." Even as she denied it, Megan knew it had to be the truth. "You didn't get it from him?"

"Oh now, Megan, you weren't to know." Distress showed in his eyes and seemed to weaken his voice. "He especially didn't want you to know."

"Why?" she demanded. "Why did you do it?"

"It just sort of happened, Meg." Pop reached out to pat her hand in his old, soothing fashion. "He was here, I was telling him about the repairs and getting a loan, and he offered. It seemed like the perfect solution." He fiddled with his shoestrings. "Banks poke around and take all that time for paperwork, and he isn't charging me nearly as much interest. I thought you'd be happy about that…" He trailed off.

"Is everything in writing?" she asked, deadly calm.

"Of course." Pop assumed a vaguely injured air. "Katch said it didn't matter, but I know how fussy you are, so I had papers drawn up, nice and legal."

"Didn't matter," she repeated softly. "And what did you use as collateral?"

"The park, naturally."

"Naturally," she repeated. Fury bubbled in the single word. "I bet he loved that."

"Now, don't you worry, Megan. Everything's coming along just fine. The repairs are going well, and we'll be opening right on schedule. Besides," he added with a sigh, "you weren't even supposed to know. Katch wanted it that way."

"Oh, I'm sure he did," she said bitterly. "I'm sure he did."

Turning, she darted away. Pop watched her streak out of sight, then hauled himself to his feet. She had the devil's own temper when she cut loose, that girl. Brushing his hands together, he grinned. That, he decided, pleased with his own maneuvering, should stir up something.

Megan brought the bike to a halt at the crest of Katch's drive, then killed the engine. She took off her helmet and clipped it on the seat. He was not, she determined, going to get away with it.

Cutting across the lawn, she marched to the front door. The knock was closer to a pound but still brought no response. Megan stuffed her hands into her pockets and scowled. Her bike sat behind his black Porsche. Ignoring amenities, she tried the knob. When it turned, she didn't hesitate. She opened the door and walked inside.

The house was quiet. Instinct told her immediately

that no one was inside. Still, she walked through the living room looking for signs of him.

A watch, wafer-thin and gold, was tossed on the glass shelves of the étagère. A Nikon camera sat on the coffee table, its back open and empty of film. A pair of disreputable tennis shoes were half under the couch. A volume of John Cheever lay beside them.

Abruptly, she realized what she had done. She'd intruded where she had no right. She was both uncomfortable and fascinated. An ashtray held the short stub of a thin cigar. After a brief struggle with her conscience, she walked toward the kitchen. She wasn't prying, she told herself, only making certain he wasn't home. After all, his car was here and the door had been unlocked.

There was a cup in the sink and a half pot of cold coffee on the stove. He had spilled some on the counter and neglected to wipe it up. Megan curtailed the instinctive move to reach for a dish towel. As she turned to leave, a low mechanical hum from outside caught her attention. She walked to the window and saw him.

He was coming from the south side of the lawn, striding behind a power mower. He was naked to the waist, with jeans low and snug at his hips. He was tanned, a deep honey gold that glistened now with the effort of manual labor. She admired the play of muscles rippling down his arms and across his back.

Stepping back from the window with a jerk, she stormed through the side kitchen door and raced across the lawn.

The flurry of movement and a flash of crimson caught his eye. Katch glanced over as Megan moved toward him in a red tailored shirt and white jeans. Squinting against the sun, he wiped the back of his hand across his brow. He reached down and shut off the mower as she came to him.

"Hello, Meg," he said lightly, but his eyes weren't as casual.

"You have nerve, Katcherton," she began. "But even I didn't think you'd take advantage of a trusting old man."

He lifted a brow and leaned against the mower's handle. "Once more," he requested, "with clarity."

"You're the type who has to poke your fingers into other people's business," she continued. "You just had to be at the park, you just had to make a magnanimous offer with your tidy little pile of money."

"Ah, a glimmer of light." He stretched his back. "I didn't think you'd be thrilled the money came from me. It seems I was right."

"You knew I'd never allow it," she declared.

"I don't believe I considered that." He leaned on the mower again, but there was nothing restful in the gesture. "You don't run Pop's life from what I've seen, Meg, and you certainly don't run mine."

She did her best to keep her tone even. "I have a great deal of interest in the park and everything that pertains to it."

"Fine, then you should be pleased that you have the money for the repairs quickly, and at a low rate of interest." His tone was cool and businesslike.

"Why?" she demanded. "Why did you lend us the money?"

"I don't," Katch said after a long, silent moment, "owe you any explanation."

"Then I'll give you one," Megan tossed back. There was passion in her voice. "You saw an opportunity and grabbed it. I suppose that's what people do in your sort of world. Take, without the least thought of the people involved."

"Perhaps I'm confused." His eyes were slate, opaque and unreadable. His voice matched them. "I was under the impression that I gave something."

"*Lent* something," Megan corrected. "With the park as collateral."

"If that's your problem, take it up with your grandfather." Katch bent down, reaching for the cord to restart the mower.

"You had no right to take advantage of him. He trusts everyone."

Katch released the cord again with a snap. "A shame it's not an inherited quality."

"I've no reason to trust you."

"And every reason, it appears, to mistrust me since the first moment." His eyes had narrowed as if in speculation. "Is it just me or a general antipathy to men?"

She refused to dignify the question with an answer. "You want the park," she began.

"Yes, and I made that clear from the beginning." Katch shoved the mower aside so that there was no obstacle between them. "I still intend to have it, but I don't need to be devious to get it. I still intend to have you." She stepped back but he was too quick. His fingers curled tightly around her upper arm. "Maybe I made a mistake by letting you go the other night."

"You didn't want me. It's just a game."

"Didn't want you?" She made another quick attempt to pull away and failed. "No, that's right, I didn't want you." He pulled her against him and her mouth was crushed and conquered. Her mind whirled with the shock of it. "I don't want you now." Before she could speak, his mouth savaged hers again. There was a taste of brutality he had never shown her. "Like I haven't wanted you for days." He pulled her to the ground.

"No," she said, frightened, "don't." But his lips were silencing hers again.

There was none of the teasing persuasion he had shown her before, no light arrogance. These were primordial demands, eliciting primordial responses from her. He would take what he wanted, his way. He plundered, dragging her with him as he raced for more. Then his lips left hers, journeying to her throat before traveling downward. Megan felt she was suffocating, suffused with heat. Her breath caught in her lungs, emerging in quick gasps or moans. His fingers ran a bruising trail over her quivering flesh. He ran his thumb over the point of her breast, back and forth, until she was beyond fear, beyond thought. His mouth came back to hers, fever hot, desperate. She murmured mindlessly, clinging to him as her body shuddered with waves of need.

Katch lifted his head, and his breath was warm and erratic on her face. Megan's lids fluttered open, revealing eyes dazed with passion, heavy with desire. Silently, she trembled. If words had been hers, she would have told him that she loved him. There was no pride in her, no shame, only soaring need and a love that was painful in its strength.

"This isn't the place for you." His voice was rough as he rolled over on his back. They lay there a moment, side by side, without touching. "And this isn't the way."

Her mind was fogged, and her blood surging. "Katch," Megan managed his name and struggled to sit up. His eyes lingered on her form, then slid up slowly to brood on her face. It was flushed and aware. She wanted to touch him but was afraid.

For a moment their eyes met. "Did I hurt you?"

She shook her head in denial. Her body ached with longing.

"Go home then." He rose, giving her a last, brief glance. "Before I do." He turned and left her.

Megan heard the slam of the kitchen door.

Chapter 8

It was difficult for Megan to cope with the two-week influx of tourists and sun seekers. They came, as they did every Easter, in droves. It was a preview of what the summer would hold. They came to bake on the beach and impress those left at home with a spring tan. They came to be battered and bounced around by the waves. They came to have fun. And what better place to find it than on white sand beaches or in an ocean with a gentle undertow and cresting waves? They came to laugh and sought their entertainment on spiraling water slides, in noisy arcades or crowded amusement parks.

For the first time in her life, Megan found herself resenting the intrusion. She wanted the quiet, the solitude that went with a resort town in its off-season. She wanted to be alone, to work, to heal. It seemed her art was the only thing she could turn to for true comfort. She was unwilling to speak of her feelings to her grandfather. There was still too much to be sorted out in her own mind. Knowing her, and her need for privacy, Pop didn't question.

The hours she spent at the park were passed mechanically. The faces she saw were all strangers. Megan resented it. She resented their enjoyment when her own life was in such turmoil. She found solace in her studio. If the light in her studio burned long past midnight, she never noticed the time. Her energy was boundless, a nervous, trembling energy that kept her going.

It was afternoon at the amusement park. At the kiddie cars Megan was taking tickets and doing her best to keep the more aggressive youngsters from trampling others. Each time the fire engines, race cars, police cruisers and ambulances were loaded, she pushed the lever which sent the caravan around in its clanging, roaring circle. Children grinned fiercely and gripped steering wheels.

One toddler rode as fire chief with eyes wide with stunned pleasure. Even though she'd been on duty nearly four hours, Megan smiled.

"Excuse me." Megan glanced over at the voice,

prepared to answer a parental question. The woman was an exquisite blonde, with a mane of hair tied back from a delicately molded face. "You're Megan, aren't you? Megan Miller?"

"Yes. May I help you?"

"I'm Jessica Delaney."

Megan wondered that she hadn't seen it instantly. "Katch's sister."

"Yes." Jessica smiled. "How clever of you—but Katch told me you were. There is a family resemblance, of course, but so few people notice it unless we're standing together."

Megan's artist eyes could see the similar bone structure beneath the surface differences. Jessica's eyes were blue, as Katch had said, and the brows above them more delicate than his, but there were the same thick lashes and long lids.

"I'm glad to meet you." Megan reached for something to say. "Are you visiting Katch?" She didn't look like a woman who would patronize amusement parks, more likely country clubs or theaters.

"For a day or so." Jessica gestured to the adjoining ride where children flew miniature piper cubs in the inevitable circle. "My family's with me. Rob, my husband." Megan smiled at a tall man with a straight shock of dark hair and an attractive, angular face. "And my girls, Erin and Laura." She nodded to the two caramel-haired girls of approximately four and six riding double in a plane.

"They're beautiful."

"We like them," Jessica said comfortably. "Katch didn't know where I might find you in the park, but he described you very accurately."

"Is he here?" Megan asked, trying without much success to sound offhanded even as her eyes scanned the crowd.

"No, he had some business to attend to."

The timer rang, signaling the ride's end. "Excuse me a moment," Megan murmured. Grateful for the interruption, she supervised the unloading and loading of children. It gave her the time she needed to steady herself. Her two final customers were Katch's nieces. Erin, the elder, smiled at her with eyes the identical shade of her uncle's.

"I'm driving," she said positively as her sister settled beside her. "She only rides."

"I do not." Laura gripped the twin steering wheel passionately.

"It runs in the family," Jessica stated from behind her. "Stubbornness." Megan hooked the last safety belt and returned to the controls. "You've probably noticed it."

Megan smiled at her. "Yes, once or twice." The lights and noise spun and circled behind her.

"I know you're busy," Jessica stated, glancing at the packed vehicles.

Megan gave a small shrug as she followed her gaze. "It's mostly a matter of making certain everyone stays strapped in and no one's unhappy."

"My little angels," Jessica said, "will insist on dashing off to the next adventure the moment the ride's over." She paused. "Could we talk after you're finished here?"

Megan frowned. "Well, yes, I suppose...I'm due relief in an hour."

"Wonderful." Jessica's smile was as charming as her brother's. "I'd like to go to your studio, if that suits you. I could meet you in an hour and a half."

"At my studio?"

"Wonderful!" Jessica said again and patted Megan's hand. "Katch gave me directions."

The timer rang again, recalling Megan to duty. As she started yet another round of junior rides she wondered why Jessica had insisted on a date in her studio.

With a furrowed brow, Megan studied herself in the bedroom mirror. Would a man who admired Jessica's soft, delicate beauty be attracted to someone who seemed to be all planes and angles? Megan shrugged her shoulders as if it didn't matter. She twirled the stem of the brush idly between her fingers. She supposed that he, like the majority of people who came here, was looking for some passing entertainment

"You are," she said softly to the woman in the glass, "such a fool." She closed her eyes, not wanting to see the reflected accusation. Because you can't let go, her mind continued ruthlessly. Because it doesn't really matter to you why he wanted you with him, just that he wanted you. And you wish, you wish with all your heart that he still did.

She shook her head, disturbing the work she had done with the brush. It was time to stop thinking of it. Jessica Delaney would be arriving any moment.

Why? Megan set down her brush and frowned into middle distance. Why was she coming? What could she possibly want? Megan still had no sensible answer. I haven't heard from Katch in two weeks, she reflected. Why should his sister suddenly want to see me?

The sound of a car pulling into the drive below interrupted her thoughts. Megan walked to the window in time to see Jessica get out of Katch's Porsche.

Megan reached the back stoop before Jessica, as she had been taking a long, leisurely look at the yard. "Hello." Megan felt awkward and rustic. She hesitated briefly before stepping away from the door.

"What a lovely place." Jessica's smile was so

like Katch's that Megan's heart lurched. "How I wish my azaleas looked like yours."

"Pop—my grandfather babies them."

"Yes." The blue eyes were warm and personal. "I've heard wonderful things about your grandfather. I'd love to meet him."

"He's still at the park." Her sense of awkwardness was fading. Charm definitely ran in the Katcherton family. "Would you like some coffee? Tea?"

"Maybe later. Let's go up to the studio, shall we?"

"If you don't mind my asking, Mrs. Delaney—"

"Jessica," she interrupted cheerfully and began to climb the open back stairs.

"Jessica," Megan agreed, "how did you know I had a studio, and that it was over the garage?"

"Oh, Katch told me," Jessica said breezily. "He tells me a great many things." She stood to the side of the door and waited for Megan to open it. "I'm very anxious to see your work. I dabble in oil from time to time."

"Do you?" Jessica's interest now made more sense. Artistic kinship.

"Badly, I'm afraid, which is a constant source of frustration to me." Again the Katcherton smile bloomed on her face.

Megan's reaction was unexpectedly sharp and swift. She fumbled for the doorknob. "I've never had much luck on canvas,'' she said quickly. She needed words, lots of words to cover what she feared was much too noticeable. ''Nothing seems to come out the way I intend,'' she continued as they entered the studio. ''It's maddening not to be able to express yourself properly. I do some airbrushing during the summer rush, but...''

Jessica wasn't listening. She moved around the room much the same way her brother had—intently, gracefully, silently. She fingered a piece here, lifted a piece there. Once, she studied a small ivory unicorn for so long, Megan fidgeted with nerves.

What was she doing? she wondered. *And why?*

Sunlight stippled the floor. Dust motes danced in the early evening light. Too late, Megan recalled the bust of Katch. One slanted beam of sun fell on it, highlighting the planes the chisel had already defined. Though it was still rough hewn and far from finished, it was unmistakably Katch. Feeling foolish, Megan walked over to stand in front of it, hoping to conceal it from Jessica's view.

''Katch was right,'' Jessica murmured. She still held the unicorn, stroking it with her fingertips. ''He invariably is. Normally that annoys me to distraction, but not this time.'' The resemblance to Katch was startling now. Megan's fingers itched to make a quick sketch even as she tried to follow the twisting roads in Jessica's conversation.

"Right about what?"

"Your extraordinary talent."

"What?" Meg's eyes widened.

"Katch told me your work was remarkable," she went on, giving the unicorn a final study before setting it down. "I agreed when I received the two pieces he sent up to me, but they were only two, after all." She picked up a chisel and tapped it absently against her palm while her eyes continued to wander. "This is astonishing."

"He sent you the sculptures he bought from me?"

"Yes, a few weeks ago. I was very impressed." Jessica set down the chisel with a clatter and moved to a nearly completed study in limestone of a woman rising from the sea. It was the piece Megan had been working on before she had set it aside to begin Katch's bust. "This is fabulous!" Jessica declared. "I'm going to have to have it as well as the unicorn. The response to the two pieces Katch sent me has been very favorable."

"I don't understand what you're talking about." Try as she might, Megan couldn't keep up with Jessica's conversation. "Whose response?"

"My clients'," said Jessica. "At my gallery in New York." She gave Megan a brilliant smile. "Didn't I tell you I run my own gallery?"

"No," Megan answered. "No, you didn't."

"I suppose I thought Katch did. I'd better start at the beginning then."

"I'd really appreciate it if you would," Megan told her, and waited until she had settled herself in the small wooden chair beside her.

"Katch sent me two of your pieces a few weeks ago," Jessica began briskly. "He wanted a professional opinion. I may only be able to dabble in oil, but I know art." She spoke with a confidence that Megan recognized. "Since I knew I'd never make it as a working artist, I put all the years of study to good use. I opened a gallery in Manhattan. *Jessica's*. Over the past six years, I've developed a rather nice clientele." She smiled. "So naturally, when my wandering brother saw your work, he sent it off to me. He always has his instincts verified by an expert, then plunges along his own way notwithstanding." She sighed indulgently. "I happen to know he was advised against building that hospital in Central Africa last year but he did it anyway. He does what he wants to."

"Hospital." Megan barely made the jump to Jessica's new train of thought.

"Yes, a children's hospital. He has a soft spot for kids." Jessica tried to speak teasingly, but the love came through. "He did some astonishing things for orphaned refugees after Vietnam. And there was the really fabulous little park he built in New South Wales.''

Megan sat dumbly. Could they possibly be speaking about the same David Katcherton? Was this the man who had brashly approached her in the local market?

She remembered with uncomfortable clarity that she had accused him of trying to cheat her grandfather. She had told herself that he was an opportunist, a man spoiled by wealth and good looks. She'd tried to tell herself he was irresponsible, undependable, a man in search of his own pleasure.

"I didn't know," she murmured. "I didn't know anything about it."

"Oh, Katch keeps a low profile when he chooses," Jessica told her. "And he chooses to have no publicity when he's doing that sort of thing. He has incredible energy and outrageous self-confidence, but he's also very warm." Her gaze slipped beyond Megan's shoulder. "But then, you appear to know him well."

For a moment, Megan regarded Jessica blankly. Then she twisted her head and saw Katch's bust. In her confusion, she had forgotten her desire to conceal it. Slowly, she turned her head back, trying to keep her voice and face passive.

"No. No, really I don't think I know him at all.

He has a fascinating face. I couldn't resist sculpting it.''

She noted a glint of understanding in Jessica's eyes. ''He's a fascinating man,'' Jessica murmured.

Megan's gaze faltered.

''I'm sorry,'' Jessica said immediately. ''I've intruded, a bad habit of mine. We won't talk about Katch. Let's talk about your showing.''

Megan lifted her eyes again. ''My what?''

''Your showing,'' Jessica repeated, dashing swiftly up a new path. ''When do you think you'll have enough pieces ready? You certainly have a tremendous start here, and Katch mentioned something about a gallery in town having some of your pieces. I think we can shoot for the fall.''

''Please, Jessica, I don't know what you're talking about.'' A note of panic slipped into Megan's voice. It was faint, almost buried, but Jessica detected it. She reached over and took both of Megan's hands. The grip was surprisingly firm.

''Megan, you have something special, something powerful. It's time to share it.'' She rose then, urging Megan up with her. ''Let's have that coffee now, shall we? And we'll talk about it.''

An hour later, Megan sat alone in the kitchen. Darkness was encroaching, but she didn't rise from the table to switch on the light. Two cups sat, her own half-filled with now cold coffee, Jessica's empty but for dregs. She tried to take her mind methodically over what had happened in the last sixty minutes.

A showing at Jessica's, an art gallery in Manhattan. New York. A public show. Of her work.

It didn't happen, she thought. I imagined it. Then she looked down at the empty cup across from her. The air still smelled faintly of Jessica's light, sophisticated scent.

Half-dazed, Megan took both cups to the sink and automatically began rinsing them. How did she talk me into it? she wondered. I was agreeing to dates and details before I had agreed to do the showing. Does anyone ever say no to a Katcherton? She sighed and looked down at her wet hands. I have to call him. The knowledge increased the sense of panic. *I have to.*

Carefully, she placed the washed cups and saucers in the drainboard. I have to thank him. Nerves fluttered in her throat, but she made a pretense, for herself, of casually drying her damp hands on the hips of her jeans. She walked to the wall phone beside the stove.

"It's simple," she whispered, then bit her lip. She cleared her throat. "All I have to do is thank him, that's all. It'll only take a minute." Megan reached for the phone, then drew her hand away. Her mind raced on with her heartbeat.

She lifted the receiver. She knew the number. Hadn't she started to dial it a dozen times during the past two weeks? She took a long breath before pushing the first digit. It would take five minutes, and then, in all probability, she'd have no reason to contact him again. It would be better if they erased the remnants of their last meeting. It would be easier if their relationship ended on a calmer, more civilized note. Megan pressed the last button and waited for the click of connection, the whisper of transmitters and the ring.

It took four rings—four long, endless rings before he picked up the phone.

"Katch." His name was barely audible. She closed her eyes.

"Meg?"

"Yes, I…" She fought herself to speak. "I hope I'm not calling you at a bad time." How trite, she thought desperately. How ordinary.

"Are you all right?" There was concern in the question.

"Yes, yes, of course." Her mind fretted for the simple, casual words she had planned to speak. "Katch, I wanted to talk to you. Your sister was here—"

"I know, she got back a few minutes ago." There was a trace of impatience in his tone. "Is anything wrong?"

"No, nothing's wrong." Her voice refused to level. Megan searched for a quick way to end the conversation.

"Are you alone?"

"Yes, I…"

"I'll be there in ten minutes."

"No." Megan ran a frustrated hand through her hair. "No, please—"

"Ten minutes," he repeated and broke the connection.

Chapter 9

Megan stared at the dead receiver for several silent moments. How had she, in a few uncompleted sentences, managed to make such a mess of things? She didn't want him to come. She never wanted to see him again. *That is a lie.*

Carefully, Megan replaced the receiver. I do want to see him, she admitted, have wanted to see him for days. It's just that I'm afraid to see him. Turning, she gazed blindly around the kitchen. The room was almost in complete darkness now. The table and chairs were dark shadows. She walked to the switch, avoiding obstacles with the knowledge of years. The room flooded with brightness. That's better, she thought, more secure in the artificial light. Coffee, she decided, needing something, anything, to occupy her hands. I'll make fresh coffee.

Megan went to the percolator and began a step-by-step preparation, but her nerves continued to jump. In a few moments, she hoped, she'd be calm again. When he arrived, she would say what she needed to say, and then they would part.

The phone rang, and she jolted, juggling the cup she held and nearly dropping it. Chiding herself, Megan set it down and answered the call.

"Hello, Megan." Pop's voice crackled jovially across the wire.

"Pop...are you still at the park?" What time is it? she wondered distractedly and glanced down at her watch.

"That's why I called. George stopped by. We're going to have dinner in town. I didn't want you to worry."

"I won't." She smiled as the band of tension around her head loosened. "I suppose you and George have a lot of fish stories to exchange."

"His have gotten bigger since he retired," Pop claimed. "Hey, why don't you run into town, sweetheart? We'll treat you."

"You two just want an audience," she accused and her smile deepened with Pop's chuckle. "But I'll pass tonight, thanks. As I recall, there's some leftover spaghetti in the fridge."

"I'll bring you back dessert." It was an old custom. For as long as Megan could remember, if Pop had dinner without her, he'd bring her back some treat. "What do you want?"

"Rainbow sherbet," she decided instantly. "Have a good time."

"I will, darling. Don't work too late."

As she hung up the phone, Megan asked herself why she hadn't told her grandfather of Katch's impending visit. Why hadn't she mentioned Jessica or the incredible plans that had been made? It has to wait until we can talk, she told herself. Really talk. It's the only way I'll be certain how he really feels— and how everything will affect him.

It's probably a bad idea. Megan began to fret, pushing a hand through her hair in agitation. It's a crazy idea. How can I go to New York and—

Her thoughts were interrupted by the glaring sweep of headlights against the kitchen window. She struggled to compose herself, going deliberately to the cupboard to close it before heading to the screen door.

Katch stepped onto the stoop as she reached for the handle. For a moment, in silence, they studied each other through the mesh. She heard the soft flutter of moths' wings on the outside light.

Finally he turned the knob and opened the door. After he had shut it quietly behind him, he reached up to touch her cheek. His hand lingered there while his eyes traveled her face.

"You sounded upset."

Megan moistened her lips. "No, no, I'm fine." She stepped back so that his palm no longer touched her skin. Slowly, his eyes on hers, Katch lowered his hand. "I'm sorry I bothered you—"

"Megan, stop it." His voice was quiet and controlled. Her eyes came back to his, a little puzzled, a little desperate. "Stop backing away from me. Stop apologizing."

Her hands fluttered once before she could control the movement. "I'm making coffee," she began. "It should be ready in a minute." She would have turned to arrange the cups and saucers, but he took her arm.

"I didn't come for coffee." His hand slid down until it encircled her wrist. Her pulse vibrated against his fingers.

"Katch, please, don't make this difficult."

Something flared in his eyes while she watched. Then it was gone, and her hand was released. "I'm sorry. I've had some difficulty the past couple of weeks dealing with what happened the last time I saw you." He noted the color that shot into her cheeks, but she kept her eyes steady. He slipped his hands into his pockets. "Megan, I'd like to make it up to you."

Megan shook her head, disturbed by the gentleness in his voice, and turned to the coffee pot.

"Don't you want to forgive me?"

The question had her turning back, her eyes darkened with distressed confusion. ''No…that is, yes, of course.''

''Of course you don't want to forgive me?'' There was a faint glimmer of a smile in his eyes and the charm was around his mouth. She could feel herself sinking.

''Yes, of course I forgive you,'' she corrected and this time did turn to the coffee. ''It's forgotten.'' He laid his hands on her shoulders, and she jumped.

''Is it?'' Katch turned her until they were again face-to-face. The glimpse of humor in his eyes was gone. ''You can't seem to abide my touching you. I don't much like thinking I frighten you.''

She made a conscious effort to relax under his hands. ''You don't frighten me, Katch,'' Megan murmured. ''You confuse me. Constantly.''

She watched his brow lift in consideration. ''I don't have any intention of confusing you. I am sorry, Megan.''

''Yes.'' She smiled, recognizing the simple sincerity. ''I know you are.''

He drew her closer. ''Can we kiss and make up then?''

Megan started to protest, but his mouth was already on hers, light and gentle. Her heart began to hammer in her throat. He made no attempt to deepen the kiss. His hands were easy on her shoulders. Against all the warnings of her mind, she relaxed

against him, inviting him to take whatever he chose.
But he took no more.

Katch drew her away, waiting until her heavy lids
fluttered open before he touched her hair. Without
speaking, he turned and paced to the window. Megan
struggled to fill the new gap.

"I wanted to talk to you about your sister." She
busied her hands with the now noisy percolator.
"Or, more accurately, about what Jessica came to
see me about."

Katch turned his head, watching her pour the coffee into the waiting cups. He walked to the refrigerator and took out the milk.

"All right." Standing beside her now, he poured
milk into one cup and, at her nod, into the second.

"Why didn't you tell me you were sending my
work to your sister?"

"I thought it best to wait until I had her opinion."
Katch sat beside Megan and cradled the cup in both
hands. "I trust her…. And I thought you'd trust her
opinion more than mine. Are you going to do the
showing? Jessica and I didn't have time to talk before you called."

She shifted in her chair, studied her coffee, then
looked directly at him. "She's very persuasive. I was
agreeing before I realized it."

"Good," Katch said simply and drank.

"I want to thank you," Meg continued in a
stronger voice, "for arranging things."

"I didn't arrange anything," he responded. "Jessica makes her own decisions, personal and professional. I simply sent her your sculptures for an opinion."

"Then I'll thank you for that, for making a move I might never have made for the hundreds of reasons which occurred to me five minutes after she'd left."

Katch shrugged. "All right, if you're determined to be grateful."

"I am," she said. "And I'm scared," she continued, "really terrified at the thought of putting my work on public display." Megan let out a shaky breath at the admission. "I may despise you when all this is over and art critics stomp all over my ego, so you'd better take the gratitude now."

Katch crossed to her, and her heart lifted dizzily, so sure was she that he would take her into his arms. He merely stroked her cheek with the back of his hand. "When you're a smashing success, you can give it to me again." He smiled at her, and the world snapped into sharp focus. Until that moment, she hadn't realized how dull everything had been without him.

"I'm so glad you came," she whispered and, unable to resist, slipped her arms around him, pressing her face into his shoulder. After a moment, he rested his hands lightly at her waist. "I'm sorry for the things I said...about the loan. I didn't mean any of it really, but I say horrible things when I lose my temper.''

''Is this your turn to be penitent?''

He made her laugh. ''Yes.'' She smiled and tilted back her head. Her arms stayed around him. He kissed her and drew away. Reluctantly, she let him slip out of her arms. Then he stood silently, staring down at her.

''What are you doing?'' she asked with a quick, self-conscious smile.

''Memorizing your face. Have you eaten?''

She shook her head, wondering why it should come as a surprise that he continued to baffle her. ''No, I was going to heat up some leftovers.''

''Unacceptable. Want a pizza?''

''*Mmm,* I'd love it, but you have company.''

''Jessica and Rob took the kids to play miniature golf. I won't be missed.'' Katch held out his hands. ''Come on.''

His eyes were smiling, and her heart was lost. ''Oh wait,'' she began even as she put her hand into his. Quickly, Megan scrawled a message on the chalkboard by the screen door.

OUT WITH KATCH

It was enough.

Chapter 10

Katch drove along Ocean Boulevard so they could creep along in the traffic filled with tourists and beachers. Car radios were turned up high and windows rolled down low. Laughter and music poured out everywhere. The lights from a twin Ferris wheel glittered red and blue in the distance. People sat out on their hotel balconies, with colorful beach towels flapping over the railings, as they watched the sluggish flow of cars and pedestrians. To the left, there were glimpses of the sea in between buildings.

Sleepily content after pizza and Chianti, Megan snuggled deeper into the soft leather seat. ''Things'll quiet down after this weekend,'' she commented. ''Until Memorial Day.''

"Do you ever feel as though you're being invaded?" Katch asked her with a gesture at the clogged traffic.

"I like the crowds," she said immediately, then laughed. "And I like the winter when the beaches are deserted. I suppose there's something about the honky-tonk that appeals to me, especially since I know I'm going to have a few isolated months in the winter."

"That's your time," Katch murmured, glancing back at her. "The time you give yourself for sculpting."

She shrugged, a bit uncomfortable with the intense look. "I do some in the summer, too—when I can. Time's something I forgot when Jessica was talking about a showing and making all those plans..." Megan trailed off, frowning. "I don't know how I can possibly get things ready."

"Not backing out, are you?"

"No, but—" The look in his eyes had her swallowing excuses. "No," she said more firmly. "I'm not backing out."

"What're you working on now?"

"I, ah..." Megan looked fixedly out the window, thinking of the half-formed bust of Katch's head. "It's just..." She shrugged and began to fiddle with the dial of the radio. "It's just a wood carving."

"Of what?"

Megan made a few inarticulate mumbles until Katch turned to grin at her. "A pirate," she decided as the light from a street lamp slanted over his face, throwing it into planes and shadows. "It's the head of a pirate."

His brow lifted at the sudden, narrow-eyed concentration with which she was studying him. "I'd like to see it."

"It's not finished," she said quickly. "I've barely got the clay model done. In any case, I might have to put it off if I'm going to get the rest of my pieces organized for your sister."

"Meg, why don't you stop worrying and just enjoy it?"

Confused, she shook her head and stared at him. "Enjoy it?"

"The show," he said, ruffling her hair.

"Oh, yes." She fought to get her thoughts back into some kind of order. "I will...after it's over," she added with a smile. "Do you think you'll be in New York, then?"

As the rhythm of the traffic picked up, he shifted into third. "I'm considering it."

"I'd like you to be there if you could arrange it." When he laughed, shaking his head, she continued, "It's just that I'm going to need all the friendly faces I can get."

"You're not going to need anything but your

sculptures,'' Katch corrected, but the amusement was still in his eyes. ''Don't you think I'd want to be around the night of your opening so that I can brag I discovered you?''

''Let's just hope we both don't live to regret it,'' Megan muttered, but he only laughed again. ''You just can't consider the possibility that you might have made a mistake,'' she accused testily.

''You can't consider the possibility that you might be successful,'' he countered.

Megan opened her mouth, then shut it again. ''Well,'' she said after a moment, ''we're both right.'' Waiting until they were stopped in traffic again, Megan touched his shoulder. ''Katch?''

''Hmm?''

''Why did you build a hospital in Central Africa?''

He turned to her then, a faint frown between his brows. ''It was needed,'' he said simply.

''Just that?'' she persisted, though she could see he wasn't pleased with her question. ''I mean, Jessica said you were advised against it, and—''

''As it happens, I have a comfortable amount of money.'' He cut her off with an annoyed movement of his shoulder. ''I do what I choose with it.'' Seeing her expression, Katch shook his head. ''There are things I want to do, that's all. Don't canonize me, Meg.''

She relaxed again and found herself brushing at the curls over his ear. "I wouldn't dream of it." He'd rather be thought of as eccentric than benevolent, she mused. And how much simpler it was to love him, knowing that one small secret. "You're much easier to like than I thought you'd be when you made a nuisance of yourself in the market."

"I tried to tell you," he pointed out. "You were too busy pretending you weren't interested."

"I wasn't interested," Megan insisted, "in the least." He turned to grin at her and she found herself laughing. "Well, not very much anyway." When he swung the car onto a side street, she looked back at him in question. "What are you doing?"

"Let's go out on the boardwalk." Expertly, he slid the Porsche into a parking space. "Maybe I'll buy you a souvenir." He was already out of the car—primed, impatient.

"Oh, I love rash promises," Megan crowed as she joined him.

"I said maybe."

"I didn't hear that part. And," she added as she laced her fingers with his, "I want something extravagant."

"Such as?" They jaywalked, maneuvering around stopped cars.

"I'll know when I see it."

The boardwalk was crowded, full of people and

light and noise. The breeze off the ocean carried the scent of salt to compete with the aroma of grilling meat from concessions. Instead of going into one of the little shops, Katch pulled Megan into an arcade.

"Big talk about presents and no delivery," Megan said in disgust as Katch exchanged bills for tokens.

"It's early yet. Here." He poured a few tokens into her hand. "Why don't you try your luck at saving the galaxy from invaders?"

With a smirk, Megan chose a machine, then slipped two tokens into the slot. "I'll go first." Pressing the start button, she took the control stick in hand and began systematically to vaporize the enemy. Brows knit, she swung her ship right and left while the machine exploded with color and noise with each hit. Amused, Katch dipped his hands into his pockets and watched her face. It was a more interesting show than the sophisticated graphics.

She chewed her bottom lip while maneuvering into position, narrowing her eyes when a laser blast headed her way. Her breath hissed through her teeth at a narrow escape. But all the while, her face held that composed, almost serious expression that was so much a part of her. Fighting gamely to avoid being blown up in cross fire, Megan's ship at last succumbed.

"Well," Katch murmured, glancing at her score

as she wiped her hands on the back of her jeans. "You're pretty good."

"You have to be," Megan returned soberly, "when you're the planet's last hope."

With a chuckle, he nudged her out of the way and took the control.

Megan acknowledged his skill as Katch began to blast away the invaders with as much regularity as she had, and a bit more dash. He likes to take chances, she mused as he narrowly missed being blown apart by laser fire in order to zap three ships in quick succession. As his score mounted, she stepped a bit closer to watch his technique.

At the brush of her arm against his, Megan noticed a quick, almost imperceptible break in his rhythm. Now, that was interesting, she reflected. Feeling an irrepressible surge of mischief, she edged slightly closer. There was another brief fluctuation in his timing. Softly, she touched her lips to his shoulder, then smiled up into his face. She heard rather than saw the explosion that marked his ship's untimely end.

Katch wasn't looking at the screen either, but at her. She saw something flash into his eyes—something hot, barely suppressed, before his hand released the control to dive into her hair.

"Cheat," he murmured.

For a moment, Megan forgot the cacophony of sound, forgot the crowds of people that milled around them. She was lost somewhere in those smoky gray eyes and her own giddy sense of power.

"Cheat?" she repeated, and her lips stayed slightly parted. "I don't know what you mean."

The hand on her hair tightened. He was struggling, she realized, surprised and excited. "I think you do," Katch said quietly. "And I think I'm going to have to be very careful now that you know just what you can do to me."

"Katch." Her gaze lowered to his mouth as the longings built. "Maybe I don't want you to be careful anymore."

Slowly, his hand slid out of her hair, over her cheek, then dropped. "All the more reason I have to be," he muttered. "Come on." He took her arm and propelled her away from the machine. "Let's play something else."

Megan flowed with his mood, content just to be with him. They pumped tokens into machines and competed fiercely—as much with each other as with the computers. Megan felt the same lighthearted ease with him that she'd experienced that night at the carnival. Spending time with him was much like a trip on one of the wild, breathless rides at the park. Quick curves, fast hills, unexpected starts and stops. No one liked the windy power of a roller coaster better than Megan.

Hands on hips, she stood back as he consistently

won coupons at Skee Ball. She watched another click off on the already lengthy strip as he tossed the ball neatly into the center hole.

"Don't you ever lose?" she demanded.

Katch tossed the next ball for another forty points. "I try not to make a habit of it. Wanna toss the last two?"

"No." She brushed imaginary lint from her shirt. "You're having such a good time showing off."

With a laugh, Katch dumped the last two balls for ninety points, then leaned over to tear off his stream of coupons. "Just for that, I might not turn these in for your souvenir."

"These?" Megan gave the ream of thin cardboard an arched-brow look. "You were supposed to *buy* me a souvenir."

"I did." He grinned, rolling them up. "Indirectly." Slipping an arm companionably around her shoulder, he walked to the center counter where prizes were displayed. "Let's see…I've got two dozen. How about one of those six-function penknives?"

"Just who's this souvenir for?" Megan asked dryly as she scanned the shelves. "I like that little silk rose." She tapped the glass counter to indicate a small lapel pin. "I have all the tools I need," she added with an impish grin.

"Okay." Katch nodded to the woman behind the

counter, then tore off all but four of the tickets. "That leaves us these. Ah…" With a quick scan of the shelves, he pointed. "That."

Thoughtfully, Megan studied the tiny shell figure the woman lifted down. It seemed to be a cross between a duck and a penguin. "What're you going to do with that?"

"Give it to you." Katch handed over the rest of the tickets. "I'm a very generous man."

"I'm overwhelmed," she murmured. Megan turned it over in the palm of her hand as Katch pinned the rose to the collar of her shirt. "But what is it?"

"It's a mallard." Draping his arm over her shoulder again, he led her out of the arcade. "I'm surprised at your attitude. I figured, as an artist, you'd recognize its aesthetic value."

"*Hmm.*" Megan took another study, then slipped it into her pocket. "Well, I do recognize a certain winsome charm. And," she added, rising on her toes to kiss his cheek, "it was sweet of you to spend all your winnings on me."

Smiling, Katch ran a finger down her nose. "Is a kiss on the cheek the best you can do?"

"For a shell penguin it is."

"It's a mallard," he reminded her.

"Whatever." Laughing, Megan slipped an arm

around his waist as they crossed the boardwalk and walked down the slope to the beach.

The moon was only a thin slice of white, but the stars were brilliant and mirrored in the water. There was a quiet swish of waves flowing and ebbing over the sand. Lovers walked here and there, arm in arm, talking quietly or not speaking at all. Children dashed along with flashlights bobbing, searching the sand and the surf for treasures.

Bending, Megan slipped out of her shoes and rolled up the hem of her jeans. In silent agreement, Katch followed suit. The water lapped cool over their ankles as they began to walk north, until the laughter and music from the boardwalk was only a background echo.

"Your sister's lovely," Megan said at length. "Just as you said."

"Jessica was always a beauty," he agreed absently. "A little hardheaded, but always a beauty."

"I saw your nieces at the park." Megan lifted her head so that the ocean breeze caught at her hair. "They had chocolate all over their faces."

"Typical." He laughed, running a hand up and down her arm as they walked. Megan felt the blood begin to hum beneath her flesh. "Before they left tonight, they were out digging for worms. I've been drafted to take them fishing tomorrow."

"You like children."

He twisted his head to glance down at her, but Megan was looking out to sea. "Yes. They're a constant adventure, aren't they?"

"I see so many of them in the park every summer, yet they never cease to amaze me." She turned back then with her slow, serious smile hovering on her lips. "And I see a fair number of harassed or long-suffering parents."

"When did you lose yours?"

He saw the flicker of surprise in her eyes before she looked down the stretch of beach again. "I was five."

"It's difficult for you to remember them."

"Yes. I have some vague memories—impressions really, I suppose. Pop has pictures, of course. When I see them, it always surprises me how young they were."

"It must have been hard on you," Katch murmured. "Growing up without them."

The gentleness in his voice had her turning back to him. They'd walked far down the beach so that the only light now came from the stars. His eyes caught the glitter of reflection as they held hers. "It would have been," Megan told him, "without Pop. He did much more than fill in." She stopped to take a step farther into the surf. The water frothed and bubbled over her skin. "One of my best memories is of him struggling to iron this pink organdy party dress. I was eight or nine, I think.'' With a shake of her head, she laughed and kicked the water. ''I can still see him.''

Katch's arms came around her waist, drawing her back against him. ''So can I.''

''He was standing there, struggling with frills and flounces—and swearing like a sailor because he didn't know I was there. I still love him for that,'' she murmured. ''For just that.''

Katch brushed his lips over the top of her hair. ''And I imagine you told him not long afterward that you didn't care much for party dresses.''

Surprised, Megan turned around. ''How did you know that?''

''I know you.'' Slowly, he traced the shape of her face with his fingertip.

Frowning, she looked beyond his shoulder. ''Am I so simple?''

''No.'' With his fingertip still on her jaw, he turned her face back to his. ''You might say I've made a study of you.''

She felt her blood begin to churn. ''Why?''

Katch shook his head and combed his fingers through her hair. ''No questions tonight,'' he said quietly. ''I don't have the answers yet.''

''No questions,'' she agreed, then rose on her toes to meet his mouth with hers.

It was a soft, exploring kiss—a kiss of renewal.

Megan could taste the gentleness. For the moment, he seemed to prize her, to find her precious and rare. He held her lightly, as though she would break at the slightest pressure. Her lips parted, and it was she who entered his mouth first, teasing his tongue with hers. His sound of pleasure warmed her. The water swayed, soft and cool, on her calves.

She ran her hands up his back, letting her strong, artist's fingers trail under his hair to caress the nape of his neck. There was tension there, and she murmured against his lips as if to soothe it. Megan felt both his resistance and the tightening of his fingers against her skin. Her body pressed more demandingly into his.

Passion began to smolder quietly. Megan knew she was drawing it from him without his complete consent. The wonder of her own power struck her like a flash. He was holding back, letting her set the pace, but she could feel the near-violence of need in him. It tempted her. She wanted to undermine his control as he had undermined hers. She wanted to make him need as blindly as she needed. It wasn't possible to make him love her, but she could make him want. If it was all she could have from him, then she would be satisfied with his desire.

Megan felt his control slipping. His arms tightened around her, drawing her close so they were silhouetted as one. The kiss grew harder, more urgent. He lifted a hand to her hair, gripping it, pulling her head back as if now he would take command. There was fire now, burning brightly. Heat rose in her, smoking through her blood. She caught his bottom lip between her teeth and heard his quiet moan. Abruptly, he drew her away.

"Meg."

She waited, having no idea what she wanted him to say. Her head was tossed back, her face open to his, her hair free to the breeze. She felt incredibly strong. His eyes were nearly black, searching her face deeply. She could feel his breath feather, warm and uneven, on her lips.

"Meg." He repeated her name, bringing his hands back to her shoulders slowly. "I have to go now."

Daring more than she would have believed possible, Megan pressed her lips to his again. Hers were soft and hungry and drew instant response from him. "Is that what you want?" she murmured. "Do you want to leave me now?"

His fingers tightened on her arms convulsively, then he pulled her away again. "You know the answer to that," he said roughly. "What are you trying to do, make me crazy?"

"Maybe." Desire still churned in her. It smoldered in her eyes as they met his. "Maybe I am."

He caught her against him, close and tight. She could feel the furious race of his heart against hers.

His control, she knew, balanced on a razor's edge. Their lips were only a whisper apart.

"There'll be a time," he said softly, "I swear it, when it'll just be you and me. Next time, the very next time, Meg. Remember it."

It took no effort to keep her eyes level with his. The power was still flowing through her. "Is that a warning?"

"Yes," he told her. "That's just what it is."

Chapter 11

It took two more days for Megan to finish the bust of Katch. She tried, when it was time, to divorce herself from emotion and judge it objectively.

She'd been right to choose wood. It was warmer than stone. With her tongue caught between her teeth, she searched for flaws in her workmanship. Megan knew without conceit it was one of her better pieces. Perhaps the best.

The face wasn't stylishly handsome, but strong and compelling. Humor was expressed in the tilt of the brows and mouth. She ran her fingertips over his lips. An incredibly expressive mouth, she mused, remembering the taste and texture. I know just how it looks when he's amused or angry or aroused. And his eyes. Hers drifted up to linger. I know how they look, how they change shades and expression with a mood. Light for pleasure, turning smoky in anger, darker in passion.

I know his face as well as my own...but I still don't know his mind. That's still a stranger. With a sigh she folded her arms on the table and lowered her chin to them.

Would he ever permit me to know him? she wondered. Tenderly, she touched a lock of the disordered hair. Jessica knows him, probably better than anyone else. If he loved someone...

What would happen if I drew up the courage to tell him that I love him? What would happen if I simply walked up to him and said *I love you?* Demanding nothing, expecting nothing. Doesn't he perhaps have the right to know? Isn't love too special, too rare to be closed up? Then Megan imagined his eyes with pity in them.

"I couldn't bear it," she murmured, lowering her forehead to Katch's wooden one. "I just couldn't bear it." A knock interrupted her soul-searching. Quickly, Megan composed her features and swiveled in her chair. "Come in."

Her grandfather entered, his fishing cap perched jauntily on his mane of white hair. "How do you feel about fresh fish for supper?" His grin told her that his early morning expedition had been a success. Megan cocked her head.

"I could probably choke down a few bites." She smiled, pleased to see his eyes sparkling and color in his cheeks. She sprang up and wound her arms around his neck as she had done as a child. "Oh, I love you, Pop!"

"Well, well." He patted her hair, both surprised and pleased. "I love you too, Megan. I guess I should bring you home trout more often."

She lifted her face from the warm curve of his neck and smiled at him. "It doesn't take much to make me happy."

His eyes sobered as he tucked her hair behind her ear. "No.... It never has." His wide, blunt hand touched her cheek. "You've given me so much pleasure over the years, Megan, so much joy. I'm going to miss you when you're in New York."

"Oh, Pop." She buried her face again and clung. "It'll only be for a month or two, then I'll be home." She could smell the cherry-flavored scent of the tobacco he carried in his breast pocket. "You could even come with me—the season'll be over."

"Meg." He stopped her rambling and drew her up so that their eyes met. "This is a start for you. Don't put restrictions on it."

Shaking her head, Megan rose to pace nervously. "I'm not. I don't know what you mean..."

"You're going to make something of yourself, something important. You have talent." Pop glanced around the room at her work until his eyes rested on the bust of Katch. "You've got a life to start. I want you to go after it at full speed."

"You make it sound as if I'm not coming home." Megan turned and, seeing where his eyes rested, clasped her hands together. "I've just finished that." She moistened her lips and struggled to keep her voice casual. "It's rather good, don't you think?"

"Yes, I think it's very good." He looked at her then. "Sit down, Megan, I need to talk to you."

She recognized the tone and tensed. Without a word, she obeyed, going to the chair across from him. Pop waited until she was settled, then studied her face carefully.

"Awhile back," he began, "I told you things change. Most of your life, it's been just the two of us. We needed each other, depended on each other. We had the park to keep a roof over our heads and to give us something to work for." His tone softened. "There hasn't been one minute in the eighteen years I've had you with me that you've been a burden. You've kept me young. I've watched you through all the stages of growing up, and each time, you've made me more proud of you. It's time for the next change."

Because her throat was dry as dust, Megan swallowed. "I don't understand what you're trying to tell me."

"It's time you moved out into the world, Megan, time I let you." Pop reached in the pocket of his shirt and took out carefully folded papers. After spreading them out, he handed them to Megan.

She hesitated before accepting them, her eyes clinging to his. The instant she saw the papers, she knew what they were. But when she read, she read each sentence, each word, until the finish. "So," she said, dry-eyed, dry-voiced. "You've sold it to him."

"When I sign the papers," Pop told her, "and you witness it." He saw the look of devastation in her eyes. "Megan, hear me out. I've given this a lot of thought." Pop took the papers and set them on the table, then gripped her hands. "Katch isn't the first to approach me about selling, and this isn't the first time I've considered it. Everything didn't fit the way I wanted before—this time it does."

"What fits?" she demanded, feeling her eyes fill.

"It's the right man, Meg, the right time." He soothed her hands, hating to watch her distress. "I knew it when all those repairs fell on me. I'm ready to let it go, to let someone younger take over so I can go fishing. That's what I want now, Megan, a boat and a rod. And he's the man I want taking over." He paused, fumbling in his pocket for a hand-kerchief to wipe his eyes. "I told you I trusted him and that still holds. Managing the park for Katch won't keep me from my fishing, and I'll have the stimulation without the headaches. And you," he continued, brushing tears from her cheeks, "you need to cut the strings. You can't do what you're meant to do if you're struggling to balance books and make payroll."

"If it's what you want," Megan began, but Pop cut her off.

"No, it has to be what you want. That's why the last lines are still blank." He looked at her with his deep-set eyes sober and quiet. "I won't sign it, Megan, unless you agree. It has to be what's best for both of us."

Megan stood again, and he released her hands to let her walk to the window. At the moment, she was unable to understand her own feelings. She knew agreeing to do a show in New York was a giant step away from the life she had led. And the park was a major part of that life. She knew in order to pursue her own career, she couldn't continue to tie herself to the business end of Joyland.

The park had been security—her responsibility, her second home—as the man behind her had been both mother and father to her. She remembered the look of weariness on his face when he had come to tell her that the park needed money. Megan knew the hours and endless demands that summer would bring.

He was entitled to live his winter years as he chose, she decided. With less worry, less responsibility. He was entitled to fish, and to sleep late and putter around his azaleas. What right did she have to deny him that because she was afraid to cut the last tie with her childhood? He was right, it was time for the change.

Slowly, she walked to her workbox and searched out a pen. Going to Pop, Megan held it out to him. "Sign it. We'll have champagne with the trout."

Pop took the pen, but kept his eyes on her. "Are you sure, Meg?"

She nodded, as sure for him as she was uncertain for herself. "Positive." She smiled and watched the answering light in his eyes before he bent over the paper.

He signed his name with a flourish, then passed her the pen so that she could witness his signature. Megan wrote her name in clear, distinct letters, not allowing her hand to tremble.

"I suppose I should call Katch," Pop mused, sighing as though a weight had been lifted. "Or take the papers to him."

"I'll take them." Carefully, Megan folded them again. "I'd like to talk to him."

"That's a good idea. Take the pickup," he suggested as she headed for the door. "It looks like rain."

Megan was calm by the time she reached Katch's house. The papers were tucked securely in the back pocket of her cutoffs. She pulled the truck behind his car and climbed out.

The air was deadly still and heavy, nearly shimmering with restrained rain. The clouds overhead were black and bulging with it. She walked to the front door and knocked as she had many days before. As before, there was no answer. She walked back down the steps and skirted the house.

There was no sign of him in the yard, no sound but the voice of the sea muffled by the tall hedges. He'd planted a willow, a young, slender one near the slope which led to the beach. The earth was still dark around it, freshly turned. Unable to resist, Megan walked to it, wanting to touch the tender young leaves. It was no taller than she, but she knew one day it would be magnificent...sweeping, graceful, a haven of shade in the summer. Instinct made her continue down the slope to the beach.

Hands in his pockets, he stood, watching the swiftly incoming tide. As if sensing her, he turned.

"I was standing here thinking of you," he said. "Did I wish you here?"

She took the papers and held them out to him.

"It's yours," she told him calmly. "Just as you wanted."

He didn't even glance down at the papers, but she saw the shift of expression in his eyes. "I'd like to talk to you, Meg. Let's go inside."

"No." She stepped back to emphasize her refusal. "There really isn't anything more to say."

"That might be true for you, but I have a great deal to say. And you're going to listen." Impatience intruded into his tone. Megan heard it as she felt the sudden gust of wind which broke the calm.

"I don't want to listen to you, Katch. This is what Pop wants, too." She thrust the papers into his hands as the first spear of lightning split the sky. "Take them, will you?"

"Megan, wait." He grabbed her arm as she turned to go. The thunder all but drowned out his words.

"I will not wait!" she tossed back, jerking her arm free. "And stop grabbing me. You have what you wanted—you don't need me anymore."

Katch swore, thrust the papers in his pocket and caught her again before she'd taken three steps. He whirled her back around. "You're not that big an idiot."

"Don't tell me how big an idiot I am." She tried to shake herself loose.

"We have to talk. I have things to say to you. It's

important.'' A gust of wind whipped violently across Megan's face.

"Don't you understand a simple no?'' she shouted at him, her voice competing with pounding surf and rising wind. She struggled against his hold. "I don't want to talk. I don't want to hear what you have to say. I don't *care* about what you have to say.''

The rain burst from the clouds and poured over them. Instantly, they were drenched.

"Tough," he retorted, every bit as angry as she. "Because you're going to hear it. Now, let's go inside."

He started to pull her across the sand, but she swung violently away and freed herself. Rain gushed down in torrents, sheeting around them. "No!" she shouted. "I won't go inside with you."

"Oh yes you will," he corrected.

"What are you going to do?" she demanded. "Drag me by the hair?"

"Don't tempt me." Katch took her hand again only to have her pull away. "All right," he said. "Enough." In a swift move that caught her off guard, he swept her up into his arms.

"Put me down." Megan wriggled and kicked, blind with fury. He ignored her, dealing with her struggles by shifting her closer and climbing the slope without any apparent effort. Lightning and thunder warred around them. "Oh, I hate you!" she claimed as he walked briskly across the lawn.

"Good. That's a start." Katch pushed open the door with his hip, then continued through the kitchen and into the living room. A trail of rain streamed behind them. Without ceremony, he dumped her on the sofa. "Sit still," he ordered before she could regain her breath, "and just be quiet a minute." He walked to the hearth. Taking a long match, he set fire to the paper waiting beneath kindling and logs. Dry wood crackled and caught almost instantly.

Regaining her breath, Megan rose and bounded for the door. Katch stopped her before her fingers touched the knob. He held her by the shoulders with her back to the door. "I warn you, Meg, my tolerance is at a very low ebb. Don't push me."

"You don't frighten me," she told him, impatiently flipping her dripping hair from her eyes.

"I'm not trying to frighten you. I'm trying to reason with you. But you're too stubborn to shut up and listen."

Her eyes widened with fresh fury. "Don't you talk to me that way! I don't have to take that."

"Yes, you do." Deftly, he reached in her right front pocket and pulled out the truck keys. "As long as I have these."

"I can walk," she tossed back as he pocketed them himself.

"In this rain?"

Megan hugged her arms as she began to shiver. "Let me have my keys."

Instead of answering, he pulled her across the room in front of the fire. "You're freezing. You'll have to get out of those wet clothes."

"I will not. You're crazy if you think I'm going to take off my clothes in your house."

"Suit yourself." He stripped off his own sopping T-shirt and tossed it angrily aside. "You're the most hardheaded, single-minded, stubborn woman I know."

"Thanks." Barely, Megan controlled the urge to sneeze. "Is that all you wanted to say?"

"No." He walked to the fire again. "That's just the beginning—there's a lot more. Sit down."

"Then maybe I'll have my say first." Chills were running over her skin, and she struggled not to tremble. "I was wrong about you in a lot of ways. You're not lazy or careless or glory-seeking. And you were certainly honest with me." She wiped water from her eyes, a mixture of rain and tears. "You told me up front that you intended to have the park, and it seems perhaps for the best. What happened between then and now is my fault for being foolish enough to let you get to me." Megan swallowed, wanting to salvage a little pride. "But then you're a difficult man to ignore. Now you have what you wanted, and it's over and done.''

"I only have part of what I wanted." Katch came to her and gathered her streaming hair in his hand. "Only part, Meg."

She looked at him, too tired to argue. "Can't you just let me be?" she asked.

"Let you be? Do you know how many times I've walked that beach at three in the morning because wanting you kept me awake and aching? Do you know how hard it was for me to let you go every time I had you in my arms?'' The fingers in her hair tightened, pulled her closer.

Her eyes were huge now while chills shivered over her skin. *What was he saying?* She couldn't risk asking, couldn't risk wondering. Abruptly, he cursed her and dragged her into his arms.

Thin wet clothes were no barrier to his hands. He molded her breasts even while his mouth ravished hers. She made no protest when he lowered her to the floor, as his fingers worked desperately at the buttons of her blouse. Her chilled wet skin turned to fire under his fingertips. His mouth was hungry, hot as it roamed to her throat and downward.

There was only the crackle of wood and the splash of rain on the windows to mix with their breathing. A log shifted in the grate.

Megan heard him take a long, deep breath. ''I'm

sorry. I wanted to talk—there are things I need to tell you. But I need you. I've kept it pent up a long time.''

Need. Her mind centered on the word. Need was infinitely different from want. Need was more personal—still apart from love—but she let her heart grip the word.

''It's all right.'' Megan started to sit up, but he leaned over her. Sparks flicked inside her at the touch of naked flesh to naked flesh. ''Katch...''

''Please, Meg. Listen to me.''

She searched his face, noting the uncharacteristically grave eyes and mouth. Whatever he had to say was important to him. ''All right,'' she said, quieter now, ready. ''I'll listen.''

''When I first saw you, the first minute, I wanted you. You know that.'' His voice was low, but without its usual calm. Something boiled just under the surface. ''The first night we were together, you intrigued me as much as you attracted me. I thought it would be a simple matter to have you...a casual, pleasant affair for a few weeks.''

''I know,'' she spoke softly, trying not to be wounded by the truth.

''No—shh.'' He lay a finger over her lips a moment. ''You don't know. It stopped being simple almost immediately. When I had you here for dinner, and you asked to stay...'' He paused, brushing wet strands of hair from her cheeks. "I couldn't let you, and I wasn't completely sure why. I wanted you—wanted you more than any woman I'd ever touched, any woman I'd ever dreamed about—but I couldn't take you."

"Katch…" Megan shook her head, not certain she was strong enough to hear the words.

"Please." She had closed her eyes, and Katch waited until she opened them again before he continued. "I tried to stay away from you, Meg. I tried to convince myself I was imagining what was happening to me. Then you were charging across the lawn, looking outraged and so beautiful I couldn't think of anything. Just looking at you took my breath away." While she lay motionless, he lifted her hand and pressed it to his lips. The gesture moved her unbearably.

"Don't," she murmured. "Please."

Katch stared into her eyes for a long moment, then released her hand. "I wanted you," he went on in a voice more calm than his eyes. "Needed you, was furious with you because of it." He rested his forehead on hers and shut his eyes. "I never wanted to hurt you, Meg—to frighten you."

Megan lay still, aware of the turmoil in him. Firelight played over the skin on his arms and back.

"It seemed impossible that I could be so involved I couldn't pull away," he continued. "But you were so tangled up in my thoughts, so wound up in my dreams. There wasn't any escape. The other night, after I'd taken you home, I finally admitted to myself I didn't want an escape. Not this time. Not from you.'' He lifted his head and looked down at her again. ''I have something for you, but first I want you to know I'd decided against buying the park until your grandfather came to me last night. I didn't want that between us, but it was what he wanted. What he thought was best for you and for himself. But if it hurts you, I'll tear the papers up.''

''No.'' Megan gave a weary sigh. ''I know it's best. It's just like losing someone you love. Even when you know it's the best thing, it still hurts.'' The outburst seemed to have driven out the fears and the pain. ''Please, I don't want you to apologize. I was wrong, coming here this way, shouting at you. Pop has every right to sell the park, and you have every right to buy it.'' She sighed, wanting explanations over. ''I suppose I felt betrayed somehow and didn't want to think it all through.''

''And now?''

''And now I'm ashamed of myself for acting like a fool.'' She managed a weak smile. ''I'd like to get up and go home. Pop'll be worried.''

''Not just yet.'' When Katch leaned back on his heels to take something from his pocket, Megan sat up, pushing her wet, tangled hair behind her. He held a box, small and thin. Briefly, he hesitated before offering it to her. Puzzled, both by the gift and by the tension she felt emanating from him, Megan opened it. Her breath caught.

It was a dark, smoky green emerald, square cut and exquisite in its simplicity. Stunned, Megan stared at it, then at Katch. She shook her head wordlessly.

"Katch." Megan shook her head again. "I don't understand...I can't accept this."

"Don't say no, Meg." Katch closed his hand over hers. "I don't handle rejection well." The words were light, but she recognized, and was puzzled by, the strain in the tone. A thought trembled in her brain, and her heart leaped with it.

She tried to be calm and keep her eyes steady on his. "I don't know what you're asking me."

His fingers tightened on hers. "Marry me. I love you."

Emotions ran riot through her. He must be joking, she thought quickly, though no hint of amusement showed in his eyes. His face was so serious, she reflected, and the words so simple. Where were the carelessly witty phrases, the glib charm? Shaken, Megan rose with the box held tightly in her hand. She needed to think.

Marriage. Never had she expected him to ask her to share a lifetime. What would life be like with him? *Like the roller coaster.* She knew it instantly. It would be a fast, furious ride, full of unexpected curves and indescribable thrills. And quiet moments too, she reflected. Precious, solitary moments which would make each new twist and turn more exciting.

Perhaps he had asked her this way, so simply, without any of the frills he could so easily provide because he was as vulnerable as she. What a thought that was! She lifted her fingers to her temple. David Katcherton vulnerable. And yet…Megan remembered what she had seen in his eyes.

I love you. The three simple words, words spoken every day by people everywhere, had changed her life forever. Megan turned, then walking back, knelt beside him. Her eyes were as grave, as searching as his. She held the box out, then spoke quickly as she saw the flicker of desperation.

"It belongs on the third finger of my left hand."

Then she was caught against him, her mouth silenced bruisingly. "Oh, Meg," he murmured her name as he rained kisses on her face. "I thought you were turning me down."

"How could I?" She wound her arms around his neck and tried to stop his roaming mouth with her own. "I love you, Katch." The words were against his lips. "Desperately, completely. I'd prepared myself for a slow death when you were ready to walk away."

"No one's going to walk away now." They lay on the floor again, and he buried his face in her rain-scented hair. "We'll go to New Orleans. A quick honeymoon before you have to come back and work on the show. In the spring, we'll go to Paris." He lifted his face and looked down on her. "I've thought about you and me in Paris, making love. I want to see your face in the morning when the light's soft."

She touched his cheek. "Soon," she whispered. "Marry me soon. I want to be with you."

He picked up the box that had fallen beside them. Drawing out the ring, he slipped it on her finger. Then, gripping her hand with his, he looked down at her.

"Consider it binding, Meg," he told her huskily. "You can't get away now."

"I'm not going anywhere." She lifted her mouth to meet his kiss.

Epilogue

Nervously, Megan twisted the emerald on her finger and tried to drink the champagne Jessica had pushed into her hand. She felt as though the smile had frozen onto her face. People, she thought. She'd never expected so many people. What was she doing, standing in a Manhattan gallery pretending she was an artist? What she wanted to do was creep into the back room and be very, very sick.

"Here now, Meg." Pop strolled over beside her, looking oddly distinguished in his best—and only—black suit. "You should try one of these—tasty little things." He held out a canapé.

"No." Megan felt her stomach roll and shook her head. "No, thanks. I'm so glad you flew up for the weekend."

"Think I'd miss my granddaughter's big night?" He ate the canapé and grinned. "How about this turnout?"

"I feel like an impostor," Megan murmured, smiling gamely as a man in a flowing cape moved past her to study one of her marble pieces.

"Never seen you look prettier." Pop plucked at the sleeve of her dress, a swirl of watercolored silk. "'Cept maybe at your wedding."

"I wasn't nearly as scared then." She made a quick scan of the crowd and found only strangers. "Where's Katch?"

"Last time I saw him he was cornered by a couple of ritzy-looking people. Didn't I hear Jessica say you were supposed to mingle?"

"Yes." Megan made a small, frustrated sound. "I don't think I can move."

"Now, Meg, I've never known you to be chicken-hearted."

With her mouth half-opened in protest, she watched him walk away. *Chicken-hearted,* she repeated silently. Straightening her shoulders, she drank some champagne. All right then, she decided, she wouldn't stand there cowering in the corner. If she was going to be shot down, she'd face it head on. Moving slowly, and with determined confidence, Megan walked toward the buffet.

"You're the artist, aren't you?"

Megan turned to face a striking old woman in diamonds and black silk. "Yes," she said with a fractional lift of her chin. "I am."

"Hmmm." The woman took Megan in with a long, sweeping glance. "I noticed the study of the girl with the sand castle isn't for sale."

"No, it's my husband's." After two months, the words still brought the familiar warmth to her blood. *Katch, my husband.* Megan's eyes darted around the room to find him.

"A pity," the woman in black commented.

"I beg your pardon?"

"I said it's a pity—I wanted it."

"You—" Stunned, Megan stared at her. "You wanted it?"

"I've purchased 'The Lovers,'" she went on as Megan only gaped. "An excellent piece, but I want to commission you to do another sand castle. I'll contact you through Jessica."

"Yes, of course." *Commission?* Megan thought numbly as she automatically offered her hand. "Thank you," she added as the woman swept away.

"Miriam Tailor Marcus," a voice whispered beside her ear. "A tough nut to crack."

Megan half turned and grabbed Katch's arm. "Katch, that woman, she—"

"Miriam Tailor Marcus," he repeated and bent down to kiss her astonished mouth. "And I heard.

I've just been modestly accepting compliments on my contribution to the art world.'' He touched the rim of his glass to hers. ''Congratulations, love.''

''They like my work?'' she whispered.

''If you hadn't been so busy trying to be invisible, you'd know you're a smashing success. Walk around with me,'' he told her as he took her hand. ''And look at all the little blue dots under your sculptures that mean SOLD.''

''They're buying?'' Megan gave a wondering laugh as she spotted sale after sale. ''They're really buying them?''

''Jessica's frantically trying to keep up. Three people've tried to buy the alabaster piece she bought from you herself—at twice what you charged her. And if you don't talk to a couple of the art critics soon, she's going to go crazy.''

''I can't believe it.''

''Believe it.'' He brought Megan's hand to his lips. ''I'm very proud of you, Meg.''

Tears welled up, threatening to brim over. ''I have to get out of here for a minute,'' she whispered. ''Please.''

Without a word, Katch maneuvered his way through the crowd, taking Megan into the storage room and shutting the door behind them.

''This is silly,'' she said immediately as the tears rolled freely down her cheeks. ''I'm an idiot. I have everything I've ever dreamed of and I'm crying in the back room. I'd have handled failure better than this."

"Megan." With a soft laugh, he gathered her close. "I love you."

"It doesn't seem real," she said with a quaver in her voice. "Not just the showing...it's everything. I see your ring on my finger and I keep wondering when I'm going to wake up. I can't believe that—"

His mouth silenced her. With a low, melting sigh, she dissolved against him. Even after all the days of her marriage, and all the intimate nights, he could still turn her to putty with only his mouth. The tears vanished as her blood began to swim. Pulling him closer, she let her hands run up the sides of his face and into his hair.

"It's real," he murmured against her mouth. "Believe it." Tilting his head, he changed the angle of the kiss and took her deeper. "It's real every night when you're in my arms, and every morning when you wake there." Katch drew her away slowly, then kissed both her damp cheeks until her lashes fluttered up. "Tonight," he said with a smile, "I'm going to make love to the newest star in the New York art world. And when she's still riding high over the reviews in the morning papers, I'm going to make love to her all over again."

"How soon can we slip away?"

Laughing, he caught her close for a hard kiss. "Don't tempt me. Jessica'd skin us both if we didn't stay until the gallery closes tonight. Now, fix your face and go bask in the admiration for a while. It's good for the soul."

"Katch." Megan stopped him before he could open the door. "There's one piece I didn't put out tonight."

Curious, he lifted a brow. "Oh?"

"Yes, well…" A faint color rose to her cheeks. "I was afraid things might not go well, and I thought I could handle the criticism. But this piece—I knew I couldn't bear to have anyone say it was a poor attempt or amateurish."

Puzzled, he slipped his hands into his pockets. "Have I seen it?"

"No." She shook her head, tossing her bangs out of her eyes. "I'd wanted to give it to you as a wedding present, but everything happened so fast and it wasn't finished. After all," she added with a grin, "we were only engaged for three days."

"Two days longer than if you'd agreed to fly to Vegas," he pointed out. "All in all, I was very patient."

"Be that as it may, I didn't have time until later to finish it. Then I was so nervous about the showing that I couldn't give it to you." She took a deep breath. "I'd like you to have it now, tonight, while I'm feeling—really feeling like an artist."

"Is it here?"

Turning around, Megan reached up on the shelf where the bust was carefully covered in cloth. Wordlessly, she handed it to him. Katch removed the cloth, then stared down into his own face.

Megan had polished the wood very lightly, wanting it to carry that not-quite-civilized aura she perceived in the model. It had his cockiness, his confidence and the warmth the artist had sensed in him before the woman had. He stared at it for so long, she felt the nerves begin to play in her stomach again. Then he looked up, eyes dark, intense.

"Meg."

"I don't want to put it out on display," she said hurriedly. "It's too personal to me. There were times," she began as she took the bust from him and ran a thumb down a cheekbone, "when I was working on the clay model, that I wanted to smash it." With a half-laugh, she set it down on a small table. "I couldn't. When I started it, I told myself the only reason I kept thinking about you was because you had the sort of face I'd like to sculpt." She lifted her eyes then to find his fixed on hers. "I fell in love with you sitting in my studio, while my hands were forming your face." Stepping forward, Megan lifted her hands and traced her fingers over the planes and bones under his flesh. "I thought I couldn't love you more than I did then. I was wrong."

"Meg." Katch brought his hands to hers, pressing her palms to his lips. "You leave me speechless."

"Just love me."

"Always."

"That just might be long enough." Megan sighed as she rested her head against his shoulder. "And I think I'll be able to handle success knowing it."

Katch slipped an arm around her waist as he opened the door. "Let's go have some more champagne. It's a night for celebrations."

* * * * *

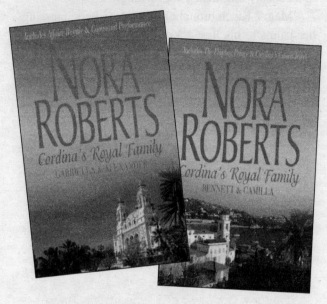

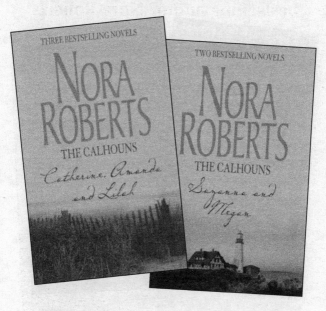

From No. 1 *New York Times* bestselling author Nora Roberts

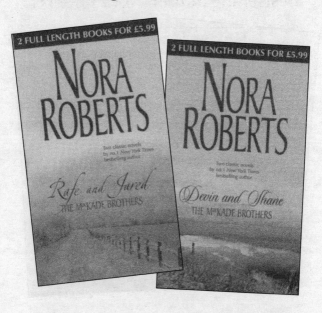

The irresistible MacKade brothers are back and once again stirring the heart of every female that crosses their path.

Rafe and Jared
Featuring *The Return of Rafe MacKade* and
The Pride of Jared MacKade

Devin and Shane
Featuring *The Heart of Devin MacKade* and
The Fall of Shane MacKade

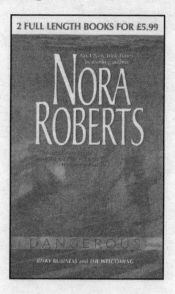

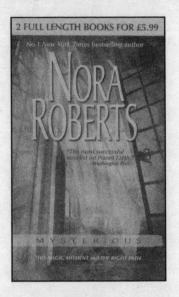